ELMORE LEONARD

OUT OF SIGHT

"Irresistible . . . Hits all the right buttons from the first page . . . A gem of perfect pacing and characterization . . . Dialogue so crisp it crackles . . . *Out of Sight* is out of sight."
Orlando Sentinel

"Nifty . . . Another page-turner from Elmore Leonard . . . Disarming romance, arresting dialogue, sly humor . . . A lean, mean character caper."
Fort Worth Star-Telegram

"Mr. Leonard weaves an absorbing story full of offbeat characters, funny incidents, vivid locales, and dialogue that jumps off the page."
New York Times

"Everything fits, everything grooves, there's not a flat scene or a wasted adjective. . . . You're in the hands of a master."
Tampa Tribune

"Elmore Leonard's writing is as lean as a good steak. *Out of Sight* is marbled with humor, unexpected turns, and snappy dialogue."
Atlanta Journal-Constitution

"*Out of Sight* is a rarity in the Leonard canon: It is a genuine love story. . . . A master of irony . . . He can write people talking the way that no one else on Earth can. . . . Leonard is on target, and when he hits the bull's-eye, he hits it cleanly."
Los Angeles Times Book Review

"At the top of his form . . . With *Out of Sight*, Leonard is at his best. . . . He freshens his customary riff—shady idealist, either cop or criminal, outsmarts everyone—with variations that yield laughs and dramatic depth. . . . The sophistication of the narrative technique is as uncompromising as that of Hemingway or Camus. . . . The romantic spark Leonard strikes between [Foley and Sisco] is credible, charming, and touching."
Fort Lauderdale Sun-Sentinel

"Clever . . . Entertaining . . . Wonderful . . . The dialogue is witty. . . . The characters are drawn with lightning speed. . . . *Out of Sight* runs with the smoothness of a Volvo on velvet."
Memphis Commercial Appeal

"As vividly written as all of Mr. Leonard's novels, this story has his signature touches of irony and black humor. . . . If you liked *Get Shorty*, you'll love Jack Foley and Karen Sisco."
Dallas Morning News

"Vintage Leonard: comical, violent, and realistic . . . You'll remember this one. . . . The characters are wonderful and quirky, the dialogue is street smart, and the thoughts and actions of those on both sides of the thin blue line seem both authentic and, ironically, in synch. . . . In *Out of Sight*, Leonard's apparently decided to make the most unlikely event that could transpire between a cop and a crook seem totally plausible. Of course, he pulls it off."

Pittsburgh Post-Gazette

"Oddball characters still crowd the pages of *Out of Sight*, but this time Leonard introduces a fresh ingredient in his usual rough guy repertoire. He adds a generous helping of Romance, with a capital 'R'. . . . It's not just peripheral romance, either. It has depth, feeling, and substance, a bittersweet, it-might-have-been flavor. Coming from tough guy Leonard, this one's mint-new, unexpected, and welcome . . . evidence of broader storytelling talents than Leonard fans might have suspected."

Buffalo News

"The oldest unsolved mystery on the books, human love, is the case to crack in *Out of Sight*. . . . Leonard pulls the old cards from his sleeve and shuffles them in a new way—the perfectly sketched minor characters, the flash-photographed locations, the blown chances and near misses and lucky guesses—and deals out the scenes and the fates. He has a page-to-page delivery that any fiction writer could study."

New York Times Book Review

"Leonard spins a rapid, engrossing story that is rich in characters. . . . Funny and sad, quirky and enlightening. *Out of Sight* is up to the high standards that Leonard fans expect and receive."

San Antonio Express-News

"Elmore Leonard is the unrivaled
master of crime fiction. . . . *Out of Sight* has all the
wonders we expect from him—bad guys with brains,
heartless villains, a tough female cop, splendid description,
and the snappiest dialogue this side of the
Marx Brothers. . . . Leonard's cast of minor characters
are colorful and, in some cases, frightening.
But you'll find yourself rooting for Karen and Foley."
Albuquerque Journal

"Elmore Leonard's ear for dialogue and imagination
for plot and character make life's likable
losers endlessly entertaining."
St. Louis Post-Dispatch

"There's no denying that Leonard writes prose
that is as good as it gets: wryly funny, whiplash-plotted,
peopled with memorable characters and sly dialogue . . .
With *Out of Sight*, he's knocked another
one out of the park."
Seattle Times

"Riotous fun . . . A great book . . . Elmore Leonard
may be the last hope for the printed word. . . .
He floats you in a world as viscerally real as anything
you can soak up from the latest home theater
surround-sound gizmos, and does it with easy elegance. . . .
This is genre fiction and proud of it—never tired,
never tricked out with knickknacks and
doodads to dazzle the jaded consumer."
St. Petersburg Times

"Fast-paced, funny . . . You thought Chili Palmer
was likable. Wait till you meet Jack Foley."
Albany Times-Union

"The master is at the top of his game in *Out of Sight*—
and that's saying something. . . . The reader often finds
himself laughing out loud at how ingeniously and
naturally the writer fits all the pieces together. . . .
Out of Sight has Leonard with one hand on the wheel,
checking out the sideshow, smirking at all the tourist traps,
and pointing out the obvious in a way that makes you
realize just how much we miss when we don't pay
attention to detail the way he does."
Detroit Free Press

"Near perfection . . . *Out of Sight* is really good. . . .
The dialogue is exceptional. . . . The characters and
relationships are full of fascinating quirks. There's
violence and tenderness, moral ruin and hearts of gold. . . .
It's all just right. . . . Leonard is far and away
the best at what he does."
Dayton Daily News

"Bringing a fresh new choreography to the conventional
steps of crime fiction is Leonard's specialty. . . .
His writing is so butter-smooth, his plotting so
balletically graceful, that the inevitable payoff is still
somehow surprising even as it satisfies our expectations.
Leonard brings out all the colors and details of subplots
and minor characters without ever losing speed."
Newsday

"The bard of thriller writers . . . Leonard moves around
this quirky romance as well as he moves through
crime stories. His usual deft touch with the gritty
side of life is still there, but he makes the sweetness
work just as well. . . . It seems the more thrillers come out,
the more one appreciates Elmore Leonard."
Washington Times

About the Author

Elmore Leonard has written more than forty novels and nearly as many short stories, including such bestsellers as *Up in Honey's Room*, *The Hot Kid*, *Mr. Paradise*, *Tishomingo Blues*, *Pagan Babies*, and *Glitz*. Many of his books have been made into movies, including *Get Shorty* and *Out of Sight*. He lives with his wife, Christine, in Bloomfield Village, Michigan.

ALSO BY ELMORE LEONARD

FICTION

Road Dogs
Up in Honey's Room
The Hot Kid
The Complete Western Stories of Elmore Leonard
Mr. Paradise
When the Women Come Out to Dance
Tishomingo Blues
Pagan Babies
Be Cool
The Tonto Woman and Other Western Stories
Cuba Libre
Riding the Rap
Pronto
Rum Punch
Maximum Bob
Get Shorty
Killshot
Freaky Deaky
Touch
Bandits
Glitz
LaBrava
Stick
Cat Chaser
Split Images
City Primeval
Gold Coast
Gunsights
The Switch
The Hunted
Unknown Man No. 89
Swag
Fifty-Two Pickup
Mr. Majestyk
Forty Lashes Less One
Valdez is Coming
The Moonshine War
The Big Bounce
Hombre
Last Stand at Saber River
Escape from Five Shadows
The Law at Randado
The Bounty Hunters

NONFICTION

Elmore Leonard's 10 Rules of Writing

OUT OF SIGHT

ELMORE LEONARD

HARPER

NEW YORK • LONDON • TORONTO • SYDNEY

For Michael and Kelly

HARPER

This book is a work of fiction. The characters, incidents, and dialogue are drawn from the author's imagination and are not to be construed as real. Any resemblance to actual events or persons, living or dead, is entirely coincidental.

A hardcover edition of this book was published in 1996 by Delacorte Press, and a mass market edition was published by Dell Publishing. Delacorte Press and Dell Publishing are both divisions of Bantam Doubleday Dell Publishing Group, Inc.

FIRST HARPERTORCH EDITION PUBLISHED 2002.
FIRST HARPER PAPERBACK PUBLISHED 2009.

Library of Congress Cataloging-in-Publication Data is available upon request.

ISBN 978-0-06-174031-2

09 10 11 12 13 ID/RRD 10 9 8 7 6 5 4 3 2 1

ONE

FOLEY HAD NEVER SEEN A PRISON WHERE YOU COULD WALK right up to the fence without getting shot. He mentioned it to the guard they called Pup, making conversation: convict and guard standing in a strip of shade between the chapel and a gun tower, red-brick structures in a red-brick prison, both men looking toward the athletic field. Several hundred inmates along the fence out there were watching the game of football played without pads, both sides wearing the same correctional blue, on every play trying to pound each other into the ground.

"You know what they're doing," Foley said, "don't you? I mean besides working off their aggressions."

Pup said, "The hell you talking about?"

This was about the dumbest hack Foley had ever

met in his three falls, two state time, one federal, plus a half-dozen stays in county lockups.

"They're playing in the Super Bowl," Foley said, "pretending they're out at Sun Devil Stadium next Sunday. Both sides thinking they're the Dallas Cowboys."

Pup said, "They ain't worth shit, none of 'em."

Foley turned enough to look at the guard's profile, the peak of his cap curved around his sunglasses. Tan shirt with dark-brown epaulets that matched his pants, radio and flashlight hooked to his belt; no weapon. Foley looked at his size, head-to-head with the Pup at six-one, but from there, where Foley went pretty much straight up and down in his prison blues, the Pup had about forty pounds on him, most of it around the guard's middle, his tan shirt fitting him like skin on a sausage. Foley turned back to the game.

He watched a shifty colored guy come out for a pass and get clotheslined going for the ball, cut down by another shifty colored guy on defense. The few white guys, bikers who had the nerve and the size, played in the line and used their fists on each other, every down. No Latins in the game. They stood along the fence watching, except for two guys doing laps side by side around the field: counterclockwise, the way inmates always circled a yard here and in every prison Foley had ever heard of. The same two ran ten miles a day every day of the week. Coming to this end of the field now, getting closer, breaking stride now, walking:

José Chirino and Luis Linares, Chino and Lulu, husband and wife, both little guys, both doing a mandatory twenty-five for murder. Walking. They hadn't done anywhere near their ten miles. While they circled this end of the field and started up the side, past the cons watching the football game, they had Foley's full attention.

A minute or so passed before he said, "Some people are going out of here. What if I told you where and when?"

The Pup would be staring at him now, eyes half closed to slits behind his shades, the way he judged if a con was telling the truth or giving him a bunch of shit.

"Who we talking about?"

Foley said, "Nothing's free, Pup," still not looking at him.

"I get your liquor for you."

"And you make a good buck. No, what I need," Foley said, turning to look at him now, "is some peace of mind. This is the most fucked-up joint I've ever been in, take my word. Medium security and most of the cons here are violent offenders."

Pup said, "You being one of 'em."

"If I was I've slowed up. Look at those boys out there, that's a vicious breed of convict. Myself, it's not so much I'm violent as habitual, liable to pick up on the outside where I left off, so they'll keep me here till I'm an old man."

The Pup kept giving him his squint.

"So you turn fink?"

"It's okay," Foley said, "if you do it to insure your future. I give you the chance to stop a prison break, you make points, advance your career as a hack. I get peace of mind. I'd expect you to look out for me as long as you're here. Let me run my business, keep me off work details . . ."

The Pup was still squinting.

"How many going out?"

"I hear six."

"When?"

"Looks like tonight."

"You know who they are?"

"I do, but I won't tell you just yet. Meet me in the chapel going on five-thirty, right before evening count."

Foley waited, staring back at those slitty eyes trying to read him.

"Come on, Pup, you want to be a hero or not?"

▼▼▼

NOON DINNER, FOLEY TOOK HIS PORK BUTTS AND YAMS down the center aisle looking for Chino among all the white T-shirts and dark hair. There he was, at a table of his little-guy countrymen eating macaroni and cheese, a dish Foley has passed on in the chow line. Jesus, eating a pile of it. The guy across from Chino giving him more, scraping macaroni from his tray on to Chino's. The man's gaze raised to Foley, dark eyes beneath lumps of scar tissue, all he had to show for his career as a welterweight before age and killing a man put him out of business. Chino was close to fifty but in shape; Foley had watched him do thirty pull-ups on a bar without kicking his legs, trying to climb through the air. Chino gave him a nod but didn't make room, tell any of his people at the table to get up. Lulu sat next to him with a neat tray of macaroni and Jell-O and a cup of milk they gave inmates under twenty-one years of age to build strong, healthy bodies.

Foley ate his noon dinner at a table of outlaw bikers, cons who bought half-pint bottles of rum Foley sold for three times what he paid Pup to sneak the stuff in. He sat there listening to the outlaws having fun, comparing his rum to piss and running with it, enjoying their use of the word, speculating on what kind it was, dog piss, cat piss, how about alligator piss? They liked that one. Foley saw it had to be an uncommon kind of piss, said, "How about chicken piss?" and the table showed him bad teeth and the food they were chewing with grins and grunts of appreciation. Foley worked through his dinner and went outside to smoke a cigarette and wait for Chino.

Lulu tagging along when he came, Lulu cute as a bug with his girlish eyelashes and pouty way of looking at you. Chino had had to punch out many a suitor to keep Lulu for his own. He had told Foley Lulu wasn't a homosexual before entering this life, but had become one and was good at it. Confiding things like that after Foley told Chino he was the most aggressive welterweight he had ever seen fight. Saw him lose to Mauricio Bravo in L.A. when Foley was doing banks out there. Saw him lose to the Mexican kid, Palomino, at the Grand in Las Vegas—tough break, the TKO in the sixth when Chino's right eye closed and they stopped the fight. Foley said, "I never saw a fighter take as many shots as you did and keep coming back—outside of Rocky Balboa." Chino's record was 22 and 17, not good if you were the fighter, not bad if you admired him for staying with it as long as he did. Foley was the only Anglo the Cuban allowed to get close.

He had his arm around Lulu's shoulder as they approached, then let it slip down to hook his thumb in Lulu's belt, the next thing to having him on a leash.

Foley said, "Today's the day, huh? You excited?"

The man was cool, no expression. "I told you, man, Super Bowl Sunday."

"Yeah, but I see you moved it up."

Now a glint showed in his eyes. "Why you think is today?"

"You were out running this morning, sticking to your routine, anybody happened to notice. But you only did a couple of miles, saving yourself for the main event. Then I see you eating about ten pounds of macaroni. Carbohydrates for endurance."

"You want," Chino said, "I tole you you can come."

"I would, but I can't stand to get dirty."

"Is finish. All we do now is go out."

"You sure you're past the fence?"

"Fifteen and a half meters, one to spare."

From the covered crawl space beneath the prison chapel to the grass just beyond the razor wire perimeter fence. They had been digging since before Christmas with their hands and a broken shovel, using scrap lumber from the construction site of a new wing being added to the chapel to shore up the walls of the tunnel. It was Christmas Day Foley happened to see Chino and Lulu come out of the ficus bushes in front of the chapel, their faces streaked with black dirt, muck, but wearing clean blues. What were they doing, making out in the bushes? That wasn't Chino's style, so Foley the fight fan said, "Don't tell me about it 'less you want to." And Chino said that time to his Anglo friend, "You want to go with us?"

Foley said he didn't want any part of it—only three feet of crawl space underneath the chapel, pitch-dark in there, maybe run into fucking mole rats face-to-face. No thanks. He'd said to Chino, "Don't you know you're digging through Everglades muck? I've talked to people. They say it's wet and'll cave in on you." Chino said, yeah, that's what people thought, but the tunnel only caved in once. If they were careful, took their time, the muck stuck together and became dry and was okay. He told Foley they had dug down four feet and then out toward the fence, the tunnel a meter wide and a meter high. One man at a time dug and the muck was passed back and spread around the crawl space under there, so nobody was going to see it. They worked two at a time in dirty clothes they kept there and put on clean ones before coming out.

Foley said to Chino that Christmas Day, "If I caught on, how come none of the hacks have?"

Chino said, "I think they believe like you no one can dig a tunnel in muck. Or they don't want to crawl in there and find out. They see us dirty they think we work construction."

It was that day Chino said they were going out Super Bowl Sunday, when everyone would be watching the game, six o'clock.

But now they were going out five days early.

"You finish ahead of schedule?"

Chino looked toward the fence along the front of the yard, between the administration building and the gun tower close to the chapel. "You see what they doing, those posts out there? Putting up another fence, five meters on the other side of the one that's there. We wait until Super Bowl Sunday they could have the second fence built and we have to dig another nine ten days. So we going soon as it's dark."

"During the count."

"Sure, and when they get the wrong count," Chino said, "they have to start over. It give us some more time to get out of here. You want—I mean it—you can still come."

"I didn't help dig."

"If I say you can come, you can come."

"I appreciate the offer," Foley said, looking toward the fence and the visitors' parking area just the other side, a few cars in the front row facing this way, not twenty yards from the fence. "And it's tempting. But, man, it's a long run to civilization, a hundred miles to Miami? I'm too old to start acting crazy, try a stunt like that."

"You no older than I am."

"Yeah, but you're in shape, you and little Lulu." Foley winked at the queer and got a dirty look for no reason. "I ever make it out it won't be in state clothes or no idea where I'm going. Shit, I'm fairly new here, still feeling my way through the system."

Chino said, "You do okay, man. I'm not going to worry about you."

Foley put his hand on the little guy's shoulder. "I wish you luck, partner. You make it out, send me a postcard."

▼▼▼

SOME OF THE NEWER WHITE BOYS DOING TIME FOR DRUGS called home just about every day after noon chow. There they were lined up by the phone outside the captain's office. Foley went in to put his name on the list, came out and went to the head of the line saying, "Fellas, I got an emergency call I have to make. Y'all don't have a problem with that, do you?"

He got hard looks but no argument. These boys were fish and Foley was a celebrity hard-timer who'd robbed more banks than they'd been in to cash a check. He gave talks at AA meetings on self-respect, how to stay alive in here without taking too much shit. If you saw it coming, hit first with something heavy. Foley's choice, a foot or so of lead pipe, never a shank, a shank was crude, sneaky, it put you in the same class as the thugs and hogs. No, what you wanted to do was lay the pipe across the guy's jaw, and if you had time break his hands with it. If you didn't see the guy coming you were fucked, so keep your eyes open. It was about all you could tell these fish.

A woman's voice accepted the charge, Foley's ex-wife now living in Miami Beach. He said, "Hey, Adele, how you doing?"

She said, "Now what?" Not with any kind of attitude, asking a simple question.

Adele had divorced him while he was doing seven years at Lompoc in California and moved to Florida. Foley never once held it against her. They'd met in Vegas where she was working as a cocktail waitress in a skimpy sequined outfit, cut low on top and high up her legs from the crotch, got married one night when they were both feeling good, and it was less than a year later he went up to Lompoc. They hadn't even kept house, so to speak. A few months after he got out, Foley came to Florida and they seemed to pick up where they'd left off, drinking, going to bed . . . Adele telling him she still loved him, but please don't talk about marriage again, okay? It made Foley feel guilty that he hadn't been able to support her while in prison, and it was this feeling that got him sent up again. He robbed a Barnett bank in Lake Worth, intending to give Adele the entire proceeds—show her his heart was in the right place—but was caught and ended up at Glades doing thirty to life. It meant, the way sentencing worked now, he'd be here at least twenty-four years before he was eligible for parole. All on account of wanting to be a good guy.

He said to Adele, "You know that Super Bowl party? They changed the date. It's on tonight, six o'clock."

There was a silence on the line before Adele said, "Didn't you tell me one time calls aren't monitored?"

"I said not as a rule."

"So why don't you come right out and tell me what you're talking about?"

"Listen to Miss Smarty Mouth," Foley said, "out there in the free world."

"What's free about it? I'm looking for work."

"What happened to Mandrake the Magician?"

"Emil the Amazing. The kraut son of a bitch fired me and hired another girl, a blonde."

"He must be crazy, want to trade you in."

"Emil says I'm too old."

"To do what, watch pigeons fly out of a hat? You have that cute, amazed look down cold, in your little assistant magician outfit. You'll hook up with another one before you know it. Run an ad. Anyway, not to change the subject," Foley said, "but the reason I called . . ."

"I'm listening."

"It's today instead of Sunday. About six, like

only a few hours from now. So you'll have to get hold of Buddy, whatever he might be doing . . ."

Adele said, "And the one driving the other car."

"What're you talking about?"

"Buddy wants to use two cars."

"You said he *might*."

"Well, he's going to, so he got this guy you know from Lompoc. Glenn Michaels?"

Foley didn't say anything, picturing a young guy who wore sunglasses all the time, even watching movies.

"Cute but seedy," Adele said, "has real long hair."

But none on his body. Foley remembered the guy in the yard always working on his tan. Glenn Michaels. The guy stole expensive cars on special order and delivered them all over, even Mexico. Acted hip and told stories about women coming on to him, even movie stars, but none Foley or Buddy had ever heard of. They called him Studs.

"You met him?"

"Buddy thought I should, just in case."

"In case of what?"

"I don't know, ask him. Glenn said he thought you were real cool."

"He did, huh. Tell Buddy I see this guy wearing sunglasses I'll step on 'em. I might not even take 'em off him first."

"You're still weird," Adele said.

"A quarter to six the latest. But don't call him on your phone."

"You tell me that every time," Adele said. "Will you be careful, please? And don't get shot?"

▼▼▼

FIVE-TWENTY, FOLEY FOUND A CHILD MOLESTER THEY CALLED the Elf alone in the chapel with the lights off: a skinny white kid sitting round-shouldered by the windows, a stack of pamphlets in the pew with him. Foley turned the lights on and the kid hunched around to look at him, no doubt afraid he was about to get beat up again, the fate of guys with short eyes among a population that felt superior.

"You're gonna ruin your eyes," Foley said, "trying to read that inspirational shit in the dark. Leave, okay? I need to speak to my Redeemer in private."

Once the Elf was out the door Foley turned the lights off and went along the row of windows pulling old brown-stained shades down halfway, keeping it just light enough in here to see the shapes of the pews. He walked around to the other side of the chapel now and stepped through an opening to the wing they were adding on, the structure framed in and smelling of new wood, big open spaces where windows would be hung.

He looked around at the mess of scrap lumber the prison carpenters, not giving a shit, had wasted. A piece of two-by-four caught his eye. Foley had thought of using pipe for what he'd have to do—there was enough of it around—but he liked the way this piece of scrap wood was split and tapered to a thin end, like a baseball bat.

He picked it up, took a swing and imagined a screaming line drive sailing out to the athletic field where half the population—he could see them through the window openings—five, six hundred cons slouched around with nothing to do, not enough jobs here to keep them busy. It was going dark now, the sky showing a few last streaks of red, and there it was, the whistle: everybody back to the dorms for evening count. It would take a half hour, then another fifteen minutes to do a re-count before they'd know for sure six inmates were missing. By the time they got out the dogs, Chino and his boys would be running through sugar cane.

Strung-out lines of inmates were coming from the athletic field now, passing through a gate to the prison compound. Foley watched them thinking, You're on the clock now, boy.

In the chapel again he placed his baseball bat in one of the pews, on the seat, and took off his denim jacket to lay over it. Chino would be down there in the muck telling his boys to be patient, making sure it was dark before they came out.

Foley turned, hearing the chapel door open. He watched the Pup come in and glance around before closing the door. No weapon on him, just his radio and flashlight, the peak of his cap down on his eyes, the man anxious. His hand went to the light switch on the wall by the door and Foley said, "Leave it off." The Pup looked at him and Foley put his finger to his lips. It was happening now and he took his time.

"They're right underneath you, Pup. They dug a tunnel."

Now the guard was unhooking the radio from his belt.

Foley said, "Wait. Not just yet."

TWO

Karen left West Palm at five, drove into the sunset past miles and miles of cane and had her headlights on by the time she turned into the parking area and sat facing the prison. Her high beams showed a strip of grass, a sidewalk, another strip of grass, the fence strung with sound detectors and razor wire, dark figures in white T-shirts inside the fence, brick dorms that looked like barracks, picnic tables and a few gazebos used on visiting days. Lights were coming on, spots mounted high that showed the compound with its walks and lawns; at night it didn't look all that bad. She lit a cigarette and dialed a number on her car phone.

"Hi. Karen Sisco again. Did Ray ever get back? . . . I tried, yeah. He calls in, tell him I won't be able to meet him until about seven. Okay?"

She watched prisoners massing at the gate from

the athletic field, straggling through and then spreading out, moving toward their dorms in the spotlight beams. She picked up the phone and dialed a number.

"Dad? Karen. Will you do me a big favor?"

"Do I have to get up? I just made myself a drink."

"I'm out at Glades. I'm supposed to meet Ray Nicolet at six and I can't get hold of him."

"Which one is that, the fed, the ATF guy?"

"He *was*. Ray's with the state now, Florida Department of Law Enforcement, he switched over."

"He's still married though, huh?"

"Technically. They're separated."

"Oh, he's moved out?"

"He's about to."

"Then they're not separated, are they?"

"Will you try calling him, please? He's on the street. Tell him I'm gonna be late?" She gave her dad Ray's beeper number.

"What're you doing at Glades?"

"Serving process, a Summons and Complaint. Drive all the way out here . . ." Headlights hit Karen's rearview mirror, a car pulling into the row behind her. The lights went off, then came on again and Karen adjusted the mirror to deflect the glare. "I have to drive all the way out here because some con doing mandatory life doesn't like macaroni and cheese. He files suit, says he has no choice in what they serve and it violates his civil rights."

Her dad said, "What'd I tell you? Most of the time you'd be serving papers or working security, hanging around courtrooms, driving prisoners to hearings . . ."

"You want me to say you were right?"

"It wouldn't hurt you."

"I'm giving the West Palm office a year. They don't put me back on warrants, I quit."

"My daughter the tough babe. You know you can always step in here, work with me full time. I just got a case you'd love, the rights of the victim at stake."

"Dad . . ."

"Guy pulls a home invasion, beats up an old lady and takes her life savings she has hidden away, eighty-seven thousand, cash. They get the guy and his lawyer cuts a deal with the state attorney, two to five and the guy will come out and make full restitution. He does fifteen months, gets his release and disappears. The old lady's son hires me to find him."

Karen said, "You do, then what? The guy pulls armed robberies to pay her back?"

"See? You like it, you're thinking. Actually, the old lady's son would settle for beating the shit out of the guy."

"I have to go," Karen said.

"When am I gonna see you?"

"I'll come Sunday and watch the game with you, if you'll call Ray."

"You get dressed up for this guy?"

"I'm wearing the Chanel suit—not the new one, the one you gave me for Christmas a year ago. I *hap*pen to be wearing it."

"With the short skirt. You want him to leave home tomorrow, huh?"

"I'll see you," Karen said and hung up.

Her dad, seventy, semi-retired after forty years in the business, ran Marshall Sisco Investigations, Inc., in Coral Gables. Karen Sisco, twenty-nine, was a deputy United States marshal, recently transferred from Miami to the West Palm Beach office. She had worked surveillance jobs for her dad while in college, the University of Miami, decided she might like federal law enforcement and transferred to Florida Atlantic in Boca Raton to take their criminal justice program. Different federal agents would come to the school to give talks and recruit, FBI, DEA—Karen was smoking grass at the time, so she didn't consider Drug Enforcement an option. She thought about Secret Service, but the agents she met were so fucking secretive—ask a question and they'd go, "You'll have to check with Washington on that." She got to know a couple of marshals, nice guys, they didn't take themselves as seriously as the Bureau guys she met. So Karen went with the Marshals Service and her dad told her she was crazy, have to put up with all that bureaucratic bullshit.

Karen was five-nine in the medium heels she wore with her black Chanel suit. Her marshal's star and ID were in her handbag, on the seat with the court papers. Her pistol, a Sig Sauer .38, was in the trunk with her ballistic vest, her marshal's jacket, several pairs of handcuffs, leg irons with chains, an expandable baton, Mace, and a Remington pump-action shotgun. She had locked the pistol in the trunk so she wouldn't have to check it inside the prison. The Sig Sauer was her favorite, her evening-wear piece; she didn't want to have to worry about some guard fooling with it.

Okay, she was ready. Karen took a final draw on the cigarette and dropped it out the window. She straightened the rearview mirror to look at herself and right away turned her face from the glare: the headlights of the car behind her still on high beam.

THREE

BUDDY SAW THE MIRROR FLASH AND BLOND HAIR IN HIS headlights, a woman in the blue Chevy Caprice parked right in front of him, Florida plate.

He didn't see anyone in the other cars in the first row. Good. Cons were coming in from the athletic field, but he didn't see any hacks running around like crazy or hear any whistles blowing. That was even better. He was on time. After busting his tail to get out here he wouldn't mind relaxing for a few minutes. He still couldn't believe his luck, getting hold of Glenn with just a few hours to spare, tell him it was on. Not Sunday, today, now. Glenn wanting to know how come. Buddy said, "We don't have time to chat, okay? Pick up a car and be waiting where I showed you. Sometime after six. Glenn? A white car."

Glenn didn't see what difference it made.

"So we're fairly sure it's you," Buddy said, "not some cop sitting in an unmarked car with a radar gun. And don't wear your sunglasses."

Glenn argued about that, too, and Buddy told him, "Boy, do as I say and you'll get by."

Buddy had to hurry to pick up a car himself, a white one Foley would spot without looking all over the parking lot, then drive most of three hours to get here from the Miami area.

As minutes passed he wondered if the woman in the Chevy was sitting there waiting for Cubans to come crawling out of a hole. He knew Latins liked Chevys and this woman could be Latina herself with dyed hair. Buddy turned his head this way and that looking around, wondering if there were other cars here waiting to pick up convicts. Like a commuter station, wives come to pick up their hubbies.

The blonde was in the right spot. Foley had told Adele the second fence post from the gun tower by the chapel, that was where they'd come out.

Buddy hated gun towers, even from outside the fence, the idea of a man up there with a high-powered rifle watching every minute you're in the yard. Foley would look up at a tower and say, "Imagine hoping to see a man on the fence so you can shoot him off it. Praying for the chance. What kind of a man is that?" Buddy would say your common, garden variety hack, mean and stupid.

This was when they first met, found they'd both been doing the same kind of work and became friends for life at USP Lompoc: five miles from the Pacific Ocean and full of big-time California dopers, con men, swindlers . . . Foley would say, "Buddy, what're a couple of pros like us doing in this dog pound, associating with misfits, snitches and dysfunctional assholes?"

They got their release three months apart.

Buddy, out first, stayed in L.A. with his older sister, Regina Mary, an ex-nun who lived on welfare, drank sherry wine and went to Mass every day to pray for Buddy and the poor souls in Purgatory. When Buddy was on the road doing banks he'd call her every week and send money. In the joint all he could do was write, since Regina wouldn't accept charges if he phoned.

Foley came out with his fifty dollars gate money and took a bus to L.A. where Buddy was waiting for him in a car he'd boosted for the occasion. That same afternoon they hit a bank in Pomona—the first time either one had worked with a partner—cleared a total of fifty-six hundred from two different tellers at the same time, and drove to Las Vegas where they got laid and lost what was left of their fifty-six hundred. So they went back to L.A. and worked southern California a few months as a team: two tellers at the same time, seeing who could score more than the other without setting off alarms. Buddy sure missed his partner.

When Foley first called him about this business, Buddy was still out in California staying with his sister. He said, "For Jesus sake, what're you doing back in the can?"

"Looking for a way out," Foley said. "A judge with bugs up his ass gave me thirty years and I don't deserve to be here. It's full of morons and misfits but only medium security, if you get my drift." The reason he was in Florida, he said, he'd come to see Adele.

"Remember how she wrote the whole time we're at Lompoc?"

"After she divorced you."

"Well, I was never much of a husband. Never helped her out with expenses or paid alimony."

"How could you, making twenty cents an hour?"

"I know, but I felt I owed her something."

"So you did a bank in Florida," Buddy said.

"It reminded me of the time in Pasadena, I come out and the goddamn car wouldn't start."

"You talked about it for seven years," Buddy said, "wondering why you didn't leave the engine running. Don't tell me the same thing happened in Florida."

"No, but it was like that. Like my two biggest falls were on account of cars, for Christ sake."

"You got in an accident?"

Foley said, "I'll tell you about it when I see you."

From then on it was Adele who called, always from a pay phone, to speak about this business with the Cubans.

By the time a date was set, Buddy had motored out from California and rented a one-bedroom unit in the Shalamar Apartments in Hallandale. It was on the ocean, just north of Miami.

Then Adele had called to say it was tonight and, man, he'd have to *move*. Got Glenn off his ass, then went out to look for a car and found the ideal getaway vehicle in a Dania strip mall: white Cadillac Sedan DeVille Concours. Buddy was about to jimmy the door when he saw a woman coming from Winn-Dixie, middle-aged, wearing pearls and high heels in the afternoon, but pushing the cart full of groceries herself, so she wouldn't have to tip a carryout boy, some poor Haitian who'd come here in a rowboat. Buddy stuck the jimmy in his pants, against the small of his back. He waited until the woman was opening her trunk before coming forward with, "Here, lemme help you with those, ma'am." She didn't seem too sure about it, but let him load the groceries in the trunk and take the key out of the lock. The woman said, "I didn't ask for your help, so don't expect a tip."

Buddy waved it off. "That's okay, ma'am." He said, "I'll just take your car." Got in and drove off.

The woman might've yelled at him, but with the windows shut and the air on high he didn't hear a thing. It was the first time he'd ever picked up a car this way, sort of like what they called car-jacking.

A quarter to six. If it was going to happen the way Foley said, it should be any second now. Almost all the cons were in from the athletic field, a few stragglers coming along in no hurry, moving through the spotlights.

Now Buddy was watching the woman in the Chevy again. He saw her hand come out the window to drop a cigarette and it made him think she *did* know about the break and was getting ready. He saw her other hand raise, inside the car, to the mirror and saw his headlights flash on the mirror again, the same way it happened before, when he first arrived. Moments later the Chevy's lights were turned off. Buddy was pretty sure she'd be getting out of the car now.

He waited, anxious to see what she looked like.

FOUR

FOLEY WATCHED THE PUP CREEP UP THE AISLE TOWARD THE front of the chapel, eyes on the floor, no doubt listening for sounds from below. Sure enough, he said, "I don't hear nothing."

"They're not digging now, Pup, they're done. Six of 'em in the tunnel as we speak, ready to go." Foley thought of something he might need to know and said, "What do you say when you're reporting a break?"

"That's an amber alert," Pup said. "You sure they're down there?"

"I saw 'em duck into the crawl space."

"Where's the tunnel come out?"

"Second fence post from the tower out there. Go on, take a look."

Pup turned his back, walked up the aisle and across the front of the pews to a window. Lights in the compound reflected on the glass and turned the shades a dirty yellow. Pup said, "I don't see nothing there."

Foley, picking up his jacket with the two-by-four baseball bat, moving through the pews to the window aisle, said, "You will directly. Keep watching."

Pup said, "They's nobody in tower six this time of day—if they do come out."

Foley said, "You think they don't know that?" moving up behind Pup, seeing the guard shirt stretched tight across the man's back, a lot of heft to him. Foley let his jacket slip to the floor; he held the two-by-four in his left hand now, down against his leg.

Pup said, "There some car headlights out there . . ." Now he was pulling his radio from his belt saying "Jesus Christ . . ." Saying into the radio, "Man outside the fence! By tower six!" Nothing about it being an amber alert—too excited. Foley edged in closer to see the car headlights in the parking lot shining on the fence, a dark-blue car and a white one behind it that had to be Buddy, bless his heart. Foley on his toes now looking at freedom, feeling it—man, right there—as the Pup was identifying himself, saying this was Officer Pupko and where he was, sending out the word too soon, before Foley was ready. He saw a figure by the fence now, lit blue in the headlights, as Pup was yelling into his radio, "I'm looking at him, for Christ sake!"

Foley took a moment to remind himself not to hold back, to follow through. Hold back, you make a mess. He got the angle he wanted, stepped in like he was going for a high hard one and laid the two-by-four smack against the side of Pup's head. Dropped him clean with the one swing, bounced him off the window frame and down without a sound coming from him. Foley took another look outside, saw two figures now by the fence, before he stooped down to get Pup undressed. Undo his shirt buttons and then roll him facedown, the Pup alive but dead weight. Man, it was work getting the shirt off, Pup not helping any. Foley quick put it on over his T-shirt. He heard a car horn blowing now, somebody leaning on it, maybe Buddy trying to tell him something. Like come on, *move*. He saw he wouldn't have time for the pants; he'd have to chance his prison blue wouldn't be noticed in the dark. Foley squared Pup's cap, too small for him, tight over his eyes, picked up the flashlight and slipped out the front door into the ficus bushes.

▼▼▼

KAREN HAD THE COURT PAPERS IN HER HAND, READY TO GET out of the car. She saw prisoners still coming in from the athletic field, passing left to right in her view, all of them some distance from the fence. She opened the car door . . .

Wait a minute.

One of the guys, a figure she hadn't noticed before this moment, was right by the fence. Close enough to touch it. The guy crouched . . . or on his hands and knees. Karen popped on her headlights again and saw him clearly.

Not crouched.

The guy was coming out of the *ground*.

On *this* side of the fence.

Reaching down now as head and shoulders appeared and another one came out of the ground.

Right in front of her. Not twenty yards from the car. Two guys breaking out and no siren or whistle going off, prisoners still crossing the compound, not even aware . . .

Karen leaned on the horn, held it down and saw the two guys by the fence, both Latins, looking into her headlights, poised there for a moment before taking off in the dark, down the fence that ran along the athletic field. By the time the third one appeared, came out of the hole followed by another convict on his heels, Karen was out of the car.

▼▼▼

BUDDY DIDN'T SEE THEM RIGHT AWAY. THE WOMAN COMmenced blowing her horn and that got him sitting up. He still didn't realize the break was on until the woman was out of the car and he saw her looking off to the left, along the fence. By the time he saw the two cons they were running away from the fence, cutting across the road that came in from the highway, the two all of a sudden in a spotlight beam that angled out from the tower at the far end of the athletic field, the spotlight following them, its beam holding, and now the sound of rifle reports were coming from out there, the guard in the far tower trying to gun them down as they ran for an orange grove and disappeared from sight. When Buddy looked for the woman again she was right in front of him—her blond hair in his headlights, long slim legs, hell, a *girl*—at the trunk of her car raising the lid.

Buddy's first thought, She's gonna put a con in there, help him escape.

He watched her duck her head in the trunk and come out with a holstered pistol, what looked like some kind of automatic.

Jesus, even ready to shoot their way out.

But then she threw the pistol in the trunk, ducked in there again and came out this time racking a pump-action shotgun. Buddy watched her hurry to the front of her car and raise the shotgun, looking off, but the two cons were gone. Now a whistle was blowing inside the compound.

Buddy saw convicts in there gathering, looking

this way, hundreds of them bunched in groups, but no hacks in sight. He told himself he'd better get out of the car, be ready. Whether he wanted to or not.

Once he was out he saw the girl, still by the front of her car, had the shotgun on two more cons, both filthy dirty, standing by the hole they must've come out of, the girl telling them to get their hands in the air. She sure as hell wasn't here to help anybody escape. So who was she? Buddy could see the two cons making up their minds, couple of Latinos, already edging away—shit, they'd come this far. They looked out at that spotlight sweeping around in the dark, then looked the other way, along the fence toward the main gate, to see armed hacks coming out on the run, and that decided it for the two cons. They took off toward the road. Buddy saw the woman, this good-looking girl in a short skirt, put her pump gun on them and knew she couldn't miss, but she didn't fire. No, the hacks coming from the main gate, five of them with rifles and shotguns, they beat her to it, opened up all at once and kept firing and Buddy saw the two convicts cut down as they ran. The hacks were looking this way now; they couldn't miss seeing the girl standing there in her headlights, but they didn't bother with her—Buddy realizing they knew who she was. They were more interested in the hole the convicts had come out of. Now they were standing by it peering in, edging closer with their weapons ready, then all stepped back at once, bumping into each other.

A head appeared wearing a guard's baseball cap, head and shoulders now coming out of the hole, the guy saying something to them, his face beneath the cap smeared with muck, shaking his head now, excited. One of the hacks was speaking into his radio. Another extended his rifle for the one in the hole to grab the barrel and get pulled out. But the one in the hole kept yelling and pointing out at the dark, toward the orange grove. Finally when the hacks moved off they checked the two convicts they'd shot, kicked at them to see if they were still alive and then kept going, and the one in the hole climbed out.

Buddy knew it was Foley, taking his time now to put on a show, standing with his hands on his hips like an honest-to-God hack, that serious cap down on his eyes. Buddy moved up to his headlights, raising his arm and waving at Foley to come on, and saw the girl turn enough to put the shotgun on him. Buddy raised the palm of his hand to her saying, "It's okay, honey, we're good guys." Buddy wanting to appear calm, wanting to believe he'd have no problem with this cute-looking blonde—maybe a probation officer, though he didn't think probation officers were ever armed.

She said, "What're you doing here?" Not so much asking, putting it to him the way cops did when they were already pretty sure of what you were doing. She glanced around to include Foley. She knew, all right, but with the two of them to watch was too late making her move. She saw Foley coming at her filthy dirty, like a creature out of the swamp, giving Buddy time to take her around the neck. She fought him, jabbing him in the gut with the butt end of the shotgun, before Foley got in there to wrench it from her grip. They dragged her to the rear end of the Chevy, the trunk lid still up, and crouched there as some hacks came running along the fence past the dark gun tower and crossed the road toward the orange grove. Pretty soon they heard bursts of gunfire, then silence.

Foley said, "I bet that's all the hacks they send out. Otherwise nobody's left to mind the store."

Buddy said, "Why don't we talk about it later."

He turned his head to see Foley and the young woman staring at each other in the Cadillac headlights, neither one seeming mad or scared, Foley saying to her, "Why you're just a girl. What do you do for a living you pack a shotgun?"

She said to him, "I'm a federal marshal and you're under arrest, both of you guys."

Foley kept staring like he was giving the situation serious thought, deciding now what to do with her, Jesus, a U.S. marshal. But what he said was, "I bet I smell, don't I?" And then he said, "Listen, you hop in the trunk and we'll get out of here."

FIVE

KAREN THOUGHT THEY'D PUT HER INSIDE AND LEAVE AND she felt around to find her handgun, quick, the Sig Sauer, before they closed the trunk lid and she'd have to kick at it and yell until someone let her out. There, she felt the holster, slipped the pistol out and closed her hand around the grip ready to go for it, six hollow points in the magazine and one in the throat, ready to come around shooting if she had to. But now the one in the filthy guard uniform gave her a shove and was getting in with her—she couldn't believe it—crawling in to wedge her between the wall of the trunk and his body pressed against her back, like they were cuddled up in bed, the guy bringing his arm around now to hold her to him, and she didn't have room to turn and stick the gun in his face.

The trunk lid came down and they were in darkness, total, not a crack or pinpoint of light showing, dead silent until the engine came to life, the car moving now, turning out of the lot to the road that went out to the highway. Karen pictured it, remembering the orange grove and a maintenance building, then farther along the road frame houses and yards where some of the prison personnel lived.

His voice in the dark, breathing on her, said, "You comfy?"

The con acting cool, nothing to lose. Karen was holding the Sig Sauer between her thighs, protecting it, her skirt hiked up around her hips. She said, "If I could have a little more room . . ."

"There isn't any."

She wondered if she could get her feet against the front wall, push off hard and twist at the same time and shove the gun into him.

Maybe. But then what?

She said, "I'm not much of a hostage if no one knows I'm here."

She felt his hand move over her shoulder and down her arm.

"You aren't a hostage, you're my zoo-zoo, my treat after five months of servitude. Somebody pleasant and smells good for a change. I'm sorry if I smell like a sewer, it's the muck I had to crawl through, all that decayed matter."

She felt him moving, squirming around to get comfortable.

"You sure have a lot of shit in here. What's all this stuff? Handcuffs, chains . . . What's this can?"

"For your breath," Karen said. "You could use it. Squirt some in your mouth."

"You devil, it's Mace, huh? What've you got here, a billy? Use it on poor unfortunate offenders . . . Where's your gun, your pistol?"

"In my bag, in the car." She felt his hand slip from her arm to her hip and rest there and she said, "You know you don't have a chance of making it. Guards are out here already, they'll stop the car."

"They're off in the cane by now chasing Cubans."

His tone quiet, unhurried, and it surprised her.

"I timed it to slip between the cracks, you might say. I was even gonna blow the whistle myself if I had to, send out the amber alert, get them running around in confusion for when I came out of the hole. Boy, it stunk in there."

"I believe it," Karen said. "You've ruined a thirty-five-hundred-dollar suit my dad gave me."

She felt his hand move down her thigh, fingertips brushing her pantyhose, the way her skirt was pushed up.

"I bet you look great in it, too. Tell me why in the world you ever became a federal marshal, Jesus. My experience with marshals, they're all beefy guys, like your big-city dicks."

"The idea of going after guys like you," Karen said, "appealed to me."

"To prove something? What're you, one of those women's rights activists, out to bust some balls? I haven't been close to a woman like you in months, good-looking, smart . . . I think, man, here's my reward for doing without, leading a clean, celibate life in there, and you turn out to be a ballbuster. Tell me it ain't so."

"How would you know if I'm smart or not?"

"See? Putting me in my place, that's the same as ballbusting. I should've known you're a militant female, girl who packs, hauls all this crime-stopping equipment around . . . But, listen, just 'cause I've done without doesn't mean I'm gonna force myself on you. I've never done that in my life."

It amazed her, the guy trying to make a good impression. "You wouldn't have time anyway," Karen said. "We come to a roadblock they'll run the car, find out in about five seconds who it belongs to."

His voice breathing on her said, "If they get set up in time, which I doubt. Even if they do they'll be looking for Cubans, little fellas with black hair, not a big redneck driving a Chevy. I'm leaving this trip in the hands of my Lord and Savior and my old pal Buddy. He's pure redneck. You know how you tell? He never takes his shirt off."

Feeling free and talkative. Karen kept quiet.

"I mean in the sun, like when we're in the yard. Joint out in sunny California only a few miles from the ocean, never once took his shirt off. Has one of those farmer tans. You see Buddy in the shower, his face and arms have color but his body's pure white. Good guy, though, wrote to his sister ever week without fail. He'd tell her what the weather was like. She'd write back and tell about her weather, which wasn't that different. His sister used to be one of those nuns who never spoke. Buddy says she still doesn't talk much, but now she drinks."

Riding in the trunk of a car with an escaped convict, chatting, passing the time, the car bumping over back roads, the floor beneath them hard, ungiving. Finally when they picked up speed and were moving in a straight line, Karen believed they were on 441 now, heading for West Palm and probably the interstate. Not the turnpike, you couldn't get on it from 441. She felt his hand patting her thigh, inches from her hand gripping the Sig Sauer.

She said, "Buddy. That's his given name?"

"One I gave him, yeah."

"Well, what's yours? It'll be in the paper tomorrow anyway."

He said, "Jack Foley. You've probably heard of me."

"Why, are you famous?"

"The time I was convicted in California? They said, 'How about telling us some of the other banks you've done?' This was the FBI. They gave me immunity from prosecution, just wanting to close the case files on whatever I could give them. I started listing the ones I could remember. After I was done they checked and said I'd robbed more banks than anyone in the computer."

"How many was it?"

"Tell you the truth, I don't know."

"About how many?"

"Well, going back thirty years, subtract nine years state and federal time served, starting with Angola. You know where it is? Lou'siana. I started out driving for my uncle Cully when I was eighteen, right out of high school. Cully and a guy use to work with him, they went in a bank in Slidell, over by the Mississippi line? The guy with Cully jumps the counter to get to the tellers and breaks his leg. All three of us went up. I did twenty-two months and learned how to fight for my life. Cully did twenty-seven years before he came out and died not too long after in Charity Hospital, I think trying to make up for all the good times he'd missed. My other fall, I did seven years, that was at Lompoc. I don't mean the place where some of Nixon's people went, Haldeman, some of those guys. That was Lompoc FPC, federal prison camp, the one they used to call Club Fed. No fence, no guys with shanks or razor blades stuck in toothbrush handles. The worst that could happen to you, some guy hits you over the head with a tennis racquet."

"I know the difference," Karen said. "You were in Lompoc USP, the federal penitentiary. I've delivered people there."

"Handcuffed to some moron?"

"We have our own plane. It still isn't any fun."

"The fog'd come in off the ocean," Foley said, "roll in and just sit there in the yard, sometimes past noon. So that's nine years, Angola and Lompoc. Add county time awaiting hearings, and that hole we just left, that's more'n a decade of correctional living. I'm forty-seven years old and I'm not doing any more time."

Karen said, "You're sure about that?"

"If I go back I do a full thirty years, no time off. Could you imagine looking at that?"

"I don't have to," Karen said, "I don't rob banks."

"If it turns out I get shot down like a dog it'll be in the street, not off a goddamn fence."

"You must see yourself as some kind of desperado."

He said, "I don't know," and was quiet for several moments. "I never actually thought of myself that way." He paused again. "Unless I did without knowing it. Like some of those boys of yesteryear.

Clyde Barrow—you ever see pictures of him, the way he wore his hat? You could tell he had that don't-give-a-shit air about him."

"I don't recall his hat," Karen said, "but I've seen pictures of him lying dead, shot by Texas Rangers. Did you know he didn't have his shoes on?"

"Is that right?"

"They put a hundred and eighty-seven bullet holes in Clyde, Bonnie Parker and the car they were driving. Bonnie was eating a sandwich."

"You're full of interesting facts, aren't you?"

"It was in May 1934, near Gibsland, Louisiana."

"That's north Lou'siana," Foley said, "a long way from New Orleans, where I was born and raised. Once you leave the Big Easy you may as well be in Arkansas, where Buddy's from originally. He went up to Detroit to work in an auto plant once, but didn't care for it, moved to California. I remember seeing the movie—it was after I got out of Angola and started doing banks on my own. That part where they got shot? Warren Beatty and . . . I can't think of her name."

"Faye Dunaway. I loved her in *Network*."

"Yeah, she was good. I liked the guy saying he wasn't gonna take any more shit from anybody."

"Peter Finch," Karen said.

"Yeah, right. Anyway, that scene where Warren Beatty and Faye Dunaway get shot? I remember thinking at the time, it wouldn't be a bad way to go, if you have to."

"Bleeding on a county road," Karen said.

"It wasn't pretty after," Foley said, "no, but if you were in that car—eating a sandwich—you wouldn't have known what hit you."

"How'd you get the guard uniform?"

"Took it off a hack."

"You killed him?"

"No, hit him over the head—the most ignorant man I ever met in my life." He paused and said, "I should talk, after the stunt I pulled to get sent up this time. I'd just done a Barnett bank in Lake Worth. I'm on a side street waiting to turn left on Dixie Highway . . . It's a long story. The only reason I was even in Florida I was visiting somebody." He paused and said, "I better keep quiet."

"You robbed the bank," Karen said, "in your own car?"

"I wasn't that dumb. No, but then I got in a situation with the car . . . The dumbest thing I've ever done."

She felt Foley's fingertips moving idly on her thigh, his voice, quiet and close to her, saying, "You're sure easy to talk to. I wonder—say we met under different circumstances and got to talking—I wonder what would happen."

"Nothing," Karen said.

"I mean if you didn't know who I was."

"You'd tell me, wouldn't you?"

"See, that's what I mean you're easy to talk to. There isn't any bullshit, you speak your mind. Here you are locked up in the dark with a guy who's filthy, smells like a sewer, just busted out of prison and you don't even seem like you're scared. Are you?"

"Of course I am."

"You don't act like it."

"What do you want me to do, scream? I don't think it would help much."

Foley let his breath out and she felt it on her neck, almost like a sigh. He said, "I still think if we met under different circumstances, like in a bar . . ."

Karen said, "You have to be kidding."

After that, for a few miles, neither of them spoke until Foley said, "Another one Faye Dunaway was in I liked, *Three Days of the Condor*."

"With Robert Redford," Karen said, "when he was young. I *loved* it, the lines were so good. Faye Dunaway says—it's the next morning after they've slept together, even though she barely knows him, he asks if she'll do him a favor? And she says, 'Have I ever denied you anything?' "

Foley said, "Yeah . . ." and she waited for him to go on, but now the car was slowing down, coasting, then bumping along the shoulder of the road to a stop.

Karen got ready.

Foley said, "I don't know anymore'n you where we are."

Still out in the country, Karen was sure of that. Maybe halfway to West Palm, or a little more.

She heard the other one, Buddy, outside, say, "You still alive in there?"

The trunk lid raised.

Karen felt Foley's hands on her, then didn't feel them and heard him say, out of the trunk now, "Where in the hell are we?"

And heard Buddy say, "That's the turnpike up there. Glenn's waiting with a car."

Glenn.

Karen said the name to herself and stored it away.

As Foley was saying, "How do we get to it?"

"Over there, through the bushes." Buddy's voice. "You have to climb up the bank."

And now Foley, sounding closer this time, saying, "Come on out of there."

Karen pushed off, rolled from her right side to her left bringing up the Sig Sauer in both hands to put it on them, both standing in the opening, in the dark but right there, close. She said, "Get your hands up and turn around. *Now.*"

They were moving as she heard Foley say, "Shit," and saw the trunk lid coming down on her as she fired the .38 point-blank, fired again and fired again through the trunk lid slamming shut, locking her in with the deafening sound, again in the close dark.

They had moved so fast in opposite directions she didn't think she'd hit either one. She listened, but didn't hear a sound now, pretty sure they were getting her shotgun from the car and would be right back.

SIX

BUDDY SAID HE FORGOT SHE HAD A PIECE IN THERE—ALL that was going on—even saw her throw it back in the trunk when she brought out the shotgun. He said to Foley they may as well leave her, they were leaving the car and had to leave her someplace anyway, what was the difference where?

It was already set in Foley's mind she was going with them. He wasn't finished talking to her. He wanted to sit down with her in a nice place and talk like regular people. Start over, let her get a look at him cleaned up. Even if he had time he wouldn't be able to explain *why* he wanted to talk to her some more, that wasn't clear in his mind, so all he said was, "She's going with us."

Buddy gave him a funny look, a frown. He said, "Jesus Christ, what were you doing in there? I can understand you need to get laid, but you have Adele, don't you?"

"Get the shotgun," Foley said, "and her purse. I'd like to know who she is."

"I already looked," Buddy said. "Her name's Karen Sisco, like the Cisco Kid only spelled different, S-i-s-c-o."

Foley said, "Karen Sisco," nodding a couple of times. "I wonder if she's ever called that, the Sisco Kid."

Headlights would come at them from the direction of West Palm and they'd keep to the narrow space between the car and the concrete abutment of the overpass. A sheriff's office green-and-white went screaming past, gumballs flashing, then another one and another, a string of green-and-whites in the space of a minute, going out to chase after escaped convicts. No time for a car sitting dark under an overpass.

When the road quieted down Foley stepped up to the Chevy's trunk, keeping to the side of it, and banged on the sheet metal once with his fist.

"Karen? Be a good girl now, you hear? I'm gonna let you out."

Foley jumped at the sound of a pistol shot, muffled from inside the trunk but real, the bullet ripping through metal.

He yelled at her, "You're putting holes in your

car!" and looked up to see Buddy, with the shotgun and a black leather handbag, staring at him.

Foley took a moment to settle down before saying, "We're not leaving you. I'm gonna open the trunk enough for you to throw the gun out. Okay? You shoot—Buddy's got your shotgun, he says he'll shoot back if you do and I can't stop him. So it's up to you." Foley put his hand out and Buddy, still looking at him funny, gave him the keys.

They heard a voice yell "Hey!" Not from the trunk, a clear sound coming from somewhere above them.

"It's me, Glenn."

Foley stepped out in the open, Buddy close behind. They looked up to see a figure, head and shoulders against the evening sky, leaning on the concrete overpass rail.

"Hey, Jack, good to see you, man. The fuck're you guys shooting at?"

Buddy raised his voice saying, "We'll be there in a minute."

"I don't mean to complain," Glenn said, "but you know how long I've been here? Florida Highway Patrol comes by I'm fucked."

Foley looked at Buddy. "Do we need him?"

"Three green-and-whites saw us," Buddy said. "One of 'em starts thinking, What's that car doing there? Ties it to the break and turns around . . . We got to get out of here."

Foley, looking up at the overpass again, said, "Hey, Studs?" sounding surprised. "We thought you were somebody else."

Glenn straightened, tossing his hair out of his face. "Man, I haven't heard that since Lompoc."

Foley waited.

Glenn said, "You guys . . ." shaking his head now. "I'm risking my ass for you and I don't even know why."

"Sure you do," Foley said, making the effort to sound pleasant. "We're your heroes."

He walked back to the Chevy and banged on the trunk.

"You coming out?"

Foley stuck the key in the lock, standing right in front of the trunk, and turned to Buddy. Buddy walked up to the trunk and racked the pump on the shotgun. Foley said, close to the sheet metal, "You hear that?"

He turned the key and raised the trunk lid.

Karen, hunched in there, extended her arm, her hand holding the Sig Sauer auto by the barrel. She said, "You win, Jack."

Buddy gave him another funny look.

▼▼▼

IF HE LEANED OUT OVER THE RAIL GLENN COULD SEE PART OF the open trunk, Foley reaching a hand in to help someone get out. Jesus, a girl. Standing by the car now smoothing her skirt, touching her hair. Guy busts out of stir and picks up a girl? Now they were crossing the ditch into weeds and some bushes; he wouldn't see them again until they came up the grade. Or, she worked at the prison and Foley grabbed her, used her as a shield going out.

Glenn thought about it returning to the car he'd left on the grassy side of the road, trouble lights blinking just in case: a black Audi sedan he'd taken up to 137 miles an hour when he first hit the turnpike at Palm Beach Gardens.

Or, Buddy brought her for Foley and he was so horny he couldn't wait, gave her a jump in the trunk of the car. Not in the backseat with Buddy watching. It was a possibility. Except these two guys never lost their cool or acted crazy.

Glenn had gotten to know them at Lompoc USP, a twenty-four-year-old fish looking around for any reasonably intelligent guys who read books or at least weren't fucking morons. Buddy asked him what he was doing and Glenn said networking, trying to find out who he should know and who he should stay away from. Buddy said he meant how much time was he doing. Oh, two to five, Glenn said, for grand theft auto, but it looked now like he was doing the whole five. He didn't explain that until later. What he told them was he stole Porsche and Mercedes top-of-the-line models he picked up on special order and delivered anywhere in the U.S. with clean titles. He told them he'd spot the car a customer wanted and use a slim jim or lemon pop to get in, a slap hammer to yank the ignition, a side kick to extract steering column locks and usually liquid nitrogen to freeze the alarm system.

See if that impressed them.

Foley said between him and Buddy they'd boosted three to four hundred cars in their time, but never sold any or kept them for more than a couple of hours.

These were cool guys for hicks, both fairly tall and stringy, Buddy with dark curly hair that was always slicked back—he kept a comb in his pocket—and looked wet. Foley's light-brown hair was short and thick enough he could do okay combing it with his fingers. Foley smoked cigarettes, Buddy dipped Skoal, stuck it behind his lower lip. They didn't seem in great shape—they'd rather watch than work out—but both had that hard-boned look, like they'd worked construction or in oil fields all their lives instead of robbing banks. Easygoing but looked you right in the fucking eye when you spoke to them or they had something to say.

Glenn stayed close to them and was never seriously approached by any perverts or butt fuckers. Foley said, "Don't take it up 'less you think you might like it." Buddy said, "What you do, just say no, then kill the guy." They watched each other's backs and never had any trouble they weren't able to stare down, giving ill-tempered assholes a calm look that said, Fuck with us, man, at your own risk.

Glenn believed they let him hang around because he was from L.A., West Hollywood, he knew what was happening, had even spent a couple of years at Berkeley but never copped a superior attitude. He'd tell them stories about when he was in the car-detailing business and got laid a lot: how he'd work on cars at these multimillion-dollar homes in Beverly Hills and wait for the lady of the house to make the move. Get asked in for a cold drink, a dip in the pool? It happened, man, more often than you'd think, couple of times even with movie stars. This was when they started calling him Studs.

One day in the yard Glenn said, "I'm gonna tell you guys something only one other person here knows about. I was originally at FPC, the camp over there? And was transferred here with another guy for trying to escape."

See what they thought.

"You know Maurice Miller in the boxing program they call Snoopy? Fights lightweight? He was at FPC doing a gig for fraud, I think credit cards. Anyway, we went out one night jogging, like Snoopy's doing road work and I'm his trainer. We made it almost all the way to Vandenberg and got picked up by air base MPs. They thought we were a-wol."

Buddy asked him was he nuts? Do an easy two or even less of his two-to-five at the country club, cable TV, salad bar in the chow hall, and he'd be out. Now he'd have to do the whole five.

"In an altogether different kind of mind-fucking incarceration," Glenn said. "I knew if we didn't make it Snoopy and I'd get sent here or some other max joint. There're some scary fucking slams you can get sent to, Marion, Lewisburg . . . Maybe I was pumped, a little overanxious, but at the time I didn't worry about getting caught. See, what happened, I got next to a guy over at FPC doing three years on a felony-conspiracy thing, strictly white collar. He got the three years and was fined—listen to this—fifty million dollars and wrote 'em a fucking check. Like that, fifty mil, signed his name."

Foley said, "One of the Wall Street scammers," and he was right. He said, "I remember reading about the guy. Went up for insider trading. Paid off snitch brokers to give him information on stock deals before they went down. Like takeovers." Telling this to Buddy, who didn't know shit. "A company buys out another company and the bought company's stock goes up. So if you have the inside scoop, you know it's gonna happen, you buy in just before it goes up and then sell when the stock peaks."

This fucking guy Foley, never even went to college.

"That's basically what he did," Glenn said, "made a fortune."

"Everybody thought the guy was a genius," Foley said, "till they found out he made it the old-fashioned way, he stole it."

"Anyway," Glenn said, "here's a multimillionaire making eleven cents an hour mopping floors, sweeping the tennis courts . . . Guy that used to be on the phone he said eighteen hours a day, had over a hundred extensions in his office, now has to stand in line to make a call. But the thing I'm getting at, the guy loved to talk."

"Yeah, to the U.S. attorney," Foley said. "He rolled over on all the snitches he was doing business with and got 'em brought up. I can't think of the guy's name."

Glenn waited.

And Foley said, "Ripley. Richard Ripley. Called Dick the Ripper on account of how he ripped off the stock market. Big good-looking guy, but I think he wore a rug."

"Not at FPC," Glenn said. "He was vain, though. What he talked about most of the time, outside of the market, was himself, and I listened. Anybody that can write a check for fifty mil, he says *any-*

thing, I'm all fucking ears. See, my bunk was right above his. I was polite, I played kiss-ass to a degree, I'd stand in the phone line for him; we're out gardening I'd do the stoop work and let him rake . . . All this time he's talking about what a high roller he is and I'm taking it all in. I learn he's got money in foreign banks, plus, around five mil in hard cash, *plus*, loose diamonds and gold coins, a shitload of coins worth around four bills each. The man actually told me, five mil in cash. He said, quote, 'Where I can put my hands on it anytime I want.' Nothing to it."

Foley said, "He keeps it at home?"

Buddy said, "Yeah, where's the guy live?"

Glenn hesitated and Foley said, "He must've been getting out soon."

"He's out now. It was in the paper."

"I mean when you and Snoopy jogged away from FPC. You mentioned you were anxious. It sounds like you wanted to get to Ripley's house before he got his release. Is that it, you couldn't wait?"

"You might say I was highly motivated," Glenn said. "Five mil sitting there waiting? All I have to do is walk out? No fence, no gun towers. The only thing to stop anybody from leaving is a sign that says Off Limits. Man, once I was pumped up—listen, they would've had to fucking chain me to a wall to keep me there."

"But you didn't make it," Foley said, "you and Snoopy. You know he was Maurice 'Mad Dog' Miller back when he was a pro? Now you pet him he goes down."

"I didn't bring him along as a bodyguard," Glenn said. "Maurice happens to live in Detroit, the same place Ripley has his home. No, the Snoop isn't any protection, but he knows the Motor City."

"So does Buddy," Foley said, "if a guide's all you need."

Neither one of them showing much interest, that time in the yard at Lompoc USP, five years ago.

▼▼▼

GLENN GOT HIS RELEASE AND MOVED TO FLORIDA, SECOND only to California in the number of cars stolen, but better: car thieves were hustled through the system and hardly ever had to do time. So if he ever wanted to get back in the business . . .

He tried to keep in touch with the bank robbers, still at Lompoc, wrote to them a few times but never heard back, not a word. So when Buddy called a few weeks ago it came as a total surprise.

Buddy saying it was a good thing he'd hung on to the letters and wasn't it a small world: he'd just arrived in Florida and Foley was here, out at GCI the past five months. The way Buddy put it, "He don't like it there and sees a way to bust out. If you aren't doing anything, you want to drive one of the cars? Take a few hours of your time is all."

If he wasn't doing anything.

Glenn said, well, he'd been up to Detroit on a deal, but at the moment was free. He said, "Yeah, I think I can make it." You had to be as cool as these guys.

"De-troit," Buddy said, "I spent three years on the line up there at Chrysler Jefferson till I went crazy and had to quit. Let me ask you—you don't see a problem might come out of delivering your special orders?"

"I'm not in that business anymore," Glenn said. "No, I went there to look up a friend. You remember Dick the Ripper we used to talk about, the Wall Street crook?"

"Wrote a check for fifty million," Buddy said, "you bet I remember him."

"My first visit I look up Snoopy. Maurice Miller at Lompoc, the lightweight?"

"He isn't brain-dead yet?"

"He's a manager now, for some club fighters. I gave him a hundred to check out Ripley for me, where he lives and all. See, I never did tell the Snoop, even back at Lompoc, exactly what it was about, so he wouldn't know enough to try on his own. The next time I go up the Snoop's gonna show me where Ripley lives and maybe where he's got an office."

Buddy said, "How's a punchy little colored guy find all that out?"

"He's a crook," Glenn said, surprised Buddy would ask. "He's into credit cards, bank fraud with bogus checks, the Snoop knows his way around."

"That's interesting," Buddy said, "but what I need to know is if you're clean. You been into anything else?"

Glenn hesitated. "I wasn't what you'd call *in*to anything, no."

"But what?"

He hesitated again.

And Buddy said, "Take your time."

"Okay. DEA happened to pull a raid on a house in Lake Worth. Nobody's home. They look around, find ten keys of base in the garage, actually in a Mercedes that happens to have my prints on the steering wheel and partials on the door handle. I'm picked up, I tell them there's no fucking way my prints could be on that car, and I say I want a lawyer. But then after a while I realize they *could* be my prints, and you know how they got there? Parking cars. Two nights a week I worked valet at a place, Charlie's Crab, and I must've parked the Mercedes sometime during the previous weekend. I tell the DEA guys, they give me their fucking bored look. Ten days I'm locked up, have to appear twice in federal court. The first time's a bond hearing, a joke, like I can post a hundred grand. The next one's like a show-cause hearing. Okay, but by this time the public defender has actually checked and found out the car was at Charlie's Crab the night before; they still have the ticket with the license number on it. The magistrate, a lovely, intelligent woman, dismissed the charge and ate the ass out of the assistant U.S. attorney for being overzealous."

Buddy said, "Nothing else pending?"

"Nothing. How about if I go see Foley?"

"You don't want your name on the visitors list out there. Sit tight till you hear from me."

"You talk to him," Glenn said, "see if he remembers Dick the Ripper. I'd still like you guys to go in with me. You think you might be interested?"

Buddy didn't comment right out and say if they would or not.

Glenn had seen him three times since that phone call. At a bar in West Palm near Glenn's apartment. A hotel in Miami Beach, a dump, where Foley's ex-wife lived. Adele. About forty but not bad looking. Glenn stopped by to see her another time that had nothing to do with the great escape: see if he could get her to put out without begging or buying her dinner. And the third time when Buddy drove him out to Glades Correctional, showed the route he'd take once he had Foley in the car, and where Glenn would be waiting with the second car.

Right here.

Twenty minutes with the Audi parked off to the

side of the turnpike's southbound lanes, trouble lights blinking, a note stuck in the side window that said GONE TO GET GAS, Glenn waiting now among scrub pines and palmettos a good fifty feet from the car. If any approaching headlights turned out to be a trooper, Glenn would be out of there, through the trees and down the grade—about where they should be coming up now, with the girl Foley must've used as a hostage. But what good was she doing him now? He should've left her in the trunk of the car. A few more minutes passed before he heard them coming.

SEVEN

KAREN TOLD FOLEY, CLIMBING THE BANK IN THE DARK, IT would be a lot easier if he'd quit hanging onto her. He let go of her arm and dropped back a couple of steps saying he was only trying to help, so she wouldn't slip in the weeds and fall. Karen said, "You mean and ruin my good suit?" The back and the sleeves stained with his muck, the skirt snagging now in the brush. He said he didn't want her to hurt herself. Karen hoped she'd be able to tell about it later. The conversation in a trunk full of handcuffs and tactical gear with a bank robber escaped convict who wondered if it would be different if they'd met in a bar. Like a first date, getting to know one another. Her dad would love it. "And then what happened?"

That was a good question.

▼▼▼

FOLEY STAYED BEHIND HER NOW LOOKING AT HER SLIM FIGure, her legs at eye level in the short skirt that hiked up on her, tight against her rear end as she climbed the grade. Buddy was up ahead. Foley said, "Have your clothes cleaned and send me the bill," wanting to say something to her, keep it light, but he felt awkward with her now, tense.

She said, "I'll send it to you at Glades."

Still not acting scared.

They reached the top of the grade to move through the scrub and now he could see the car, amber lights blinking. He didn't see Glenn until he heard him.

"Jesus, what'd you crawl through, a sewer?"

Standing at the edge of the trees with Buddy saying to him then, "That's a white car?"

"What's the difference? It's the only one here."

Glenn had on sunglasses and a limp, ratty-looking raincoat that hung long on him, open, over a T-shirt and jeans cut off at the knees.

Foley said, "Take your sunglasses off," his tone mild, Karen Sisco standing only a few feet away.

"I see better with them on," Glenn said.

"I'd take 'em off," Foley said, "before they get stepped on." He was aware of Karen turning to look at him, but kept his eyes on Glenn, who gave a shrug, took the glasses off and stuck them in his jeans.

"Wait in the car," Foley said.

Glenn didn't move. He said, "You're out in civilization now, man, ease up."

"I'd like you to go wait in the car," Foley said. "How's that? Take her with you and put her in back."

Glenn said, "In the trunk?"

"The backseat."

"What do you need her for?"

Foley stared at him, waiting.

Glenn said, "Busting out of stir can fuck up your nerves, can't it? I know, I've been there. But I'm hanging my ass out for you, man. I don't need any get-in-the-car shit. I'm here, but I don't fucking have to *be* here."

Buddy said, "Be cool, Studs. Are you cool? Go on, quit talking so much."

"Studs," Glenn said. "Now we're old pals again, back in the yard at Lompoc. How come that seems like such a long time ago?" He motioned to Karen saying, "Come on, have to do what I'm told."

She walked past Foley without looking at him and he said, "Wait a minute," to Glenn. "Let me have your raincoat." He said, "Somebody forgot to bring me clean clothes," looking at Buddy with a straight face.

He didn't get it. He said, "I brought 'em, they're

back at Glades in the Cadillac. You wanted to take her car . . ."

And Karen said, "You can blame me if you want. I don't mind."

What Foley wanted was to tell them he was kidding, for Christ sake, he wasn't blaming anyone, he was trying to lighten up, get rid of this awkward feeling he had. And since he couldn't do that he kept his mouth shut and watched Karen walk over to Glenn as he was slipping the raincoat off.

Glenn saying, "Here you are, sir," folding the raincoat once and then rolling it up. He threw the coat to land in the weeds at Foley's feet. Glenn got his sunglasses out of his jeans then, put them on and took Karen by the arm toward the car.

Foley watching them.

Close to him Buddy said, "What's wrong with you?"

Foley didn't answer, watching Glenn and Karen standing by the car now, Glenn talking to her, Karen as tall as he was, facing him, listening, Glenn looking back this way before opening the door. Now Karen looked over, ducked her head and got in the backseat.

▼▼▼

SHE WATCHED GLENN WALK AROUND THE FRONT OF THE CAR to the other side, open the door and slide in behind the wheel, the inside light on, Karen getting a look at him before he pulled the door closed. Glenn half turned now, laying his arm along the top of the seats. He hunched a little to look out the side window, running his hand through his hair.

"Like I said, I walked away from a prison myself one time, out in California, so I know what it can do to your nerves, being a wanted fugitive. But if he thinks he can talk to me like that . . . Shit, I've been here over a half hour watching headlights coming this way, hoping to Christ they don't stop and it's the Florida Highway Patrol, if you think that's fun. I even smoked a doob lurking there in the fucking bushes. I wouldn't mind another one, either, right now. How about you?" He turned his head enough to look at her, at the same time running his fingers through his hair. "You must be scared shitless, get in a situation like this. You heard me ask him what he's gonna do with you? He wouldn't say. You know why? He doesn't know himself. In stir, he's as cool as they come; but you get a guy like that outside, now he's a fugitive, he's too fucking wired to think straight. Is he gonna let you go or shoot you? It's too bad, but I guess you were in the wrong fucking place at the wrong time. I imagine you just got offa work . . ." He turned to stare out the window again.

Karen leaned forward to have a look. She saw them against the dark foliage, one holding her shotgun, the other, Foley—it looked like he was unbuttoning his shirt, working at it, his head lowered. They seemed to be talking.

"What I mean is you can be the man inside," Glenn said, still watching them, Karen sitting back now, "but out in the world, if you don't know where you're going, man, you're fucked. I came out, took a trip up north and I had something laid out. I mean something big. The kind, one score, you retire. I'd go do it right now, except it's so fucking cold up there in January." He paused for a moment and said, "You know what he's doing? Taking off that filthy uniform. He's gonna put my raincoat on and ruin it. I bought it at a flea market out in West Broward, ten bucks. It's old but, shit, it's a genuine mackintosh. Now I'll have to have it cleaned. It didn't do me much good in Detroit, I froze my ass off and that was in November. California, all the time I was out there I never even *owned* a raincoat. Come to sunny Florida—I wasn't here for Andrew, but everybody was talking about it so much, and then the end of last summer it started raining like hell, the beginning of hurricane season, so I bought a raincoat. That flea market, any time you go out there it's full of Haitians buying all kinds of shit, radios that don't work, clothes, even canned goods. I'm not kidding."

Karen said, "Glenn?"

His head turned and she was looking at his designer shades, small oval lenses in a gold wire frame.

"You don't remember me, do you?"

She watched him hesitate, uncertain.

He said, "It couldn't have been out at Glades, if that's what you're thinking. I was never out there."

Karen shook her head.

He raised his hand to stroke his hair away from his face. "But you're sure we've met, huh?"

"A couple of times."

"Is that right? Where?"

"Last fall," Karen said, "I drove you from the Palm Beach county jail to the federal courthouse, twice. You're Glenn Michaels. I never forget anyone I've cuffed and shackled."

He didn't move or say a word, staring at her now like he'd been turned to stone.

Karen said, "Let's think for a minute, Glenn, see if we can work this out. Is there a gun in the car?"

▼▼▼

FOLEY HAD HIS HEAD DOWN, CHIN ON HIS CHEST, FINGERS working at a button caked with muck. Buddy, watching him, said, "You're pulling at it. If you want to do that—here." He laid the shotgun in the grass, came up to take the guard shirt in his two hands and ripped it open, popping buttons and tearing the shirt. He wiped his hands on his khaki pants as Foley threw the shirt in the bushes, picked up the raincoat and put it on.

"Why you brought Glenn," Foley said, "I'll never know."

"Since I got so many friends here," Buddy said. "He came through and you treat him like shit."

"He wants something. It's the only reason he's here. He gets picked up doing one of his cars, he'll make a deal and give us up."

"He talks too much, that's all."

"That's what I'm saying."

"Get rid of the cap."

"I don't know why, but every time he opens his mouth I want to punch him out."

"He ain't the problem, Jack."

"Look. I couldn't leave her in the trunk. And that's all I can tell you."

"You don't want to leave her here, either."

"She's *in* the car. You want to go or stand here talking about it?"

"I have a choice? Okay, first take your head out of your ass, then tell me why you want to bring her."

Buddy waited.

"You gonna tell me?"

"It's hard to explain," Foley said.

▼▼▼

She touched his arm, leaning in close like she was creeping up on him and Glenn turned away, all the way around to look straight ahead, get out of her face, Jesus, and try to *think*. He wanted to know what Foley and Buddy were doing, if they were coming, but didn't want to look to find out. He had planned to tell them, when they got in the car, he'd had the Audi up to one-thirty-seven in less than half a mile; German iron, it *cruised*, man . . . She said his name.

She said, "Glenn, don't think, okay?" Knowing that's what he was trying to do. She said, "Just listen. You're in a tough spot, but I think I can help you."

He said, "Hey, wait a minute . . ." but didn't know what to say after that. She asked him again if there was a gun in the car. The way she put it this time, "Do we have a gun in the car?" *We*. Like they were together in this. He remembered her voice now from before, riding in the GMC van. She had a nice voice and never raised it, not even when she was in some moron's face who was giving her a hard time. He remembered you could bullshit with her about different things, this girl no older than he was. She said his name again.

She said, "Glenn, Foley's not going to make it. You said yourself he's too fucking wired to think straight. And if he goes down . . . Glenn, you go with him." She touched his shoulder and he jumped. She said, "If I had hair like yours, all that body, I'd never have to put it up." She said, "I can understand if you and Foley are close . . ."

"We're *not*. I'm helping him, yeah . . ."

She stopped him. "Wait. *Have* you helped him, Glenn? At this point, technically, I doubt you could be charged with aiding a fugitive. So you still have a choice." She said, "You can help him and risk going down again, get cuffed and shackled, hope to God you pull a reasonable judge, not some hard-on. Or, if you want to play it another way . . ."

She paused and Glenn said, "How?"

▼▼▼

"ALL THE TIME WE'RE IN THE TRUNK," FOLEY SAID, "WE'RE talking, we're getting along, you might say."

Buddy said, "Jesus Christ," turning his head, as if he didn't want to hear it.

"Listen to me, all right? I kept wondering if she and I had met, you know, under normal circumstances like at a cocktail lounge . . ." He stopped, running out of words, Buddy staring at him again.

"You want to take her up to my place," Buddy said, "and get cleaned up? You come out of the bathroom with your after-shave on and she goes, 'Oh, I had you all wrong'?"

"I want to talk to her again, that's all."

Buddy kept staring at him.

"You're too late, Jack. You're what you are, clean or dirty. The best either of us can do is look at nice pretty girls and think, well, if we had done it different . . ."

Foley began to say—he wasn't sure what, *something*; repeat himself, not wanting to give up? He heard Glenn start the car and looked over to see the headlights pop on.

"He wants to go," Buddy said, "get out of here, and I don't blame him."

They walked toward the car.

Then stopped and watched as it took off, tires squealing as the rubber hit pavement. They watched the taillights until they were out of sight down the turnpike, neither of them saying a word.

EIGHT

At good Samaritan they told Karen she was lucky, all she had was a concussion, but they'd keep her here till tomorrow, do a few more tests to make sure.

Her dad came with newspapers and magazines to camp here and watch over his little girl. Milt Dancey, her supervisor, came up from Miami to stand by her bed for two hours. Flowers came. Ray Nicolet came, he kissed Karen on the cheek and touched her hair but could only stay a few minutes; he was on the Violent Crimes Task Force hunting the escapees. More flowers came. When Daniel Burdon, FBI special agent, arrived he asked her dad to please wait outside, they had some business to do here. He had in his hand a copy of the statement Karen had dictated to a court reporter that morning. It was midafternoon now, sunny outside, the private room pleasant enough, flower arrangements gathering along the window ledge.

Burdon asked her, "What's in the IV?"

"I think just glucose."

"You sweet enough, Karen. Tell me how you got the bump on your head."

"Isn't that my report?"

"Read it," Milt said. "That's why you have a copy."

"I *have* read it. What I want is to hear Karen tell it, if it's all right with her," Burdon said. "I don't give a shit if it's all right with you, Milt, or it isn't all right. You don't even have to be in the room. This is my investigation."

Karen's gaze moved from the black special agent who looked like a lawyer to the overweight old-boy marshal who was all cop, and said, "Don't hit him, Milt, Daniel's being important. I don't mind."

Burdon smiled at her. "I love the way you talk, Karen, like you one of the boys. So tell me what happened. You tried to grab the wheel—where was this?"

"Coming to the Okeechobee exit. I wanted to get to a phone and thought of the tollbooth. We went off the exit ramp, down the grade and I guess hit the abutment."

"Must not've had your seat belt on."

Milt said, "For Christ sake . . ."

"No, but I did think about it," Karen said, "once

I was in the front seat. I climbed over . . ." Swung her leg over the seat in the tight skirt and told Glenn not to look. Actually told him that, Don't look. And smiled for just a moment remembering it. Burdon was frowning at her. She said, "Glenn had it up to a hundred and twenty, blowing past cars . . . I don't mean when we went off the road. As soon as I saw the exit and grabbed the wheel, he hit the brakes. We were going about fifty when we went off."

"When he had it up to speed," Burdon said, "where was he going in such a hurry?"

"He didn't know, he was running, getting away. I tried to talk to him. I said, 'Look, if you come in with me you'll be okay. You haven't really done anything yet.' "

Burdon said, "Hadn't *done* anything? The man conspired to aid a fugitive and he's driving a stolen car."

"I told him not to worry about the car; you have to be brought up on grand theft at least three times before you go down, and even then it isn't a sure thing. Forty thousand cars stolen last year in Dade County, three thousand arrests and half of them never went to court."

"Recite all those stats to him," Burdon said, "it sounds like you're aiding and abetting."

"I wanted to bring him in."

"After you piled up, you didn't see him?"

"The next thing I knew, the paramedics were taking me out of the car."

"And nobody else saw him," Burdon said, "that we know of."

Milt stepped in again. "That's all. Leave her alone now."

Burdon raised his hand to the marshal without looking at him. "There a couple of points I keep wondering about have to do with the two guys that grabbed you. Buddy is it? And this fella Jack Foley. I looked him up, I swear the man must've robbed two hundred banks in his time."

Karen said, "Really?" Impressed, but sounding tired. "I asked him how many, he said he wasn't sure. He's been doing it since he was eighteen."

"You talked to him, uh?"

"In the trunk, yeah."

"What'd you talk about?"

"Oh . . . different things, prison, movies."

"This fella has you hostage, you talk about movies?"

"It was an unusual experience," Karen said, looking right at Burdon, the dude Bureau man in his neat gray suit, pale blue shirt and necktie. "But I wasn't a hostage."

"What were you then?"

"I was his treat after five months of servitude."

Burdon frowned. "He assaulted you, sexually?"

"I wasn't that kind of a treat," Karen said.

Now Burdon was studying her lying there in her hospital gown, sheet up to her chest, something dripping from the IV into her arm. Maybe he didn't know where to go with it now, and Karen felt no desire to help him.

"Wanted to be close to a woman, so he crawled in the trunk with you."

"I don't know," Karen said, looking up at Burdon, standing ten feet tall by the bed.

He said, "Foley made me think of that fella Carl Tillman, the one you were seeing, it turns out the same time he was doing banks. You recall that? I said at the time it was a highly unusual situation, find out a U.S. marshal's fucking a bank robber." He smiled, just a little. "See, then you let this guy Foley get away, I couldn't help but wonder, you know?"

"What?"

"If bank robbers turn you on."

"You're serious."

"Maybe. I'm not sure I am or not."

"When I was seeing Carl Tillman, I didn't know he robbed banks."

"Yeah, but I had enough reason to believe he did, and I told you. So you had to at least suspect him."

Karen said, "And what happened to Carl?"

Burdon smiled again. "The time came, you shot him. But you didn't shoot Foley or the guy with him. They're unarmed, you had a shotgun and you let them throw you in the trunk. Okay, now you got your Sig in your hand. You say in the report you couldn't turn around, he had you pinned down. But when the trunk opened, how come you didn't cap the two guys then?"

Karen said, "Is that what you would've done?"

"You say in the report Glenn didn't have a gun, but you let him get away."

Karen said, "Daniel, you're not carrying, are you?"

He hesitated. "How do you know that?"

"What do you work on most of the time, fraud? You go after crooked bookkeepers?"

"Karen, I've been with the Bureau fifteen years, on all kinds of investigations."

"Have you ever shot a man? How many times have you been primary through the door?"

"I have to qualify, is that it?"

"You have to know what you're talking about."

She watched him shrug and start to turn away, smoothing the front of his gray double-breasted suit. He paused and said, "We'll talk another time, Karen. All right? I'd like to know why Foley put you in that second car when he didn't need you anymore."

"You'll have to ask him," Karen said.

"Sounds to me he liked having you around. I'll see you, Karen." Burdon turned and walked out.

A few moments later her dad came in as Milt

Dancey was saying, "The white man's Burdon. That's what we call him in Miami."

Her dad said, "That's what everybody calls him in Miami, Miami Beach, the Metro-Dade guys. He's got a knack for pissing people off."

"Yeah, but he's got style," Karen said. "You notice that suit he had on?"

"That combination," her dad said, "it reminded me of the way Fred Astaire used to dress, the shirt and tie the same shade. There was a guy with style, Fred Astaire." He said, "How you feeling? You hungry, you want something to eat? How about a beer? I can go out and get some."

"Tomorrow," Karen said. "I'm not supposed to do anything for at least a week. I was wondering, how about if I stay with you a few days? We'd finally have time to talk."

"About what?" Her dad cocked his head looking at her. "These guys you let get away? You want to use me, don't you? Get me to work for nothing."

"You're my *dad*."

"So?"

▼▼▼

FOLEY HELD IN HIS HAND A CREDIT APPLICATION BROCHURE that said on the cover in bold letters:

LOOKING FOR MONEY?

YOU'VE COME TO THE RIGHT PLACE.

There were headings inside the piece that mentioned auto loans, home loans, lifestyle loans, but nothing about getting-out-of-town loans. Foley folded the brochure and put it in his pocket. Now he continued to study the bank layout, standing at the glasstop counter in the middle of the floor, where the forms were kept. There were tellers at three of the five windows, cameras mounted high on the wall behind them, no security guard in sight, a customer leaving and one coming in, a guy in a suit with an attaché case. Foley watched him move through the gate into the fenced-off business area at the front of the bank, where one of the executives rose from his desk, shook the guy's hand and they both sat down. As the guy began opening his case, Foley, wearing a brand-new Marlins baseball cap and sunglasses, crossed to the teller window where a nameplate on the counter said this young woman with a pile of dark hair smiling at him was Loretta.

She said, "How can I help you, sir?"

Foley said, "Loretta, you see that guy talking to your manager, has his case open?"

She said, "That's Mr. Guindon, one of our assistant managers. Our manager is Mr. Schoen, but he's not in today."

"But you see the guy," Foley said, "with the attaché case?"

Loretta looked over. "Yes?"

"That's my partner. He has a gun in there. And if you don't do exactly what I tell you, or you give me any kind of a problem, I'll look over at my partner and he'll shoot your Mr. Guindon between the eyes. Now take one of those big envelopes and put as many hundreds, fifties and twenties as you can pack into it. Nothing with bank straps or rubber bands, I don't want any dye packs, I don't want any bait money. Start with the second drawer and then the one over there, under the computer. Come on, Loretta, let's go. Don't be nervous, the key's right there next to you. No bills off the bottom of the drawer. That's the way, you're doing fine. The twenties go in if there's room. Smile, so you won't look like you're being held up. Here, give me the twenties, I'll put 'em in my pocket. Okay, I haven't had to give my partner a sign; that's good. Now, he's gonna wait thirty seconds till after I'm out the door, make sure you haven't slipped me a dye pack or set off the alarm. If you have, he's gonna shoot Mr. Guindon between the eyes. Okay? I think that'll do it. Thank you, Loretta, and have a nice day."

Foley walked out the front entrance with his head lowered and his knees bent. Some banks put a mark on the doorway at six feet, so the teller, watching the guy go out, can estimate his height.

Buddy was waiting for him across Collins Avenue in a black Honda. Foley got in and as they drove off Buddy said, "You're a better man than I am, Gunga Din. Bust out one day and back to work the next."

"Lompoc," Foley said, "you picked me up and we did the bank in Pomona the same day." He was quiet then, looking out the window at pink hotels, white ones, yellow ones, all past their prime but still doing business. He said, "I always feel a letdown after."

"Once you start breathing again," Buddy said. Foley handed him the brochure he'd taken and Buddy smiled. " 'Looking for money? You've come to the right place.' They got that right. It's like they're asking for it. I can't figure out how nine out of ten bank robbers get caught."

"They talk about it," Foley said, "or do something dumb, call attention to themselves. The time I did the bank in Lake Worth for Adele and ended up in Glades? I drove away from the bank and cut through side streets till I came to Dixie Highway. I'm waiting for traffic to clear so I can make a left, I hear this car behind me revving its engine, guy in a red Firebird Trans Am, can't wait. He backs up about ten feet, guns it, cuts around me, tires screaming—it's like he thinks I'm one of those retirees, takes forever to make a turn. I'd just robbed a fucking bank and this guy in the Firebird's showing me what a hotdog he is."

"So you went after him," Buddy said.

"I made the left and *tore* after him. Caught him about a mile down the road and came up on the driver's side, close, seeing how close I could come while I stared at him, gave him the look. He pulled ahead, I came up again and this time I gave him a nudge, sideswiped him. I was in a Honda, I think just like this one."

"I read it's the number one choice of car thieves," Buddy said, "your Honda."

"Yeah, I read that, too. Anyway, what happened, when I sideswiped the guy I blew a tire and fucked up the steering, the car kept going to the right, so I had to pull over. The guy in the Firebird—I don't think he had any idea what this was about—he's gone. I wasn't there two minutes a sheriff's radio car pulls up. 'What seems to be the trouble, sir?' No trouble, I just robbed a bank and my fucking car broke down. Outside of that . . . He's checking my license when he gets a report about the bank—somebody spotted the car—so the next time I see him he's pointing a big chromed-up Smith and Wesson in my face. The only time I can ever remember losing my temper like that and I draw thirty to life."

"Time goes by," Buddy said, "you'll think it's a funny story."

"If I'm still around."

"I'll tell my sister, see if she laughs," Buddy said. "I have to think of things to say to her before making the weekly call, otherwise we have these long pauses."

"Between your weather reports," Foley said.

Going over the causeway at Haulover Cut, Foley threw his brand-new Marlins baseball cap out the window. A few minutes later they dropped the Honda off at a strip mall and picked up Buddy's car—an '89 Olds Cutlass Supreme in faded maroon he'd paid cash for in L.A., costing him, Buddy said, a bank job and change.

▼▼▼

FOLEY SAT IN THE MIDDLE OF AN IMITATION DANISH SOFA IN a room with bare white walls, a TV set and house plants Buddy had bought. The currency from the bank, counted now, was on the coffee table in a single neat stack he could press into a wad that would be not much more than two inches thick. Foley raised his voice to tell Buddy, out on the concrete balcony reading the paper, "Thirty-seven eighty. That Loretta's all right." He got up and walked out into the sunshine. "She could lose some weight, though, do something with her hair."

Buddy said, "You see your picture? They pass this one around you can go anywhere you want, nobody'll know you."

"The straight-ahead mug shot, I wasn't feeling my best that day, I look like some kind of terrorist.

The one of Chino, he must've been thirty pounds heavier then." Foley was looking down at the newspaper Buddy held open, at the seven head-shots in a row across the front page, beneath a color photo of the red-brick prison. "Chirino, that's Chino. He must've put the weight on right after he quit fighting, then got back in shape to make his run. Linares, the cute one, that's Lulu, Chino's girl-friend."

"They're the only two made it," Buddy said. " 'Four were shot down outside the fence in a hail of gunfire.' All doing twenty-five to life for murder. Your pal Chino, it says he hacked a guy to death with a machete."

"He was in a bind," Foley said, "owed a lot of money and got forced into throwing a fight. Only he didn't go down in the fourth, when he's sup-pose to—couldn't bring himself to do it, fighting this white kid—and waited till the sixth. Not only the guy wouldn't pay him, the promoter, Chino says the dive fucked up his chance of ever going for the title. A few years later he's done. So he got a machete, went to the Fifth Street Gym, Miami Beach, and used it on the promoter."

Buddy said, "Linares . . ."

"That's Lulu."

"Yeah. It says he had an argument with his roommate over a bag of marijuana and shot him nine times in the head with a MAC-10. Jesus."

"While the guy was sleeping," Foley said. "I think there was more to it than the grass. Like jealousy. Chino says Lulu was straight before he met him, but I don't believe it. He was too good at being a girl."

"It says they're concentrating the search for him and Chirino in Miami's Little Havana."

"Where're they looking for me?"

"I haven't come to you."

Foley put on his sunglasses. He moved to the concrete railing to look out at the ocean and the beach and, directly below, the building's patio and pool area, seven floors down, everything pink and white.

"They mention Pupko? That's the guard gave me his shirt."

Buddy looked up from the paper. "I thought you read this."

"I skimmed it. The diagram of where they tunneled out from the chapel's pretty accurate."

"Here it is, Pupko. Says he was overpowered by the escapees. 'Suspicious when he saw them going in the chapel, Pupko confronted the inmates . . .' Wanted to know why they weren't in their dorm for the evening count. 'While he was held immobile Pupko was struck repeatedly by inmate John Michael Foley'—there you are—'using a two-by-four from the construction site. Foley later made his escape in Pupko's uniform.' It says you were doing thirty for armed robbery."

"I wasn't armed that time. I didn't hit the guard repeatedly, either. One swing, he went down. Chino reads that, he's gonna get the wrong idea."

"FBI, sheriff's office, Florida Department of Law Enforcement are all out looking for you, but it doesn't say where. They think you may 'flee the country.' "

"I've had to run like hell a few times," Foley said, "but I don't think I've done any fleeing. You ever flee?"

"Yeah, I read one time I fled the scene of a robbery. I don't see anything about Glenn."

Foley waited, watching him now.

"They found the girl's Chevy, at the Holiday Inn on Southern, right where we left it. Nothing about the car we picked up there. It says the Chevrolet was taken from the GCI parking lot . . ."

"Nothing about Karen?"

"I'm coming to it. 'The car, property of the U.S. Marshals Service . . .' Here. 'Deputy Marshal Karen Sisco had driven from her office in West Palm Beach to GCI to serve a Summons and Complaint filed by one of the inmates.' It doesn't say anything about . . . No, here it is. 'Authorities believe Foley used the car in his escape and left it at the Holiday Inn.' "

"Where he took a hot shower and went to bed,"

Foley said. "Why don't they know we took her with us? Maybe they do, but for some reason they're not saying."

"There's nothing about me," Buddy said. "No mention of aiding in the escape. How come? I mean if she got away the cops'd know about me, right?"

"She got away from *us*, yeah."

But what happened after she drove off with Glenn?

He had thought about her last night, trying to fall asleep on the hard sofa, and had thought about her all day. Now he was thinking about her again, looking out at the ocean.

Buddy said, "It's pretty here, isn't it? If you like looking at views. I don't think you should go out anymore. I mean for a couple of weeks, anyway. You got the need to do a bank out of your system. Fell off your horse and got right back on. I was thinking we could hire a boat to take us to the Bahamas for a while. Get one right at the Haulover docks, a fishing boat. Pay the skipper the going rate. How's that sound to you?"

"I'd like to know where Glenn is," Foley said, "and what happened to Karen."

"I imagine somewhere along the line he threw her out of the car and kept going. It's what I would've done."

"You don't think she took him in?"

"How would she do that?"

"It's her business. Has Glenn ever been here?"

"I never told him where I live or gave him my phone number."

"How about Adele?"

"She has my number, yeah, but never called me on her phone."

"If they have Glenn, once he starts talking he'll never stop. He'll give Adele up in a minute."

Buddy said, "As soon as they check you out they'll see you were married and divorced. They get Adele's name, either one, her date of birth, they've got her. That's a given. I even told her, if Foley makes it they'll be around to see you. She said, 'What do I know?' You can put your money on Adele."

"I was thinking," Foley said, "you could give Glenn a call. If he did get away and feels safe . . ."

"And if he didn't get away and they hung a wire on his line . . ."

"We could call the West Palm marshal's office."

"For what?"

"See if Karen's there."

"She is, what's that tell us?"

"She's okay, he didn't—you know—do anything to her."

"What if they have that kind of hookup—it gives 'em the number of anybody that calls?"

"Use a pay phone."

"You're still thinking about her."

"I want to know what happened."

Buddy folded the paper and got up. He said, "I'll see what I can do," and left the apartment.

▼▼▼

WHEN THEY CAME IN LAST NIGHT AN OLD WOMAN ASKED IF they were delivering her oxygen. Foley thought he was in a nursing home—all the old ladies and a few skinny old guys sitting around the lobby. In the elevator Buddy said, "They'll stop me and want to know if I'm the laundry man, or am I from the dry cleaners or the grocery store. They're outside on the patio, they're in the lobby, they're like birds sitting on a telephone line watching everything that's going on. Can you imagine bringing that girl marshal through there and up seven floors and not cause some attention? You're no problem. They understand somebody wearing a raincoat. They put on their raincoats any time they see a cloud. Over their beaded sweaters. I've never seen so many beaded sweaters in one place in my life."

Foley said to him last night, "But you still would've let me bring her if I had my way. I'm sorry I acted like an asshole. I think I'm over it."

"I might've acted the same way," Buddy said. "She was the first real girl you'd seen in five months and, man, she smelled good, didn't she?"

Last night and all day today Foley kept seeing her in different ways: in the headlights before putting her in the trunk, her face up close, when she came out of the trunk showing her legs and when she stood there in the road, her body in profile, her nice tight rear end in that short skirt; and seeing her close from behind as they climbed the grade. Those pictures of her kept popping into his head and he would take his time looking at them. He never thought of her in a sexual way, like picturing her naked or wondering what her bush looked like. He would remember the feel of her, though, his hand on her arm, on her thigh with her skirt pushed up. He could hear her voice, too, saying, "Why, are you famous?" Saying, "Are you kidding?" And coming out of the trunk, "You win, Jack." That was his favorite. "You win, Jack." He played that one over and over. She said, "Buddy. Is that his given name?" Because he'd slipped and said Buddy was driving. Talking too much. Then had tried to cover by saying it was the name he'd given him. What else did he tell her he shouldn't have? Karen listening to every word. Alert the whole time. Smarter than he was. Smarter than Glenn, the college boy. Foley was sure she had talked Glenn into taking off. Glenn too long there alone, waiting, scared to death. But she couldn't still be with Glenn. Could she? If she took him in it would be in the paper. If she didn't take him in—what happened?

▼▼▼

BUDDY WASN'T GONE LONG. HE CAME OUT TO THE BALCONY where Foley was taking the sun and sat down in one of the plastic deck chairs.

"I called Glenn. The little fella's answering machine came on saying he was out and leave a message, but I didn't speak to it."

"I wouldn't either," Foley said. "Hear yourself talking and nobody's there. How about the marshal's office?"

"I asked was Karen there; they said she's on leave, won't be back till next week."

"Last seen flying down the turnpike," Foley said, "and the next day goes on her vacation. How come I knew she wouldn't be there?"

"I guess 'cause you think too much," Buddy said. "You realize what you're doing? Worrying about a person that works in law enforcement. You want to sit down and have cocktails with a girl that tried to shoot you. You hear what I'm saying?"

Foley said, "I should never've got you into this."

"I had my eyes open," Buddy said. "Listen, you want to go to the Bahamas or not? It's up to you."

It made sense. Foley nodded, saying, "It would be a change. We have enough cash . . . Thirty-seven eighty, that's not bad. I used the one, the guy talking to the bank manager's my partner. Guy's an accomplice and doesn't even know it."

"I heard about one," Buddy said, "the guy tells a joke to get the teller relaxed. Then hands her a note that says, 'This is no joke. Give me all your big bills.' "

"That's pretty good." Foley nodded again and seemed to be thinking about it. Finally he said, "You know, after a while it gets to be the same old thing. You try to come up with ways to make it interesting."

"Like any job, sure, it gets boring," Buddy said. "But there other trades, like burglary, home invasion . . ."

Foley shook his head. "I couldn't be a burglar, it's too sneaky. And it's hard work. You pick up TV sets, you need a truck. You swipe jewelry you have to know if it's worth anything."

"Home invasion they're home," Buddy said. "You bust in, it's like a holdup. Or we could do supermarkets, liquor stores."

"Then you might as well stick to banks," Foley said, "a holdup's a holdup." He got up from his chair to look out at the ocean again. "I'd sure like to know what happened."

"Well, Glenn'd be the one to talk to," Buddy said. "If they caught him it'd be in the paper, so he must be hiding out. Or, he might've gone up to Detroit again." Now Buddy was nodding. "When I first spoke to him he'd been up there checking things out. You remember the Wall Street crook, Dick the Ripper? That's where he lives."

"Ripley," Foley said, "sure, I remember him, with the five mil walking-around money. Glenn's still talking about that?"

"He wanted to visit you at Glades, see if you're interested."

"I might *be*, now. So you think Glenn's in Detroit?"

"If he ain't locked up. He sure isn't hanging around here. Not after leaving us out on the highway."

"I'm not mad at him," Foley said. "I don't think any less of him than I ever did. No, but if he's up there and has it worked out . . ."

"He got hold of Snoopy Miller. You recall how he was taking Snoopy with him that time? He isn't fighting no more, Glenn says he's managing some guys. I figure all we'd have to do is find out where they hold fights and there's Snoopy."

"He takes us to Glenn," Foley said, "and we help him rip off the Ripper. That the idea?"

Buddy said, "If you don't mind breaking into the man's home."

"It's the sneaking around in the dark never appealed to me much," Foley said. "But you never know if you're gonna like something or not till you try it. I never tried okra, even living in New Orleans, till I was a grown man. Now I never see it."

"Look at it another way," Buddy said, "there's nothing like work to take your mind off your worries."

NINE

HER DAD, READING THE PAPER, SAID, "THEY'RE FINALLY OFfering a reward, ten grand for information leading to the arrest . . ."

The doorbell rang.

"That's on each one. Somebody could make thirty grand."

Karen got up. Leaving the room she heard her dad say, "He's late," and something about missing his program. It was eight-fifty in the evening of the third day following the escape. She opened the door for Ray Nicolet, smiling at her in the porch light. He said he couldn't find the house, all the trees and vegetation, and came in saying, "It's like a jungle out there."

"It *is* a jungle," Karen said. "I asked my dad if he remembers what the house looks like. He said, 'Yeah, it's white.' "

"He needs a gardener."

"He has gardeners, he likes the seclusion. When my mom was alive you could see the house from the street. She was outside every day trimming, weeding."

"So, you having a nice visit?"

"He took the week off so we'd have time together. So far he's played golf every day. He watches *Jeopardy!* during dinner and English murder mysteries after. Inspector Morse, Wexford . . . You never see a MAC-10 or blood on the walls." She told Ray this bringing him through the dark house to a screened sitting room of chairs and sofas slipcovered in green and red hibiscus patterns.

Her dad sat in soft lamplight with the paper. Outside, beyond the garden and a sweep of lawn, was the fifth fairway of the Leucadendra Country Club. Karen said, "Dad? Ray Nicolet?" Watching them shake hands she said, "Ray's with the Violent Crimes Task Force, working on the prison break."

"I see that," her dad said, and Ray turned to Karen holding his jacket open to show the task force inscription on his T-shirt in red, her dad saying, "In case no one knows what he does."

Ray said, "The reason I'm late—"

Got that far as her dad said, "Ray, answer a question for me."

Karen felt her body tense; but then decided it was okay. Her dad had the paper open looking for a story; he wasn't going to ask Ray about his personal life, his marriage, separation, was he still living at home, any of that.

"Here it is. It says in the headline, ' "I slept with a murderer," says shaken Miami woman.' She lives in Little Havana. The guy comes to her door, says he's a rafter, just made it here from Cuba and doesn't know anybody or have a place to stay. She fixes him pork chops and rice, the next thing you know they're making love on the sofa. She says he was very gentle."

"I spoke to her," Ray said. "The guy told her he missed his little girl and she felt sorry for him."

Her dad said, "That's how you score now?" He looked at the paper again. "Listen to this. 'Afterward, she went to sleep in the bedroom with her children.' She says, quote, ' "I don't allow any man other than my husband in our bed." ' The husband's out of town, working. The next morning she fixes the guy Kellogg's Corn Flakes for breakfast and sends one of the kids to the store to get him a can of Colgate shaving cream, regular scent."

"You see it," Karen said, "as a testimonial, an ad. Escaped con swears by Colgate shaving cream."

"Regular scent," her dad said. "No, I was wondering how they know this guy's Chirino."

"From her description of him," Ray said, "down to his tattoos, a bee on each forearm. Stings like a bee—the guy was a fighter before he went up. The woman also said he stole her husband's gun, a twenty-two pistol, and some of his clothes." Ray said, "But listen, I have to tell you the latest."

"Wait." Karen's dad held up his hand. "The woman's married. She goes to bed with this guy because he misses his little girl and then tells the world about it. But you don't reveal her name, you protect her. It sounds like you're saying it's okay as long as her husband doesn't find out about it. Like the guy who cheats on his wife saying what she doesn't know won't hurt her."

Her dad picked up his drink and Karen said, "Why don't we let Ray tell us what's going on, okay?"

"I'm pretty sure it'll be on the news tonight," Ray said. "We got one of them."

Her dad put his drink down. "No kidding. Where was this?"

"Out in West Dade, near the turnpike."

"As soon as I saw you offering a reward . . ."

Karen said, "Dad."

". . . I said to myself, those guys are done, it's over."

Karen said, "*Dad.*"

He looked up at her.

She said to Ray, "Was it Foley?"

▼▼▼

THEY'D HAD TO RUN ALMOST FIVE MILES ALONG THE CANE before they came to the gas station on 27, climbed in the back of an empty truck, a big semi-trailer, and came all the way here that night to find this place called *el Hueco,* the Hole: hidden away in the weeds, a camp of vagrants, men who lived in shacks made from things thrown away, sheets of plywood, corrugated metal, old doors, seats from cars—all the men here Cuban; there were no women. Chino said he was from a raft that broke up but came ashore, thanks to Holy Mary Mother of God. He said he didn't know the other one who came—wearing the same clothes he did—and tried not to be seen with Lulu, telling him, "Don't follow me anymore. Stay away." By the third day the two of them worth twenty thousand dollars to any vagrant who could read a newspaper and think yes, maybe, why not, and walk one mile to the highway police.

It was Lulu who came to him this morning with the newspaper and accused him of being with the woman, showing him in the paper where the woman said she slept with a murderer. Chino said yes, of course, he went to find a woman; it had been eight years since he was with one. And Lulu said, "You've been with *me.*" Hurt. But also with the anger beyond reason of a jealous woman. Perhaps the same way he was when he shot his roommate nine times in the head with a machine gun.

Chino gave Lulu a shirt and a pair of pants from the woman's house and told him he'd see him later, when it was dark. Now he went to talk to a man who prepared café Cubano and smoked Cohiba panatelas listening to Radio Mambi on his ghetto box; a man named Santiago who trained fighting cocks, the roosters with their thighs shaved he kept behind chicken wire in cages; a man who had been here since Mariel, the boatlift, and knew this world. Chino said to him, "You know the one you've seen speaking to me? He's a homosexual."

"I believe it," Santiago said.

"I know he's also a murderer and wants to kill me for a personal reason. But I can't go to the police, they know me from another time. But if you go and tell them where to find the homosexual, they'll give you ten thousand dollars. Do you understand what I'm telling you?"

"Clearly," Santiago said.

▼▼▼

"OUR PHONE NUMBER AND THE ADDRESS OF THE COMMAND post on NW 27th were in the paper, so the guy knew where to come."

Ray Nicolet sat at one end of the sofa now, close to Karen's dad. Ray would look up at Karen, standing—she wouldn't sit down—in her jeans and shirt hanging out, and then look at her old man sipping his drink as Ray told them:

"The guy, his name's Santiago, walks in with a dead cigar in his mouth and says he can give us two of the escaped convicts, they're hiding out in this squatters' camp way the other side of the airport. I'd been there before, raiding cockfights; it's like a junkyard with banana trees. We showed him a mess of pictures. He points to Chirino and Linares and goes, 'Him and him. When do I get my twenty-thousand dollars?' We told him to sit tight, we'd be right back. By six-thirty we're out there, FDLE, FBI, Metro-Dade, local cops; there were even guys from Fish and Game. Once we were in position, helicopters came in and lit up the camp like a football field. You heard roosters, you heard these people yelling in Spanish scared to death, they're coming out of the shanties with their hands up. The order was, you see anybody run, give them a warning, and if they don't stop on a dime, shoot. Linares ran right into a Metro-Dade cop, kept running and was popped four times. We looked all over for Chirino, under every rock, you might say, but he wasn't there. Linares died on the way to Jackson Memorial."

Karen got out a cigarette and picked up the lighter on the table next to her dad's chair. He was asking Ray, "Did you pay the guy the reward?"

"Yeah, as soon as we got back."

"What do you do, write a check?"

"No, we paid it in cash. It was late, the banks were closed—I asked Santiago if he wanted to keep the money in our safe till tomorrow. You kidding? No way. Skinny old guy with dark skin, he looked like a chicken. He walked out with the ten grand in a shopping bag."

Karen drew on her cigarette and blew the smoke out. "Foley hadn't been there?"

"This place was strictly Cuban," Ray said. "If Foley had a ride he must have his own agenda. He's the only one seems to know what he's doing."

▼▼▼

THE LATE TV NEWS BECAME WEATHER REPORTS AND BUDDY clicked the remote to turn off the set, on a stand surrounded by plants. Foley and Buddy, on the imitation Danish sofa, didn't move.

"What do you think?"

"I thought Chino would have a better place to hide. It looked like a hobo jungle."

"They said he wasn't there."

"If Lulu was, he was. He got out. You know what I'm wondering?" Foley said. "If he thinks I set him up. See, he asked me if I want to go with him. I said no, but didn't tell him I'd made my own plans."

"Why not?"

"It wasn't any of his business. But now he reads the paper, he sees I'm out. He knows it didn't happen the way Pup said—all of us ganging up on him in the chapel. He's gonna ask himself what I was doing there with Pup. Did I tell him they were going out? I did, but it was to get Pup in the chapel, for his uniform. It wasn't like they would've all made it if Pup hadn't been there and seen them. As soon as they're out you know they're gonna be spotted—the hack in tower seven, or they touch the fence, the shaker wire sets off the alarm . . ."

"He's running for his life," Buddy said, "he doesn't give a shit about you."

"Unless he thinks I snitched him out. He does, he'll come looking. It's the way those guys are, they're big on revenge."

"Yeah, but he'll never find you. How could he?"

"Maybe through Adele."

"He knows where she lives?"

"I didn't tell him, no. But we were talking one time, sipping rum and confiding, you might say. He tells me how he came here from Cuba, twelve years old, born in '47. He tells me how he always wanted to be a fighter, might've had a chance at a title and blew it when he took the dive, all that. I mentioned Adele, told him how I did the bank so I could give her some money, how I got caught fucking around with the guy in the Firebird . . ."

Buddy said, "If you didn't tell him where she lives—she's not in the phone book . . ."

"No, but I mentioned she worked for a magician and Chino got interested. Yeah? How does he saw the woman in half? He saw a show in Vegas when he was fighting out there. How is the woman in the cage changed into a tiger? Does Adele ever get changed into an animal? He wanted to meet her. Or get a look at her if she ever came to visit."

Buddy got up. "I'm gonna get a Diet Pepsi. You want one? Or a beer?"

Foley shook his head. Buddy started for the kitchen and stopped.

"You tell him the magician's name?"

"Emil the Amazing," Foley said. "Yeah, I think I did. You want to call Adele for me, just in case?"

"What do I tell her?"

"Don't talk to any Cubans."

"Her phone'll be wired."

"She knows your voice?"

"I'm pretty sure."

"Just say it and hang up."

▼▼▼

AS SOON AS IT WAS DARK CHINO HAD WALKED AWAY FROM the camp, down the road to 12th Street and then east past open fields to the Café Cuba Libre sitting by itself. Santiago had told him this was where he came to get drunk and Chino believed he would come this evening to celebrate becoming rich. He bought six bottles of Polar and took them across the street to wait in the trees. Wait for this cockfighter the way he had waited in the Fifth Street Gym for the fight promoter. His life coming to this because of countless reasons, all beyond his control.

His hands had been broken too many times.

He never had time to train properly.

He never had a manager who could influence the right promoters.

He never had gauze for his hands; he had to use cotton wraps and wash them every day when he trained.

What else?

He had never owned a hooded running suit.

The big one. He had never had people handling him who cared. The cutman should have told him not to clear his nose after taking the shot in the eye from Palomino. Blowing his nose put pressure on the blood vessels, the eye became swollen and closed and the fucking referee stopped the fight, the one in Vegas Jack Foley saw, or said he did. You couldn't be sure, since Foley was a liar who pretended to be a friend. It was all the bad luck and then blowing his nose that time. If he didn't blow his nose he would have beaten Carlos Palomino and then would have had shots at Cuevas and Benitez, Duran, Curry, anyone, and wouldn't have had to take the dive with the white kid he could have beaten lefthanded, thirty-nine years old.

In the trees across from the Cuba Libre he drank one of the beers, waited, and began to drink another. The gun he had taken from the woman's house was a Ruger .22 with a long barrel, he believed a target pistol, not a high-caliber gun, but it should be enough. At exactly seven-thirty he heard the police helicopters and saw the searchlight beams shining down on what would be the squatters' camp over there, about a mile away. He wasn't sure if he heard gunfire, maybe. He continued to wait, drinking the beer slowly to make it last. Three hours passed before he saw Santiago's pickup, the truck so old Chino didn't know what kind it was, coming from the direction of Miami. He walked across the street, the pistol in his belt beneath the woman's husband's shirt. The truck was in front of the café now, among a few cars parked there, Santiago getting out, locking the door. Chino called to him and Santiago turned. In the streetlight and in the red neon that said Cuba Libre, Chino saw the man's look of surprise change immediately to innocence, wide-eyed now, ready, even smiling a little.

"They pay you?"

"It was as you said."

"Where is it?"

"Oh, you think I have it? No, I left it in their safe for tonight. They said tomorrow I can have it."

Chino turned his head to look in the pickup truck. "What do you have in that bag?" It was on the floor of the passenger side.

"Only some things I bought."

Chino said, "Do you want a beer?"

He had never seen a man appear so grateful, Santiago saying, "Yes, indeed," smiling again, turning to go in the café.

Chino took the man's frail arm in his hand. "Not in there. I have some I already paid for. Why waste it." He brought Santiago across the street, the man saying no, let's go to the bar, it would be his treat. Saying, listen, he was going to give Chino half the reward; he was going to surprise him with it, tomorrow. When they were in the trees Chino said, "I'm going to use your truck." Santiago said, of course, anytime. Chino said, "Where are the keys?" Santiago said here, in his jacket. It was a black nylon with a hood that hung down in back.

Chino said, "Take it off." Santiago said it was his, whatever he wanted. He turned to look across the street at the café in red neon, at the cars and the pickup truck in front, people inside but no one coming out, as he took off the jacket. Chino, behind him, drew the pistol from his belt. He shot Santiago in the back of the head and shot him twice again lying on the ground.

Chino walked to the truck with the jacket covering the gun in his hand, got in and drove toward Miami to find a telephone book.

TEN

"SHE GOES BY ADELE DELISI NOW," KAREN SAID, "HER maiden name. Married Foley in Las Vegas in '86 and filed for divorce the next year in Los Angeles County. Adele's forty-two. She lives in the Normandie on Collins Avenue, in the South Beach area."

They were at the kitchen table: Karen having a cigarette and a cup of coffee. Her dad, in one of his golf outfits, was having breakfast, a cheese and jelly sandwich on French bread and coffee, before leaving for the club.

"Anybody check her phone records?"

"Six times in the past month Adele accepted collect calls from GCI, the last one the day of the escape. But she never visited him the five months he was there."

"Didn't want her name on the list."

"Burdon asked why he kept calling her. She said because he was depressed. She said she hadn't seen him in eight years."

"She's in on it," Karen's dad said.

"I think so too. Foley told me the reason he came to Florida was to visit someone, and then dropped it. He said, 'I better keep quiet.' "

"He called *her*. Who did she call?"

"Her sister-in-law, Ann; she's a disc jockey, I think in Canada. And a magician she worked for, Emil something."

"The Amazing, a third-rate act," her dad said, eating his sandwich, sipping his black coffee. "The amazing thing about Emil is he's still around. Works with pigeons."

"Talking to Burdon she referred to Emil as that kraut son of a bitch. He let her go right before Christmas and hired a younger girl. Adele's been surveilled since the day after the escape, but hasn't gone anywhere to speak of. She put an ad in the *Herald,* in the personals, to get another job with a magician. Good luck, huh? Burdon says they've trapped her line and hung a wire."

"I bet she knows it, too. Why don't you go talk to her?"

"I was thinking about it. I mentioned it to Burdon, he said he has all the help he needs."

"Why don't you talk to her anyway. Do it right, she'll tell you things she wouldn't tell Burdon. Pay attention to how she talks about Foley, her tone. Tell her you think he's a nice guy. No, first tell her about being in the trunk with him, in the dark for half an hour, and see how she takes it. If she's in on it, what does she get for all the aggravation, cops breathing on her? I bet nothing. So she still likes him enough to stick her neck out. You think that's possible? What kind of a guy is he?"

"He's pretty laid-back, confident."

"Cocky?"

"No, but he was surprised I hadn't heard of him. Maybe I should have."

"He remind you of that guy Tillman?"

"Not at all."

"Remember calling me? You'd been out with him I think three times. You tell me the guy's a bank robber suspect and you don't know what to do. I told you to get another boyfriend."

"You said, if I want to know if it's true, ask him."

"Yeah, bring up the subject, see how he reacts. If he breaks out in a sweat, call for backup. But this guy Foley, you know he's dirty and you still want to see him again."

"I want to bust his ass, put him in shackles."

"Yeah, okay. Don't overdo it. Your pride's hurt, you were armed and he took you. That bothers you, I can understand how you feel. But you're also curious about the man. Last night, twice you asked your married boyfriend Nicolet about him. You were concerned, but didn't want to show it."

"My married boyfriend—setting him up with that news story so you could talk about infidelity. I couldn't believe it. Yes, I could. That's why I never brought my boyfriends home, you interrogated them. Mom used to yell at you for that all the time."

"Your mother never raised her voice, God rest her soul. She'd give me the look. No, what I was doing, I'd screen your boyfriends and tell you which ones were jerks, help you weed out the guys who were unfit. Take this guy Nicolet, he's okay, I guess, but he's a cowboy. The mag stuck in his jeans . . . You like the wild ones, don't you? You know I've always said there's a thin line between the cowboy cops and the armed robbers, all those guys that love to pack. Maybe that accounts for your interest in Foley, the old pro bank robber."

"He *kid*napped me."

"Yeah, but you talked all the way from GCI to the turnpike. It sounds more like a first date than a kidnapping. You ever hear of the Stockholm syndrome?"

"Now wait a minute," Karen said.

"The bank robbery in Stockholm," her dad said, "two guys, one of them's name—I can't think of it."

"Olufsson," Karen said.

Her dad winked at her. "You know what I'm talking about. They're trapped in the bank, in there a few days holding the women hostage. They come out, three of the women say they're in love with this Olufsson."

"I wasn't a hostage," Karen said. "We were in the trunk together maybe a half hour."

"I don't know, this Foley sounds a lot like Olufsson. Talk to his ex-wife, see what she says about him."

"I know what he is, an habitual offender, a con."

"Before, you said he was laid-back, confident, like you admired him."

Karen watched her dad bite through the crust of the French bread, eating his cheese and jelly sandwich, making her want one. She watched him sip his coffee, head lowered over the table. He looked somewhat like a short Walter Matthau. Once when he had a subject under surveillance and was waiting in his car, two women rushed up to him saying, "My God, it's Walter Matthau!" The subject came out of a bar and drove off before her dad could get away from the two women.

He said, "I know what I wanted to ask you. How come there's no mention of Glenn Michaels in any of the news stories?"

"Burdon says Glenn isn't anyone's business but theirs, the Bureau. I told him what Glenn said in the car about working on a score up north, a big one. Burdon wanted to know where up north. I said, well, Glenn mentioned freezing his ass off in Detroit last November. You could try there. This morning he called to say no one named Glenn Michaels flew from here to anywhere in November. I said maybe he drove. Burdon said don't worry about it."

"He didn't say, 'Don't worry your pretty head'?"

"Yeah, he did."

"And that makes you want to kick him in the crotch."

"No, it makes me want to bring in Glenn. I already want Foley. Buddy, if he's around."

"Pour me a half a cup, would you, please. And tell me what we know about Buddy."

"Not much," Karen said, getting up. She came back to the table with the coffee, served her dad and sat down again. "He's about Foley's age, has a sister who used to be a nun, but we don't know where she lives. He and Foley were both at Lompoc and probably met there. And that's where Glenn got to know them. Burdon's gonna call the prison, see if they can come up with a name, someone who was a friend of Foley's."

"They'll be lucky if anybody remembers Foley. What's the population out there, a couple thousand?"

"About sixteen hundred, the last time I went out."

"They expect some administrative hack or a trusty to go through the computer hoping to find a *Buddy*? Even if they knew his first name—when did he come in? How many years would the search have to cover? You don't know that unless you know his sentence. You imagine calling out to that penitentiary and asking, 'Say, any of you people remember a con named Buddy?' " He sipped his coffee, getting it all, and said, "Listen, I have to run."

Karen watched him get up from the table to stand looking out the kitchen window at the fairway, hiking up his yellow slacks that drooped in the can.

She said, "I asked Foley if Buddy was his given name and he said yeah, he gave it to him. But what if it's his real name?"

Her dad turned to look at her and seemed for a moment surprised. "Where's he from, originally?"

"Arkansas."

"I don't know—but now that I think about it, Buddy might be the key, the one to work on. He risks everything, including his life, to help some guy he jailed with. What does he get out of it? He does it as a friend or because there's a payoff? You see what I mean?"

"Either way," Karen said, "Foley owes him."

"So whatever Buddy wants to do next," her dad

said, "the chances are Foley will go along. Find Buddy and you've got him."

"If we knew Buddy's name."

"You gave me an idea. But listen, I got to get out of here, I'm late already."

Karen followed him to the door that opened into the garage. "Dad, come on. How do we find him?"

He held the door open and turned to look at her. "It might work, it might not. I'll tell you as soon as I get back."

"You'll tell me about your golf game for an hour."

The door closed.

Every drive that stayed on the fairway, every chip to the green, his specialty, any long putts that dropped in—his Jack Daniel's on the rocks next to him. He exaggerated, he even cheated . . . But he knew how to find people; it was his business. Karen turned to the sink. Should she do the dishes?

Or go talk to Adele Delisi?

▼▼▼

BUDDY HAD CALLED HER THREE DIFFERENT TIMES THIS MORNING, she was never home. When he came back the last time Foley said it didn't matter, he was going to see her. Buddy told him he was crazy and Foley said he'd made up his mind.

"You know they'll have people watching the hotel."

"To see if she leaves. You think they're gonna check everybody that goes in?"

"Why take the chance?"

"I owe her."

"You haven't given her a dime in eight years. Now all of a sudden . . ."

"I'm not talking about owing her money, this is different. I kept thinking about it last night trying to get to sleep on this sofa, this board. I wouldn't be here if it wasn't for Adele."

"That's right, you wouldn't have done the bank and got sent up."

"She helped get me out. The least I can do is try to see her. If I can't, I can't, but I have to try."

"I won't drive you."

"I'll get there."

"They'll spot you on the street."

"You said yourself I don't look like my mug shot. That's all they have to go on."

"That you know of. Your picture's been around, man. I used to see it in banks before I ever knew you."

"I'll go as a tourist. Wear shorts, a straw beach hat, hang a camera around my neck. Wear socks with sandals . . . Can you fix me up?"

ELEVEN

ADELE SPENT THE MORNING ON THE ART DECO HOTEL STRIP going from one to the next, ten blocks of sidewalk tables and tourists, stopping at each café and bar to ask the hostess if she would do her a huge huge favor. Even the ones she knew slightly would take the three-by-five card like it had ka-ka on it and glance at it, never changing their expressions, as Adele explained it was a version of an ad she'd placed in the *Herald*. But it was so tiny in the paper she thought if she could get some of these, you know, displayed around the beach . . . The hostesses said sorry, and handed the card back, or yeah, okay, and dropped it on their reservation stand. The card read:

LIKE MAGIC!

Call 673-7925 and out pops Adele!

Experienced magician's assistant!
Expert with doves and all forms
of legerdemain!

Walking along 10th toward Collins Avenue she paused to look back and saw the guy tailing her come to a stop at the alley. He stood looking around as though he might be lost. The tail across the street had stopped and was tying his shoelaces. She wondered why they bothered. Adele waved to the one across the street and continued on to Collins. The next two, another pair of serious, clean-cut types, were in a car, one of them reading the paper. Every day there was some mention of Jack on the news and in the paper, "still at large" along with one of the Cubans, but not a word about Buddy or Glenn Michaels, so the two-car escape plan must've worked. The time Glenn came alone to visit, a few days before the break, he'd sat with his vodka and tonic posing, playing with his hair, waiting for her to make the move while he talked about himself, letting her know what a cool guy he was and how he planned to use Jack and Buddy later, for a job he had lined up. Five minutes with Glenn, she understood why Jack didn't want him, why he said on the phone that last time he'd take the guy's sunglasses off and step on them. She said to him, "You know who you remind me of? That freeloader who lived in O.J.'s guesthouse, the instant celebrity with the hair." Glenn said, "Yeah? Really?" taking it as a compliment. The best thing to do with Glenn Michaels, she decided, would be to put him in Emil the Amazing's vanishing box and lose his ass.

She came to the Normandie in a row of pastel-colored apartment hotels and nodded to the old ladies on the porch, waiting out their lives. Crossing the lobby she said hi to Sheldon behind the desk and he showed her his bad teeth. At least he smiled. None of the tight-assed hostesses on the strip smiled or gave her one fucking word of encouragement.

Adele went up the stairs to the second floor and into her apartment done in blond furniture from fifty years ago, Miami Beach Moderne, with sailboats and palm trees on the limp curtains. She turned on the window air conditioner. Every time she looked out now she hoped to God she wouldn't see Jack across the street, like in a movie: leaning against a post he lights a cigarette and looks up at the window. Jack posed too, but was good at it.

She dropped the LIKE MAGIC! three-by-five cards she had left over on the glasstop dining table and stood looking down at them. *Expert with doves and all forms of legerdemain*. Expert at cleaning up dove shit in the dressing rooms. A natural at standing with one four-inch heel precisely in front of the other, smiling, glowing, her arm rising in a graceful gesture to the birds flying out of Emil's filthy coat.

What she should do, hell, advertise herself as a magician and play birthdays, schools, company parties, that kind of thing; prisons, why not? She could do rope tricks: cut and restore, threading the needle, the coat-escape using volunteers. She could do handkerchief tricks: Fatima the dancer, the serpentine silk, the dissolving knot. She could do card tricks: the Hindu shuffle, overhand shuffle, the doubt lift, the glide . . .

The phone rang, on the desk by the window.

She could do sealed envelopes: the Gypsy mind reader, impossible penetrations . . .

"Hi, this is Adele speaking."

A male voice said, "Oh, is this Adele?" with an accent, Cuban, or one of those.

"Yes, it is. Are you calling in answer to my ad in the paper?"

"No, I don't see it."

"You picked up one of my announcements? You must have been right behind me when I passed them out."

"I talk to the guy you work for, Emil?"

"Oh, uh-huh. Yeah, I was Emil's box-jumper for almost four years."

"You were his what, his box? . . ."

"His assistant. What did he say about me?"

"He tole me your number and where you live.

See, I'm looking for an assistant and would like to speak to you."

"May I ask, sir, do you perform in the Miami area?"

"Yes, around here. I was a mayishan in Cuba before I come here. Manuel the Mayishan was my name. Let me ask you something. You do the sawing of the box in half trick with you inside?"

Adele paused. "Yes?"

"How do you do that trick?"

"How do you *do* it?"

"Forgive me. I ask you this wanting to be sure you are experience."

"Well, I've seen it performed both ways," Adele said, " 'thin sawing' or the old Selbit method, if that's what you mean."

There was a silence before the Cuban voice said, "Yes, I see you know what you doing. I would like to come speak to you about working for me."

Adele said, "Well . . ." She said, "Why don't I meet you at the Cardozo, on the porch? You know where it is?"

"Yes, but you don't want me to come where you live?"

"I have to go out anyway. I can meet you in an hour. Will that be all right?"

He took a moment before saying, "Yes, all right."

And Adele hung up.

How do you do the sawing of the box in half

trick? . . . Was he serious? He didn't know a box-jumper was an assistant. Maybe mayishans in Cuba called them something else.

The phone rang.

She'd wear shorts, show off her legs.

"Hi, this is Adele speaking."

Whoever it was hung up.

▼▼▼

BUDDY CAME OUT OF WOLFIE'S AND GOT IN THE CAR.

"She's home."

He turned south on to Collins and didn't say another word until they had gone ten blocks and were passing the Normandie.

"There it is. You see the guy sitting on the porch? The old ladies and one guy? You know they'll have a couple more in a car."

Foley was looking around. "I didn't notice any."

"You *know* they're there."

"I'll keep my eyes open."

Buddy turned right on 10th and right again into the alley to pass behind the row of hotels. He said, "Nobody hanging out back here, that's good." They came to 11th at the end of the alley and Buddy stopped.

He said to Foley, "You bring the gun?"

Foley lifted the straw bag from his lap. "In here, with my suntan lotion and beach towel."

"You giving her some cash?"

"What I got the other day."

Buddy nodded, staring at Foley, studying him. "I still think you ought to wear a hat."

"All the shots of me in banks I have a hat on, or a cap. I doubt anyone's seen me without one."

"Look at your watch," Buddy said. "It's eleven-twenty. I'll be back here in half an hour, at ten of twelve. You don't show, I'll be back here at twelve-twenty. You still don't show I'll see you in thirty years."

▼▼▼

THIS CAFÉ WAS RUN BY PUERTO RICANS—CHINO COULD tell by the way they spoke—but it was okay. The coffee was Cubano and they didn't bother him sitting at the counter or looking out the front window through the backward words on the glass and seeing the hotel almost directly across the street, the Normandie, four stories high. Jack Foley's former wife was on the second floor, in 208, maybe a room in front and she was looking out the window as he looked at the hotel. He had phoned from here. He didn't like the plan of meeting her on the porch of the Cardozo Hotel, people there, people passing by. He'd have this coffee and a little more and go up to her room to talk to her in private. What could she do?

▼▼▼

FOLEY WALKED FROM THE ALLEY TO COLLINS AVENUE AND stopped on the corner to watch cars creeping by in both directions, tourists taking in South Beach, or looking for a place to park. He started walking toward the hotel in the middle of the block, taking his time. Buddy was right, there'd be a car somewhere close by with two guys in it. He watched a car up ahead pull away from the curb and a Honda nose into the parking space, a woman at the wheel. He wondered if they used women on surveillance. What he'd do, walk in the hotel. If the guy on the porch followed him in, he'd start talking to whoever was behind the desk about rates for next season. Make up a story. As if he could see a room or use the men's, hang around until he could slip upstairs. He didn't think the guy on the porch would pay any attention to him. He was approaching the Honda now, the woman out of the car, standing at the parking meter in profile, feeling her pockets for change:

Blond hair, tan jacket and shoulder bag, long legs in slim jeans and heels—plain, pink medium heels that caught his eye, pink shoes, a nice touch with the jeans. The hair, the profile, made him think of Karen Sisco.

She turned from the parking meter and he was looking at Karen Sisco—it *was*, right there, not ten feet away, it was Karen—looking at him now, waiting. She said, "You wouldn't happen to have change, would you, for a dollar?"

Foley shifted the straw bag to his left hand, still looking at her, telling himself to keep going, don't stop, don't say a word. But he did, he said, "Sorry." He was past her now without breaking stride, holding to the same unhurried pace, glancing around at signs, the sights, the people, but not looking back, telling himself to keep walking. It was her, all of a sudden right in front of him. He saw her and saw her eyes and for a moment, the way she was looking at him . . . He told himself if he looked back he'd be turned into a convict on the spot, in state blue, so don't even think of looking back. You saw her again and that's it. All you get.

▼▼▼

KAREN WATCHED HIM WALK PAST THE NORMANDIE, PAST THE women on the porch, the agent sitting there now. She thought, No, it couldn't be. She saw Foley's face streaked with muck in bright headlights, the guard's cap hiding his eyes. She saw his mug shot in her mind like all the mug shots she'd ever seen, a criminal offender with a number, not this guy in his color-coordinated orange and bright ocher beach outfit carrying a straw bag, dark socks with those thick leather sandals. She had almost smiled and said hi, how're you doing, her hand going to her bag. In that moment sure it was Foley. But his eyes gave no sign that he knew her and he said, "Sorry," without much expression and kept going. She waited for him to look back. She waited until he was all the way to the end of the block, crossing the street, and when he still didn't look back, she felt a letdown, disappointment, believing that if it was Foley he would have looked back. Or he might even have stopped and said something to her. It wouldn't make sense, but didn't have to; it was a feeling she had, so it was okay. Like if she were to make a *T* with her two hands, or he would, calling for a time-out, to give them a few minutes to finish what began in the trunk of the car. It would be okay then to say hi, how're you doing? Oh, not too bad. They stand there talking, polite to each other. That was some experience. Yes, it was. Well, we made it. He might say something about her shooting at him and she'd say yeah, well, you know . . . . You have time for a drink? I guess we have a few minutes. They walk over to the beach, sit at a table and talk for a while, say whatever comes to mind, have another drink, talk about movies . . . Maybe. Why not? There would be no way to predict what they'd talk about, they'd just talk until their time was up. Well, okay then, back to work. She gets up and walks away, and if she were to look back he wouldn't be there. It would be over with, out of the way. The next time she saw him—and she would try hard to make it happen—she'd cuff his hands behind his back and take him in.

Karen walked down to the Normandie. As a courtesy she stopped at the porch railing to show the agent, a young guy she didn't know, her ID and marshal's star, saying she was going up to see Adele. The agent said, "Does Burdon know about this?"

Karen said, "Don't worry about it," started to turn away and said, "You wouldn't have a quarter, would you, for the meter?"

▼▼▼

ALL THE WAY DOWN COLLINS TO 5TH STREET FOLEY WOULD stop to look at store windows, menus displayed on cafés, until he was sure Karen wasn't following him, hadn't recognized him after all. Foley thinking, That was close. But with more of an empty feeling than a sense of relief.

She'd be talking to Adele now. That had to be the reason she was down here. He realized that if she had come only a few minutes later and found him in 208, it would've gotten Adele charged with a first-class felony, aiding a fugitive. So quit fooling around. Leave.

But not a minute later he was thinking of going

back, walking up Collins on the other side of the street to wait across from her car, the Honda, and get another look at her when she came out of the hotel.

He said to himself, Jesus Christ, where are you, back in grade school? You just discovered girls?

Foley turned the corner at 5th and turned again into the alley to walk back that way, by himself, past trash cans and grease smells coming from the café kitchens, seeing Karen in her slim jeans and looking at possibilities again. Like if he were to cross the street just as she's getting in her car. Walk up to her and say . . .

If she didn't recognize him he could walk up to her and say *some*thing, anything. He thought of things to say to bank tellers, make it up on the spot before he asked for the money. I sure like your hair, Irene? Is that the latest style? Or, mmmmm, your perfume sure smells nice. What's it called?

He could tell Karen he liked her shoes. I just wanted to tell you I like those shoes you have on.

And she'd look down at them—the way bank tellers touched their hair when he told them it was nice. She'd look down and he'd walk away.

And then she'd look up again wondering who the moron in the beach outfit was.

When he got to 11th Buddy was waiting.

"Well?"

"We got to get out of town."

Buddy said, "Now you're talking."

"We drive or what?"

"We drive. I wouldn't mind taking off right now."

"What about our stuff? I just bought new shoes."

"We're gonna need winter clothes," Buddy said, "before we drive into a fucking snowstorm. Coats, gloves . . . We could go to a mall."

"And then stop off, get my shoes and stuff."

Buddy turned out of the alley heading for Collins. "We'll drive up to Lauderdale, Galleria mall, that's the place, get us a couple of heavy coats."

"Overcoats?"

"If you want, or a parka."

"I don't think I ever owned an overcoat."

"You've never been to De-troit. January, man, you freeze your nuts off."

Foley said, "You sure you want to go?"

TWELVE

ADELE HAD THE CHAIN ON THE DOOR AND SPOKE TO KAREN through the narrow opening. "I've already told the FBI anything I know about it I saw on TV or read in the paper. I haven't heard from Jack or have any idea where he is. Why would I? We've been divorced eight years."

"He talked about you," Karen said, "in the car."

Adele hesitated. "You were with them?"

"You might say I got in the way," Karen said, "so they put me in the trunk of my car. Then Jack got in with me. I thought the FBI might've told you."

"You were both in the trunk?"

"From Glades to the turnpike. But then as soon as I was in Glenn's car he took off, left them standing there." Karen watched Adele's face in the opening, freshly made up, heavy on the eye shadow and lip gloss. "They didn't tell you that, either?"

"They didn't *tell* me anything, they asked questions."

"But you know what I'm talking about? Glenn driving the second car?"

Adele stared. She said, "I know a Glenn." The door closed and opened again, all the way. "I'm getting ready to go out. You can come in if you want, sit down for a minute. Would you like a Diet Coke?"

Karen said no thanks, looking around at the art deco resort-hotel decor. She turned a chair from the glasstop table and sat down as Adele came out of the kitchenette with a Diet Coke and a pack of cigarettes: Adele wearing a polyester makeup coat hanging partly open, panties but no bra, and clear-plastic mules. Karen saw her as a size 10, her body soft and white, a bit plump but good legs, dark curly hair . . . She said to Karen, "Those are cute shoes. The kind of jobs I get, I have to wear these killer spikes, they ruin your feet." She walked away and came back with an ashtray. "When you were in the trunk with Jack . . ."

Karen waited while she lighted a cigarette.

"He didn't hurt you or anything, did he?"

"You mean, did he try to jump me? No, but he was kind of talkative."

Adele sat down at the other end of the table. "You mentioned, he said something about me?"

Karen was ready. "He said the reason he came to Florida was to see you. So I guess you spent some time together."

"Well, yeah, before he was arrested."

"But you didn't visit him in prison."

"He didn't want me to."

"Why not?"

"I don't know. He was different after he was sentenced, looking at thirty years."

"But you spoke to him on the phone."

"He'd call every once in a while."

"He called the day he escaped," Karen said.

Adele stared at her. "He did? I don't remember. What else did he say about me?"

Karen had to think of something.

"He said he wished the two of you could start over, live a normal life."

"Bless his heart. I'll say one thing for Jack, he was never ugly or mean, or drank too much. His idea of a normal life, though, was robbing banks. It's all he's ever done."

"Did you know that when you married him?"

"He said he was a card player, how he made his money. I could live with that. Or he'd come home with a bundle and say he was out to the track, Santa Anita, and I suppose sometimes he was, he liked to gamble. I never knew he robbed banks till he got caught with that car that wouldn't start—if you can imagine something like that happening, comes out of the bank and the car won't start. I did go see him at Lompoc—I guess you know he did time there—to tell him I was filing for divorce. He said"—Adele shrugged—"okay. Jack's so easygoing. He was fun, but never what you'd call a real husband."

"He met Buddy at Lompoc," Karen said.

"Yeah, and Glenn, the creep." She squinted at Karen through cigarette smoke. "Why isn't there anything about him in the paper?"

"They don't know where he is," Karen said, "and I guess they don't want to have to admit it." She said, "It looks like Glenn took off by himself."

"The weasel. You know what I wish? You could put him away and forget about Jack. He doesn't deserve thirty years."

"I'd give anything to find Glenn," Karen said. "I had him in custody once; he sure loves to talk."

"Yeah, about himself, what a cool guy he is. He said he's lined up a job and was gonna use Jack and Buddy. Fat fucking chance."

"What kind of job?"

"He didn't say." Adele paused to smoke. "The only reason I met him, he was a friend of Jack's at one time, and that's all I'm saying."

"And I guess you met Buddy."

"You can guess all you want, I can't help you. I

have to finish dressing anyway, I'm seeing a man about a job. He claims he's a magician, only he's Latin and I have my doubts about him. You know I worked for a magician?"

"Emil the Amazing?"

"Yeah, the prick. This guy that called, he goes, 'How do you do that sawing of the woman in half trick?' I go, 'Are you kidding?' I should've said it's not a trick it's an illusion. He said he was testing me to see if I was experienced."

"What I can't figure out," Karen said, "is how the two halves of the box can be separated while you're in it, and you see your head in one and your feet in the other, moving."

"It's magic," Adele said.

"Or the one, the girl gets in the cage," Karen said, "it's covered, the cover comes off—"

"You spin the cage around first," Adele said.

"You spin the cage around, the cover comes off and the girl's gone and there's a tiger inside."

"Emil does it with a lion."

"Get out of here."

"A male we'd rent for the evening. An old one, but still had a lot of teeth."

"How do you do it?"

Adele shook her head. "I can't tell you, it would be unethical."

"I'm just curious," Karen said, "I won't tell anybody."

Adele said, "Have you ever heard or read about how illusions are done? No, because it's a secret. It's the *way* they're done, that's what it's all about. *How* isn't that interesting."

"Did you ever tell Jack?"

Adele took time to draw on her cigarette. "Once in a while he'd ask. I might've told him about some of the easy ones."

"How do you do the switch with the lion?"

"If I tell you, you'll be disappointed. It's always simpler than it looks."

"Come on, just that one. I won't ask you about anything else."

"No more about Jack or those guys?"

"I'll leave you alone," Karen said.

"You promise you won't tell anyone?"

"I swear. Cross my heart," Karen said, facing Adele sitting at the end of the table. Karen saw her about to speak and saw her jump at the sound of three quick raps on the door, three and three more and a voice then from outside, in the hole.

"Adele? I want to speak with you, please."

Sounding far away.

Karen watched Adele turn her head.

"Who is it?"

"I'm the man call you about work."

"I said I'd meet you."

"Look, I'm here. Open the door."

"I'm not dressed."

He said, "Listen to me." And in a lower voice, "I'm a good frien' of Jack Foley."

Karen got to her feet, bringing her bag to the edge of the table. She saw Adele staring at her and said, "Ask him his name."

Adele turned her head again, the rest of her rigid, upright in the chair, her cigarette held in front of her between two fingers.

"Who are you?"

There was a pause.

"José Chirino."

Karen brought her Beretta out of the bag.

"Or maybe you hear Jack Foley call me Chino. I'm the same person."

Karen moved along the table to Adele. She said, barely above a whisper, "Tell him to wait in the hall, you have to get dressed. Say it loud, raise your voice."

She did, yelled it out and her words covered the sound of Karen racking the slide on the 9-millimeter pistol.

The voice outside the door said, "Tell me where is Jack Foley, I don't bother you no more."

Karen said, "Tell him you don't know."

She did, and Chino said, "Listen, I'm the one help Jack escape from prison. He tole me, I can't find him to see you."

"I said I don't know where he is."

"Listen, why don't you open this fucking door. Okay? So we can speak."

Staring at Karen, Adele said, "Go away, or I'll call the police."

"Why you want to do that, to a frien'?"

Adele didn't answer and there was a silence.

Now he said, "Okay, you don't want to help me, I'm leaving."

Adele started to get up and Karen put her hand on her shoulder.

"I'm going now," Chino said. "I see you maybe some time, okay? Bye bye."

In her whisper Karen said, "Go in the bedroom and close the door." She waited until Adele was crossing the room before she moved to the apartment door and put her left hand on the knob.

Karen turned it, held the lock open and looked over her shoulder. Adele, in her makeup coat and plastic mules, was watching from the bedroom doorway. Karen motioned to her, waving the Beretta, to get in there, go on. But Adele didn't move. She stood watching and it was too late now to say anything to her. Karen brought the door toward her, opening it a few inches, listening, then stepped aside, out of the way, a moment before the door banged open and Chino, a solid figure in black, was in the room, Chino going for Adele and was past the table when he stopped, glanced around and then turned to Karen and she saw the gun in his right hand, the .22 pistol, its slender barrel pointing down, close to his leg. Karen brought up the Beretta in two hands, cocked it and put the front sight on his chest.

She said, "Lay it on the table and turn around."

Chino raised his left hand to her saying, "Wait," frowning. "You not Adele?"

"I'm a federal marshal," Karen said, "and you're under arrest. Put the gun on the table. I mean *now*."

"For what? I haven' done nothing. If you not Adele," Chino said, "this must be Adele, uh?" He turned to face her.

And now Karen was looking at him in profile, the pistol in his right hand, away from her. She glanced at Adele. "Go in the room."

Adele didn't move, staring at Chino.

"Do it. And close the door."

Adele started to turn as Chino said, "No, I come to see you." He raised the pistol, aiming it point-blank at Adele, and she stopped.

Karen said, "Put it down or I'll shoot."

She watched him look past his shoulder at her, raising his eyebrows, saying, "Oh, is that right? You going to shoot me? Nice girl like you?" Smiling at her as he said, "No, I don't think so."

That little smile hooked her.

Karen said, "You don't huh?" and started toward him and saw his expression change, the smile gone, saw him glance at Adele, still holding the pistol on her, then look back this way again at Karen moving toward him, Karen saying, "You can live or die," as she reached him and put the Beretta in his face, the muzzle inches from his eyes. "It's up to you."

His eyes closed for a moment and opened, looking at Karen's eyes past the muzzle.

"You wouldn't shoot me . . . Would you?"

She said, "What do you want to bet?"

He said, "I could walk out of here."

She said, "If you move, if you look at her again, you're dead."

They stared at each other. She saw him let his breath out, his shoulders sag and saw him lower his arm and heard the pistol hit the carpet and she almost looked down, but continued to stare at his face, his eyes dull now, beyond hope.

"Turn around and put your hands on the edge of the desk."

When he was leaning against it, off balance, Karen raised his jacket, felt around his waist from behind and, when she was finished, kicked his feet out from under him. Chino dropped to his knees, grabbing for the desk and hitting his head on the edge. He looked up at her in pain.

"I think you would shoot me."

Karen picked up his gun and told him to lie facedown on the floor. She stepped around him to the desk, punched a number on the phone and looked over at Adele staring at her.

"Daniel Burdon, please. Karen Sisco."

She waited, Adele still watching her, then turned to the window as she said, "Daniel? I've got a proposition for you."

THIRTEEN

"I SAID TO BURDON, 'IF I GET CHIRINO, WILL YOU PUT ME ON the task force? I can work it out with my boss if you okay it.' "

Her dad said, "You didn't tell him you had the guy?"

"I felt I had to make a deal first."

Her dad said, "My little girl."

They were on the patio with Jack Daniel's over ice, the sun going down. Her dad had told her often enough it was Walter Huston's favorite time of day in *The Virginian* and Walter was right. This evening he didn't mention it.

"Burdon naturally was suspicious. He said, 'Girl, are you trying to run some kind of game on me?' I said, 'All you have to say is yes or no.' He said, 'You come up with the Cuban you can call your shot.' He got there about twenty minutes later. He took one look at Chirino and got his surveillance guys to take him away. He had to ask how I got an escaped con to lie on the floor, but didn't act surprised or make a big deal about it."

"You sandbagged him," her dad said. "I don't think I'd be civil with you either."

"He had to decide what kind of attitude to have, how to treat me, and he wasn't sure yet. He talked to Adele, asked her a lot of questions. She was pretty cool about the whole thing. I was surprised."

"If anybody was cool," her dad said, and raised his glass to her.

Karen sipped her drink. Her eyes raised to her dad and she said, "Once you're into it and you're pumped up and you know who the guy is and you know you can't give him one fucking inch . . . He has the choice, you don't."

"You tell that to Burdon?"

"No, but he said, 'Let's go have us a cold beverage and talk some.' We went over to the Cardozo for about an hour."

"What's he drink, water?"

"Yeah, Evian, one of those. He warmed up. For the first time since I've known him he came down from heaven and acted like a normal guy. He asked me if I would've shot Chirino if he didn't drop the gun. I said yes and he said he believed it. He wanted to have dinner. He's asked me before, but always made it sound like he was making my day. Wow, I get to go out with Daniel Burdon. I turn him down and he thinks it's a racial thing with me. When I was in college almost every black guy who asked me out was like that. I'd say no thanks, 'cause the guy was an idiot or an asshole or had bad breath, and he'd accuse me of being racist."

"What's Burdon's problem?"

"He thinks he's irresistible. He wants to get me in bed, that's all, and I don't see any future in it. Ray Nicolet is the same way, he's getting around to it. All those macho guys . . . Jesus, give me a break."

Her dad said, "I don't want to know everything, okay?" He sipped his drink looking out at the lawn. After a bit he said, "How come we don't play catch anymore?"

She smiled at him. "Anytime you want. How's your arm?"

"I don't know, it's been so long."

Twelve years old she had her own glove, a Dave Concepcion model, and they'd throw a hardball at each other out on the lawn.

"You discovered boys and quit playing ball."

"I didn't want to show them up."

"You could've, too, you had an arm. You never threw like a girl."

They were quiet for a while in the last of the day's light. Her dad said, "I don't want to lose you.

I think I'm gonna live forever and I need my daughter around. I lost your mother, that's enough." There was a silence again. This time he said, "You're too smart to pack a gun and deal with felons. You're too smart and you're too nice a person."

Karen got up, went over to his chair and kissed him and stayed there, hunched over, her arm around his shoulders. She said, "I didn't go out with Burdon 'cause I wanted to stay home with you. Before that, the plan was to see Adele and come right home and be waiting for you. You know why?"

"Because you love your dad."

"Because I love you and because you have an idea how to find Buddy."

"You gave me the idea. Remember you said what if Buddy's his real name?"

Karen got up. "And it is?"

"No, but it was something to go on."

Karen turned to sit on the wrought-iron cocktail table, facing him now.

"I called my main source." Her dad paused to sip his drink.

And Karen said, "Gregg, the computer whiz. Just tell me, okay, don't drag it out."

"That's what I'm doing"—acting a little offended—"I'm telling you. I called Gregg, I said, 'What can you do with this combination? Your search criteria's the name Buddy, bank robbery or armed robbery, and California between 1970 and 1990.' I told him Buddy got out of Lompoc either this year or last year, but we don't know how long he was in."

Karen lit a cigarette. Her dad took it from her, for himself, and she had to light another one.

"You happen to have any grass?"

"I don't do that anymore. Come on, what about Buddy?"

"You start with a nickname it looks impossible, doesn't it? But if you can add a few facts, and if you're lucky . . . Gregg used, I don't know, Nexis, Lexis, one of the programs he has, and came up with Orren Edward Bragg, arrested March 22, 1985, and charged with robbing a branch of City Federal on Sepulveda in Los Angeles, three months before. And how did they find him? The way they get most of those guys, on a tip. LAPD got an anonymous call that turned out to be from the guy's sister, of all people. One of the detectives quotes her as saying, 'It was Buddy Bragg who robbed the City Federal bank and some others, too, may Almighty God forgive him.' That was the only reference to a Buddy associated with bank robbery, buried way down in the news story, and Gregg had it in about five minutes, printed it out and faxed it. It's inside."

Karen stood up and then sat down again.

"We don't know for sure, though, do we, if it's our Buddy?"

"I called Florence—you met her one time—still one of my best sources. I said, 'See if you can run an Orren Bragg for me in Dade, Broward or Palm Beach County.' I called her from the club, the same as I did Gregg. I come home, both faxes are waiting. Orren Bragg has accounts with Florida Power and Light and BellSouth. His phone number's in there too. Buddy resides in Hallandale at the Shalamar Apartments on A1A, he's in 708."

"That's our Buddy," Karen said. She stood up again.

"My sources," her dad said, "will bill you about fifty bucks each. I'll give you the invoices when they come."

Karen stood facing him, nodding and then saying, "Why do you suppose Buddy's own sister ratted him out like that?"

Her dad said, "She felt it was for his own good. Or maybe she never liked him. He was a brat, made her life miserable when they were kids."

"Foley said she was a nun, or used to be."

"I don't know," her dad said, "I always liked nuns. They're so clean. They never seem to sweat."

She finished her drink and saw her dad watching her.

"You're not thinking of calling, are you? Ask if your friend's there? Please don't tell me that."

Karen said, "Okay, I won't."

▼▼▼

IT WAS AN IDEA, THOUGH, SHE DID THINK ABOUT. CALL Buddy's number and ask for someone, a name, any name, pretty sure she'd recognize Buddy's voice, or Foley's if he answered, if he was there, and they'd tell her she had the wrong number and hang up. She was tempted, wanting to do it. But if they recognized her voice . . . She thought of asking her dad to call and decided no, go by the book. So she called Burdon. He was cool, wanting to know how she came about this information, and after she told him he said, "Karen, you're for real, aren't you? You can come along if you want." He'd stop by the home of a judge friend for a warrant, get a SWAT team together and meet her at the Shalamar Apartments as soon as they could make it. He said, "Karen"—not calling her "girl" this time—"get a key from the manager, if you would, please."

▼▼▼

KAREN WAS AWARE OF DETAILS SHE WOULD TELL HER DAD about later this evening.

The smell of sauerkraut in the manager's first-floor apartment. His watery wide-open eyes as she assured him the residents wouldn't be disturbed. Telling him this as she imagined their reaction to the SWAT team invading the place. The senior citizens in the lobby, mostly women, sweaters over their shoulders, bifocals shining, real fear in their eyes at the sight of black uniforms and jackboots, the helmets, the ballistic vests with FBI in yellow, big, on the backs of the vests, the automatic weapons at port arms, the SWAT team coming through the lobby like a troop of Darth Vaders.

She thought, No, these old people wouldn't think of Darth Vader, they'd see Nazi storm troopers coming in to haul them away, because it could have happened to some of them. She had seen old ladies in Miami with faded numbers on their arms.

Karen would tell her dad what she expected and then say she was surprised Burdon didn't make it a full-scale SWAT assault. Very surprised.

He came with eight guys in jackets and wool shirts hanging out, running shoes, half of them carrying bags that could hold tennis racquets or different kinds of athletic gear. The residents did stop what they were doing, watching television, playing gin; they had to wonder what was going on, curious, but didn't seem alarmed. Burdon posted two men outside, back and front, and sent two more up to seven to cover both ends of the hall. He said to Karen, "You ready?"

Then had to pause as a woman asked, "Are you delivering the oxygen?"

Burdon, Karen and the remaining four SWAT team agents got on the elevator. On the way up Burdon looked at them one at a time. "You're primary, you're secondary, you're point man." He said to the fourth, "You're gonna use a ram?"

He carried it in what looked like a navy seabag.

Karen said, "The manager's door is metal. You know what I mean? They might all be."

Burdon looked at her. "Yeah, you've been through doors, haven't you?"

"A ram on a metal door," Karen said, "makes an awful lot of noise for what good it does."

She'd tell her dad how you grabbed the handle on top that was like a dorsal fin, and the handle at the back end and swing the ram hard against the door. If it was wood the ram would shatter it. Metal, you might only dent it. But the fourth man also had a shotgun with a "shock-lock" round in it and that would do the job.

They reached the seventh floor and the SWAT agents took off the jackets and wool shirts they'd worn over their ballistic vests, heavy ones with a ceramic plate covering the heart area. Karen handed the key to the agent with the canvas bag. He had his shotgun out now, a Remington with a three-inch strip of metal taped to the muzzle. They approached 708.

The primary and secondary stood to the right of the door, Beretta nines held upright. The point man, who would be the third one in and would cover them, held an MP-5 submachine gun. The one with the shotgun eased the key into the lock and turned it. The door wouldn't budge, a dead bolt holding it shut. He raised the shotgun and put the strip of metal against the seam, where the lock entered the frame, the muzzle of the shotgun exactly three inches now from the dead bolt, and looked over his shoulder at Burdon and Karen. Burdon nodded. With the sound of the shotgun blast the primary hit the door going in, secondary and point went in right behind him and Karen, her ears ringing, pulled her Beretta, expecting in a moment to hear gunfire.

FOURTEEN

FOLEY SAID UNLESS YOU WANTED TO GO SKIING OR HUNTING they sure had a piss-poor selection of winter coats here. Buddy said they had some pretty nice jackets. Foley said he didn't even see any wool gloves. Buddy said well, what did you expect, we're in Florida. Foley said he expected to see some overcoats, why else did they come all the way up to this mall? Part of it was, he felt like a fool walking through stores in his orange and baby-shit yellow beach outfit, the socks and sandals. Driving back, Buddy said it looked like they'd have to wait till they got up north, say when they crossed the river from Kentucky and came to Cincinnati, Ohio.

And then said, "No, wait a minute. I know the place we should go."

They turned off 95 onto Hallandale Beach Boulevard and in a minute came to the Jewish Recycling

Center. Buddy said, "It's like the Salvation Army or St. Vincent de Paul only Jewish. It's got everything we'll need."

OVER 3,000 NEW ITEMS DAILY, the sign said on the way in. They passed through a section of home furnishings, beds, bureaus, everything from TV sets to toasters and waffle irons. Hurried through kids' clothes and a big section of women's things, narrow aisles cramped with clothes and shoppers —Christ, mink coats for only eight hundred bucks —and the constant sound of hangers clicking against metal pipe racks. They came to the men's section, aisles packed with suits, jackets, even tuxedos, and overcoats—some in the exact style Foley was looking for.

The first one he pulled off the rack was dark navy blue, double-breasted. With the sandals and no pants on it looked funny in the mirror, but he knew this was his coat. A slim cut, not at all boxy, like the coat was wearing *him*.

He put on a navy-blue single-breasted lightweight suit that had a Brooks Brothers label in it and felt good on him, the sleeves a speck short but that was all right; he'd rather have them short than too long. The pants were a perfect fit and not too shiny in the seat. He wondered what the guy did who'd owned the suit. Foley hoped he was successful. He looked at himself in the mirror, at the suit over his cotton beach coat. It looked okay, but he wanted to get a true effect, so he picked out a white dress shirt with short sleeves and a necktie that was mostly dark blue, put them on with the suit and stepped in front of the full-length mirror again to study his new image, expecting to see himself as a businessman, some kind of serious executive.

What he looked like was a guy who'd just been released from prison in a movie made about twenty years ago. Steve McQueen as Doc McCoy. Yeaaah . . . He liked it. He half turned and cocked his hip in a pose: a photo of Jack Foley taken shortly after his daring prison escape. His mind flicked to a picture of Clyde Barrow, hat cocked down on one eye, and right away saw Karen Sisco coming out of the Chevy trunk in her short skirt, and then on the street in her jeans and pink shoes. He imagined her seeing him in this suit. A semi-dark cocktail lounge. They look at each other . . .

Buddy came over in an overcoat, a double-breasted gray herringbone, saying, "What do you think?"

Foley nodded, raising his eyebrows.

Buddy said, "I always wanted one like this. I think I need a hat to go with it. I like a hat."

Foley asked how he looked and Buddy took a few moments to say, "Like a stockbroker." After that, Foley tried on a tuxedo to see what it was like.

Buddy told him now he looked like a waiter, one that drank and was always getting fired. They were having fun, two grown men playing dress-up.

▼▼▼

THERE WERE CLOTHES IN THE APARTMENT, NEW SHOES, FOOD and drink in the refrigerator, orange juice, Diet Pepsi Cola in half-gallon plastic bottles, six-packs of beer. Burdon said, "Don't anybody touch that leftover pizza, Buddy's coming back and we gonna be waiting for him. Here in the apartment and somebody in the lobby with a radio till the people go to bed. Karen, I'd like you to call Hallandale PD, ask if they have a quiet, unassuming evidence tech they can send over to dust around, do the door knobs, glasses in the kitchen, empty bottles, the handle on the toilet. Say to come in an unmarked car, please. They'll send us some little girl wants to be a police officer. Karen, you see anything interests you, or you recognize?"

"The raincoat in the hall closet, Glenn Michaels was wearing it." She paused and said, "Foley asked if he could wear it, so he could take off the shirt he had on, it was filthy."

"The guard's shirt," Burdon said, "the guy Foley assaulted with a two-by-four. So he was here. Or he still is, huh? I prefer to think of it that way, get this done. Karen, you're on my task force. Don't worry, I'll fix it with your boss. Then when this's closed we gonna have a talk, see about getting you transferred over to the Bureau."

Karen didn't say a word, she nodded and made the call to Hallandale PD. After that she began looking around the apartment again for traces of Foley, something that would tell her he was staying here.

She looked at the shoes again, dark-brown loafers, size 10, so new they hadn't been worn. She believed they were Foley's because they were by the sofa with a pair of white Nikes, same size, also new but showing some signs of wear. The shoes in the bedroom closet, two pairs, well broken in, were no doubt Buddy's. There were magazines in the living room, *Sports Illustrated, National Enquirer,* and a stack of newspapers—the *Miami Herald* and *Ft. Lauderdale Sun-Sentinel*—for the entire week, Monday, the day of the prison break, through today, Friday. Karen found Foley's mug shot in the *Herald* and stared at it, trying to see in this face what she remembered of the guy on Collins Avenue dressed for the beach. If it was Foley he might've sat right here to take the Nikes off and strap on the sandals. Going to see Adele, a high-risk move. But so was busting out of prison. He had the nerve . . . And maybe the beach outfit showed a weird sense of humor: in his own mind a disguise because, ordinarily, he would never in the world dress like a tourist. Karen's feeling was that after a half hour alone with Foley in the dark, she could say he was pretty cool, and cool guys didn't wear orange and ocher beach outfits and socks with sandals . . .

Burdon said, "We have here Mr. Orren Bragg's phone bill. Four long-distance calls last month to the same two-one-three area, that's Los Angeles. Who does he know out there, Karen?"

She shook her head.

"Well, we gonna find out. You been in the kitchen?"

"Not yet."

"There's a shoe box in the trash, looks like a receipt in it. Must be for the new shoes. You can go by the store tomorrow, see if they remember who bought them. I mean if we don't do any good here."

"But you think they're coming back," Karen said.

"Yes, indeed, and we gonna have a surprise party. I want you to take a radio, go down to the lobby and hang out with the folks. You see Foley and this guy Bragg, what do you do?"

"Call and tell you."

"And you let them come up. You understand? You don't try to make the bust yourself."

Burdon slipping back into his official mode.

Karen said, "What if they see me?"

"You don't let that happen," Burdon said. "I want them upstairs."

▼▼▼

BUDDY TURNED SOUTH OFF HALLANDALE BEACH BOULEVARD onto A1A, three blocks from the Shalamar Apartments.

He said, "It's about, roughly, fifteen hundred miles. You can do it in two days. We leave tonight and drive straight through, we get there two three o'clock Sunday morning. The bars close at two in De-troit and Sunday you can't buy any booze till noon. Give everybody a chance to go to their place of worship before they tie one on."

Foley said, "What're you trying to say?"

"You want to leave tonight or tomorrow? We leave tomorrow morning, say around seven and drive straight through, we'd get in early Sunday afternoon. The game starts at six, so we'd have plenty of time to find a place and get in some provisions. Unless you want to watch the game at a bar. You know, a sports bar, with a big screen."

"Who do you want?"

"The Steelers, and all the points I can get. Or, we could leave tonight, stop early in the morning someplace in Georgia, sleep a few hours, have a good breakfast . . . You like grits?"

"I love grits."

"Biscuits and redeye gravy?"

They were turning in at the Shalamar now, following the drive that went down to the building's underground parking area. Foley saying, "I don't care for the gravy. What I like to do is crumble up my bacon in the grits." He said, "It's up to you, whenever you want to get going."

Buddy said, "We don't want to be too leisurely about it, like we got all the time in the world." He nosed the Olds into a space near the elevator. "What do you think, leave our new duds in the car? We may as well."

▼▼▼

AN OLD GENT IN A GOLF CAP ASKED KAREN IF SHE WANTED to play gin.

Several ladies, stopping by on their way to the elevator, asked if she was a new resident.

Another, a frail little gray mouse of a woman in her eighties, leaning on a malacca cane, asked if she was visiting her mother. Karen made the mistake of saying no, her mother had passed away. Then had to gather up the radio and copy of the *National Enquirer* she'd brought from Buddy's so the woman could sit down close to her on the sofa. She took Karen's hand and began to pat it saying something about God's will, then asking what her mother had died of. Karen said non-Hodgkin's lymphoma, twelve years ago. The mouse woman said oh, gave Karen's hand a few more pats, looked around in a vague sort of way and said it was time for her pills.

Karen watched her creep off toward the elevator, the little mouse woman with her big black cane, and thought again of her mother, who would be only fifty-seven, at home, not hobbling around in a place like this; she would be outside in her straw hat and gloves, trimming, weeding, and you'd be able to see the house from the street. She told friends that and remembered telling Ray Nicolet and thought of the task force again and the SWAT team upstairs waiting and Burdon saying, "You let them come up. You don't try to make the collar yourself."

Karen looked off to the left, past a lamp next to the sofa and a giant schefflera in a planter, to the lobby's street entrance. The elevator was directly in front of her, not much more than thirty feet away.

The little gray mouse woman was still waiting, leaning on her cane.

The elevator door opened and Karen was looking at two men inside, both about the same height, facing this way. One in a dark shirt and trousers, the other . . .

The other in an orange and ocher beach outfit holding a straw bag.

Now the mouse woman was entering, feeling with her cane, one step at a time.

The one in the dark shirt and trousers reached out to help her aboard.

The one in the orange and ocher outfit continued to look straight ahead at Karen on the sofa looking back at him in the elevator's fluorescent glow lighting him and the other one like two suspects standing in a lineup. He didn't move. Not until the elevator door began to close. Then raised his hand.

He did—Karen positive now it was Foley—raise his hand to her as the door closed.

▼▼▼

THE ELEVATOR STOPPED AT THREE. THE OLD WOMAN DIDN'T move and Buddy said to her, "Is this your floor, Mother?"

She looked up at the panel of numbers, the light indicating the floor. She said, "Yes, it is."

Foley said, "It's ours, too," and turned his head to Buddy looking at him. "Karen Sisco's in the lobby. I imagine there some fellas upstairs."

They had to wait for the woman to get off, poking the floor with her cane, then eased past her, ran down the hall to the EXIT sign and took the stairs to the garage.

Once they were in the car Buddy said, "I guess we're going tonight, huh?"

Foley liked his tone. He didn't have to tell Buddy to take it easy, not be in so big a hurry to get out they'd bang into cars. Buddy said, "She'll see the elevator's going up to seven—that ought to give us some time."

They were leaving the building now, turning out into traffic.

"She saw us," Foley said, "so she'll know we got off."

Buddy said, "Well, if they know where I live, I guess they know what I drive. Should we pick up another car? This one's still got California plates on it. Or take 'em off and pick us up a Florida plate. I got a screwdriver in the glove box. They only use one license plate in Florida. I guess other states too. Stop off and lift one before we get on 95. There's a Wal-Mart over on Hallandale Beach Boulevard, has a big lot always full of cars. What do you think?"

"She looked right at me," Foley said. "She didn't yell or get excited. She didn't move."

They were on A1A in northbound traffic, a two-lane street full of headlights.

"We got one thing going for us," Buddy said, keeping an eye on his rearview mirror, "it's dark out."

"She just sat there," Foley said, "looking right at me."

FIFTEEN

HER DAD SAID, "HE WAVED TO YOU?"

"I won't swear to it," Karen said, "but I'm pretty sure he did. He raised his hand about as high as his head and it looked like, just as the elevator door closed, he waved."

It was Saturday now, seven in the evening. They had both been away from the house all day and were in the kitchen now, having a drink before going out to dinner.

"Maybe he was scratching his head."

"He was looking right at me the whole time."

"He knew you recognized him?"

"I'm sure he did. That's why I think he waved, he had nothing to lose. You know what I mean? He couldn't pretend to be someone else, I'd already seen him in that dumb beach outfit." Karen smiled just a little. "He's a pretty cool guy. You know it?"

Her dad had to be cool, too, when he was with her.

"You wave back?"

"I didn't have time. The door closed."

"I imagine you would've though." Saying it in a matter-of-fact way, going along straight-faced, not sure if he was serious or if Karen was, his darling little girl who tracked fugitives and took them to federal court.

"So what did you do next?"

"I used the radio to call Burdon. I told him Foley saw me, so he and Buddy were sure to get off the elevator. Burdon left one guy in the apartment and came down the stairs with the rest of his people to check the floors."

"What did you do?"

"Burdon told me to stay where I was. I radioed his guys outside and told them to get to the garage entrance. At that time, though, we didn't know if Buddy had a car, or if he did, what kind and where it was registered."

"They might've still been in the building."

"It's possible, but they did get out and the chances are they made it before the two outside guys got to the garage. Burdon called the Broward sheriff's office and they contacted I think Autotrak and they made Buddy's car, an eight-nine Olds registered in California to Orren Bragg. It was too late by then to lay out a grid and have local police cover it. Burdon did send out an all-points, but was sure they'd already switched plates or picked up another car."

"Burdon leave surveillance on the building?"

"Yeah, but took it off this afternoon. I stopped by DEA to look at Glenn Michaels' case file again. They had him on possession with intent but couldn't make it stick. The interesting part of Glenn's statement, he said he went up to Detroit to visit a friend and look into job opportunities—if you can believe that. They wanted to know where he stayed and who the friend was. Glenn said a guy named Maurice Miller, also known as Snoopy, a former prizefighter. I looked him up, Maurice was at Lompoc the same time Glenn was. In fact they walked out of the prison camp together—for some reason I see them holding hands. They were picked up and sent to USP Lompoc, the max prison, where Glenn met Buddy and Jack Foley. It ties in with Glenn telling me, when we were in the car together, he had a big score lined up. Then from something else he said, it had to be in Detroit. I called Burdon—you know what he said?"

"You'll have to tell me."

" 'What's this have to do with our bank robbers?' He says they're on their way to Calfornia because 'they always run to familiar ground to hide out.' "

Her dad said, "They do, huh?"

"Buddy's phone bill was in the apartment. It shows he called a number in Los Angeles at least once a week. Guess whose it is."

"His sister."

"How did you know?"

"You said guess, I guessed."

"His sister Regina Mary Bragg, the ex-nun who turned him in. Burdon called her this morning, five a.m. in Los Angeles. She said her brother was in Florida visiting a friend, but didn't know his name or have a phone number for Buddy. What I want to know," Karen said, "is why he calls his sister every week after she turned him in."

Her dad said, "Well, he doesn't seem to hold a grudge."

"I think he's basically a nice guy, does it out of kindness."

"Or maybe," her dad said, "she has some kind of nervous disorder from years of celibacy and his phone calls keep her stable."

"Foley said she drinks."

Her dad thought about it and said, "But not at five o'clock in the morning, when you say Burdon called her. If she's any kind of alcoholic she'd have been hung over and trying to think straight, careful about what she's saying."

"I guess the time to talk to her," Karen said, nodding, "is when she's into the sauce."

Now her dad was nodding. "Sometime in the evening, but not too late."

They went to Joe's Stone Crab for dinner.

▼▼▼

WHEN THEY GOT BACK KAREN STAYED IN THE KITCHEN TO call Regina Mary Bragg. Eight p.m. in Los Angeles.

Her dad went to his chair in the screened-in room to watch television, a cognac next to him on the lamp table. He moved through channels with the remote, looking, until he came to Robert Redford and Max von Sydow in the library of someone's home, the man seated at the desk. Redford is pointing what looks like a Colt .45 at him. But Max, with a Walther PPK, a much more intelligent gun, has the drop on Redford and tells him to put his gun on the desk. It reminded him of Karen having lost the Sig Sauer he gave her three Christmases ago. The day she spent in the hospital he told her if she was a good girl she might get another one for her birthday, in April. She said, "I'll get my gun back when I find Jack Foley. What I need are shoes. But don't get me anything, okay? Really." Which was what she said every year. And every year she would be his little girl again unwrapping presents, eager, taking great pleasure in it, while his pleasure was watching her. Watching Max von Sydow now walk over to the seated man and shoot him in the right temple, to Redford's amazement, and place the Walther in the man's hand. Forty years as a private investigator Marshall Sisco had never carried a gun or kept one in his office or home. None of his investigators did either, or Karen when she worked surveillance jobs for him: the cute girl following slip-and-fall and whiplash cheaters looking for insurance payoffs. They had talked about those times at dinner, Marshall trying to sell his little girl on the idea of returning to private investigating, run the office, make some real money representing big companies being sued—supermarkets and restaurants, hospitals, bike and car manufacturers . . . She wouldn't have to carry a gun or load her trunk with all that law enforcement stuff. She'd meet lawyers, doctors—nothing wrong with them necessarily if they were divorced. Why settle for some cowboy cop who drank too much and cheated on his wife? That's the way those hotshots were, all of them. Karen was a nice girl, well behaved in her own way; she listened to him at dinner, nodding a few times while picking her crab claws clean, and asked him if he thought Buddy and Foley would stick together. "Wouldn't they be better off if they split up?" He thought, What're you gonna do? His little girl was preoccupied. She'd mention Buddy, but it was Foley she had on her mind. He said to her yeah, they'd have a better chance of making it if they split up. But if Buddy had something he wanted to do and needed Foley, and since Foley owed him . . . Max von Sydow and Redford are coming out of the house now. Max turns to Redford, who has just watched him commit a murder, and says, "Can I drop you?"

▼▼▼

COMING INTO THE ROOM KAREN SAID, "*THREE DAYS OF THE Condor*, I love that movie. Do you know the title of the book it was based on?"

"Tell me."

"*Six Days of the Condor*. I spoke to Regina Mary. She has a very quiet voice—like this, barely above a whisper. 'Yes? May I help you?' E-*nun*-ciating, so I think she was definitely a little ripped. I took a shot, I said, 'Regina, this is Karen, Buddy's friend in Miami?' I said, 'He told me where he'll be staying and I wrote down the address, but now I can't find it.' I think it confused her. She said, 'Oh,' in that voice, 'I don't have any idea.' And I thought, well, that's it. But then she said"—Karen dropped her voice, getting a hushed tone—" 'He called just a while ago to let me know he's all right.' I couldn't believe it. I said he only left last night and he's there already? She said, 'Oh, no, he's in Lexington, Kentucky.' " Karen said to her dad, "Are you ready? And then she said, 'He won't be in Detroit till tomorrow.' "

Her dad was smiling at her. "Beautiful."

"I said, 'Buddy's awfully thoughtful, isn't he, to call you.' And you know what she said? 'He'd better, if he wants to save his immortal soul.' What do you suppose that means?"

"Like she's his ticket to heaven," her dad said, "so he'd better keep in touch. Regina may be out of the habit, but still has a lot of old-time nun left in her. What else did she say?"

"That was about it. I asked if the next time Buddy calls she could find out where he's staying, maybe get the phone number. She said it wasn't necessary for her to know that, he was on his honor to report to her."

"Well, nuns weren't all sweethearts," her dad said. "Regina sounds like the kind, they'd make you hold your hand out and then whack it with a ruler. Hurt like hell."

Karen sipped her drink, quiet for several moments.

"You have to tell Burdon," her dad said, "and you'd rather not. Am I right?"

Karen looked up. She said, "The FBI has warrants right now for over six thousand fugitives. What do they need two more for?"

Her dad said, "You're kidding."

Karen sipped her drink.

Her dad said, "Aren't you?"

▼▼▼

SUNDAY, IT WAS HALFTIME AT THE SUPER BOWL BY THE TIME Karen got home. She saw her dad trying to act like it didn't bother him.

"I'm sorry I'm late. What's the score?"

Her dad, with his beer and a bowl of peanuts, said, "Thirteen to seven, Dallas. It's still a game, but not as close as it looks. The Cowboys had to kick a couple of field goals when they should've gone in."

"So they can't be acting too arrogant."

"Give 'em time."

Karen said, "I went to see Burdon."

Her dad turned his head to look at her now.

"He wasn't watching the game?"

"He wanted to, but had to get rid of me first." Karen started out of the room and stopped. "Thirteen to seven, that's a total of only twenty so far. What's your bet, sixty?"

"Sixty-one, based on a final score of forty-four to seventeen, the Cowboys in control all the way."

"So they'll have to score thirty-one points for you in the second half."

"I'm not worried," her dad said. "Last year, the 49ers and the San Diego Chargers scored a total of seventy-five points. The year before, Dallas over Buffalo, they scored a total of sixty-nine. Where you going?"

"Get a beer. I'll be right back."

It gave her dad time to think about their bet. The sports book money line had the Dallas Cowboys favored over the Pittsburgh Steelers by 13½. They both wanted the Steelers to win, so they were betting on the total number of points scored, whoever came closer, Karen with 45—she had to be dreaming—her dad 61. If Karen won, she could pick out a pair of shoes at Joan & David. If her dad won, she had to come here for a week and cook dinner, all his favorites—pot roast, Swiss steak, chicken paprikash. Her dad told everybody he knew Karen cooked like a grandmother.

She came back with a long-neck Bud.

"What's going on?"

"Nothing, it's still the half. The experts are telling us what we just saw." He waited for Karen to sit down on the sofa and then offered the peanuts. "So you broke down and told Burdon they're in Detroit."

"Yeah, and he said, 'You mean it's possible Buddy is.' He's sure they've split up. Burdon's theory, Buddy knows Detroit, he used to live there, so he could've gone back to hide out. But look at Foley's record, the banks he's robbed by his own admission are all in the South, the Southwest and California."

"Burdon," her dad said, "is trying to watch the game while you're talking?"

"Standing at the door, he wouldn't let me in the house. We could *hear* the game . . . I asked if he'd send me to Detroit. Absolutely not. Out of the question. For what? He's already put out an all-points, the Detroit office knows who to look for. I said all I want to do is give them a hand. I know the guys we're looking for better than anyone on the investigation. You could pass them on the street and not know them, but I would. All you have to do is tell your office I'm coming."

"Meanwhile," her dad said, "dying to get back to the game . . ."

"Right, he said okay to get rid of me. I leave in the morning, probably stay at the Westin."

Her dad was frowning a little, shaking his head. "You report to the FBI office up there, you know how they'll treat you. A girl walks in—she's gonna tell them how to find a couple of fugitives?"

"*If* I walk in," Karen said. "I've been there, remember? Twice I had to pick up prisoners."

"So they know you."

"Not the Bureau guys," Karen said, "the Detroit cops. I have a friend now in Major Crimes, an inspector, I know will help me out."

"Married?"

"They're all married."

▼▼▼

THEY WATCHED MOST OF THE SUPER BOWL AT GALLIGAN'S, a bar on Jefferson that was a block from the Omni, where they were staying.

Foley had turned the game on in his room, Buddy brought a bottle of Jim Beam and they watched the first quarter from the chair and the bed until Foley said they should go to a bar, see the game with a crowd of people making some noise. So they walked to Galligan's, Foley hunching his shoulders in his new overcoat, and joined four other guys from out of town, stuck here over the weekend, and a woman who said she lived in Greektown but didn't look at all Greek. Blond, somewhere in her fifties. She said her name but Foley forgot it right away and she left at the half saying she had an appointment.

The only reason Foley and Buddy liked the Steelers was that they didn't like the showboating Cowboys, though they had little to strut about today. It wasn't much of a game. Final score, 27–17, Dallas.

Foley left the table to talk to the bartender.

Buddy ordered a couple more Jim Beams with a splash, for the road.

Foley came back and sat down.

"They have fights at Cobo Hall sometimes, the Palace, he says where the Pistons play, and the State Theater on Woodward Avenue. He says you can walk from here. He's never heard of Maurice Snoopy Miller. I asked him how come they don't have fights at Joe Louis Arena. He said they do, it's where the Wings play hockey. Then he said yeah, they've had title fights at the Joe, but no regular program. That's what they call it, the Joe."

"You know Louis is from here," Buddy said, "the old Brown Bomber. They have like a statue—it's just his right arm and the fist—out there on Jefferson."

"The Brown Bomber," Foley said, "it sounds racist. You have to be careful these days, you can sound like a racist without even trying. Anyway, the guy said if Snoopy Miller's in the fight game we might find him at the Kronk gym, it's where Thomas Hearns trained. I saw the Hit Man get the decision over Benitez in New Orleans, I happened to be home. I asked him where the Kronk gym was, he said he didn't know. Somewhere on the west side."

"I was an eastsider," Buddy said, turning to the window. "Look out there. You ever see so much glass in your life? All those buildings over there, like giant tubes of glass. The tallest one's the hotel, the Westin. There's a restaurant and cocktail lounge on top, something like seventy floors up, turns around real slow—you don't even feel it. You're looking out at the Motor City, have another drink, you're looking across the river at Canada. You want, we could go up there, get a good look at the city."

"From what I've seen," Foley said, "it looks deserted, like everybody left town."

"It's Sunday, Jack, everybody's home watching the game. You want to go over to the Westin, see what's there? Maybe go up to the top?"

"If we didn't have to go outside."

"It's not that cold. You know what you do? Relax your body. Don't hunch up, swing your arms, keep your blood moving and it doesn't seem as cold."

"Who told you that?"

"I think it was my sister. She knows things like that."

"Living in sunny California. That's where we oughta be, 'stead of here at the fucking North Pole."

"Wait a minute," Buddy said, "we don't have to go outside. That glass thing that goes across Jefferson, it's like a bridge you walk across from our hotel to the RenCen."

"What's the RenCen?"

"The Renaissance Center, those glass tubes over there. Tell me what you want to do."

"I don't know," Foley said. "What do you do in

Detroit on a Sunday when you can't think of anything and the banks are closed?" Foley sipped his drink. "I know where I want to go tomorrow."

"Yeah, where?"

"The Kronk gym."

SIXTEEN

THE FIRST THING MAURICE SAID TO GLENN WAS, "UH-UNH, you don't call me Snoopy. I don't answer to that Snoopy shit no more." Later on in the car he said, "I let White Boy call me Maury sometime if I'm in the mood. White Boy Bob's my all-around man, my bodyguard when I feel I need one, and my driver."

Right now he was driving the '94 Lincoln Town Car Glenn had brought from Florida and Maurice had fixed up with a Michigan license plate and what he said were clean papers, Glenn not sure now if it was his car or belonged to this dude wearing a lavender do-rag bandanna, this ex-con who used to be known as Snoopy.

White Boy didn't seem to pay any attention to Maurice and Glenn in the backseat talking about him. Driving out to the suburbs on a cold, sunless afternoon, all the way out Woodward Avenue from downtown to show Glenn Mr. Ripley's house in Bloomfield Hills.

"White Boy," Maurice said, "never made it as a pro, even though he can be a mean and vicious motherfucker. See, but if a fighter works in and gives him a good shot, White Boy's eyes cross and he don't know where he's at. I'm talking about in the ring, you understand, where you have to go by the rules. You mess with him on the street it's a whole different situation. Look at him, the shoulders, a size twenty neck on him. White Boy Bob stands six-four and goes two-fifty, can put his fist through a plaster wall. I've seen it." Maurice said, "White Boy," raising his voice, "tell Glenn the reason you went down on that burglary that time."

Glenn saw White Boy Bob look up at the mirror.

"I left my wallet in the house I robbed."

Glenn saw him grinning now in the mirror.

"Come out of his pocket," Maurice said, "as he's climbing through the window. Takes the TV, the VCR, some other shit and leaves his wallet on the floor. The police come by to see him. 'You lose this, Bob?' White Boy goes, 'Yeah, I guess I did,' not thinking where he might've left it. Got sent to Huron Valley." Maurice raised his voice again. "What was it, two years you done that time?"

"Twenty-two months."

Glenn watched him looking at the mirror and Maurice said, "Watch the road, Boy." He said to

Glenn, "I like this Town Car. We can cruise the man's neighborhood without getting the police or the private security people on our ass. Understand what I'm saying?"

Glenn said, "Sure, right, they see Bigfoot driving around a black guy wearing shades and a lavender fucking bandanna, no, they won't think anything of it."

Maurice said, "It's lilac, man, the color, and the style's made known by Deion and other defensive backs in the pros. I could be one of them living out here with doctors of my race and basketball players. Man, all you need is money. Here, this road we coming to . . . What is it, White Boy?"

"Big Beaver," White Boy said, grinning at the mirror.

"White Boy can't get over a road name Big Beaver. Okay, we come about fifteen miles from that whorehouse motel you staying at downtown. Now we in Bloomfield Hills. We go left a ways and then right. They no hills to speak of, huh, but lots of trees. Remember Lompoc, we had that nice view of trees and the warden had 'em all cut down?"

"Eucalyptus," Glenn said.

"New warden," Maurice said. "Cut down the trees and kept the yard closed till noon every day. I worked nights, see, in the bakery? Use to come off and do my training. So I couldn't do it no more, work on my legs. You don't have legs, you got no business in the ring."

White Boy said, "I let Maury hit me in the gut as hard as he can."

Maurice said, "Watch the road, Boy. Slow down, I think it's the next street . . . Yeah, Vaughan Road, nothing but money. Here come Mr. Ripley's house up on the left. Yeah, the brick wall . . . There's his drive, right there."

Glenn turned his head to look out the back window and caught sight of a slate roof, glimpses of a Tudor-style country house through the trees, a huge place, Glenn saying, "He went by too fast."

Maurice told White Boy to turn around, in that drive there, and go slow so Glenn could see the house. "Okay, now creep. Big place, huh? We come by and see people trimming, cutting the lawn, so I send White Boy to go find the boss of the crew, ask was there any work for him. The boss say no, so White Boy goes around to where this houseman is washing a car, in back, and ask can he have a drink of water from the hose. The houseman's white too, see. They get talking, White Boy ask him they any trouble with prowlers around here, car thieves and such. The houseman say they got a system, the man's sleeping and hears a sound he don't like? He press a button and every light inside and outside the house comes on. He wants to, he can press the button again, all the lights outside the house start flashing, a siren goes off and the police get a call, like a signal. The man has everything but U.S. Marines run out the garage at you. I'm thinking, we don't need none of that shit. I make up my mind, if this Ripley place is worth going into, they's only one way to do it. Which I believed from the time you first told me about Ripley was how to do it anyway."

"How?" Glenn said.

"I'll show you, soon as I get two more people I'm gonna need. Couple of young gym rats I know, hang out at the Kronk. Give 'em a hundred each they go anywhere I say."

"Wait just a fucking minute," Glenn said. "I'm letting *you* in on this, not all your friends."

"You let me in on what?" Maurice said. "You come this time and tell me, finally, the whole story, how this man has all kind of money in there, stones, gold; but that was five years ago the man told *you*. What's he got in there now? You tell me you gonna bring some people, couple old cons know what they doing. Then you say you change your mind, you ain't bringing these people."

"And you told *me*," Glenn said, "you know how to break and enter, only your expert here leaves his fucking wallet in the house."

"You learn from doing," Maurice said. "You learn where the money's at, then you do it. You don't go in a house and toss it looking for valuables, slit open the mattress, that kind of shit. They young fellas do that call the Head Bangers, go in and beat up on old ladies for money they save in a coffee can. No—the way to do it, you go in where you *know* they's money from illegal trade and the man ain't gonna tell on you. Like Mr. Ripley, you say made his from illegal trade. But what he told you, not only was it some time ago, it might've been bullshit. Understand? The one thing visible this Ripley deal has going for it, I mean we're sure of, is that big fucking house you have to be rich to live in."

"He's got it," Glenn said, "don't worry."

"Man, the only thing I'm worried about is you, if you can step up and do it. Understand? 'Stead of just talking the talk."

"Can I do *what*?"

"Walk in a house with me I got picked out. Man that lives there, a white guy, I used to sell to when I was in Young Boys, Incorporated."

"Excuse me," Glenn said, "but I don't know what the fuck you're talking about."

"Quit looking out the window and listen, you find out. Young Boys, man, we had the whole west side. This man I'm talking about would drive down to the projects, stop by my corner and I'd fix him up. Okay, now later on when I was doing business for the Chambers brothers—the ones had the crack factory?"

Glenn shook his head.

"Had girls working there cooked the rocks they called the Rockettes."

"I thought you were into credit cards."

"That was like on the side, use 'em to buy clothes, things for my house. See, but when I got ratted on and the feds wanted me for product, I had the credit cards to plead down to. Understand? They saw it as better than nothing, sent me to Lompoc and I let you talk me into escaping. Only stupid thing I ever done in my life. Okay, now this man I'm talking about . . . You know the one I mean?"

"The guy who used to buy coke off you."

"Was scag he bought off me. After while kicked it and found his happiness with crack, what I started dealing him when I worked for the Chambers brothers. But, see, the man turned around and got into dealing himself, selling to white people out this way. You with me?"

"This is a long fucking story," Glenn said, looking out the window again at shrubs, stone walls, driveways, trying to be cool, but feeling his control of the situation slipping away as Maurice took over the car and now, it seemed, was taking over the whole fucking deal, the con named Snoopy nowhere in sight.

"Look," Maurice said, "I know you cool, but don't give me no tone of voice, okay? You don't like what I'm saying, you can get out anywhere along here you want."

There it was. Still, Glenn felt he should call him on it. He said, "I think you're forgetting, this is my car. I drove it up here."

Maurice said, "Hey, shit, come on. I say I want this car, man, it's mine. You go get yourself another one. Now you gonna listen to me?"

They weren't having a discussion, Glenn realized for sure now, they were arm wrestling, Maurice showing him who was boss. Glenn, sitting there bundled up in his new wool-lined raincoat, his wool gloves and scarf, acted surprised, for what it was worth, saying, "What's all this fucking hostility about? I thought we had an understanding."

"I said you gonna listen to me or not?"

So much for the understanding.

Glenn took his time, making Maurice wait, before he said, "This guy who used to be your customer is dealing now, selling to white folks. You're thinking of a way to rip him off, knowing he won't call the cops 'cause it's money, as you say, from illegal trade," Glenn getting just a hint of a bored tone in there. He glanced at Maurice in his silk bandanna, sitting there like some fucking African prince. "What else?"

"You either stupid or you showing me some nerve," Maurice said. "Okay, we gonna find out how much you actually have."

▼▼▼

A YOUNG WOMAN NAMED MARCIE NOLAN, THE POLICE BEAT reporter for the *Free Press*, spotted Karen Sisco going into 1300 Beaubien, Detroit Police headquarters. Marcie was coming back from lunch at a Greektown restaurant, two blocks away, approaching 1300 when she saw Karen. But by the time Marcie got to the lobby and through the metal detector, Karen was in an elevator on her way up to . . . Well, she could be seeing one of the brass on the third floor, or someone in the Homicide section on five or Major Crimes on seven. If Karen was picking up a prisoner she'd eventually end up on nine, where the holding cells were located. Unless her prisoner was across the street, in the Wayne County jail. Marcie Nolan went up to her office on the second floor, a partitioned room she shared with the *News* beat reporter, and called an assistant editor at the *Free Press*.

She said, "Hi, it's Marcie," eager to tell about Karen Sisco, the federal marshal she got to know in Miami when she was at the *Herald*, but had to answer questions first. No, they still weren't giving out information. All they seemed to have was the witness report of four guys in a blue van. Two of the women were here this morning for show-ups. She said they had to release the suspect they'd brought in. "But listen, there's a U.S. marshal here from Miami, Karen Sisco . . . I don't know yet, I have to find her. She's probably picking up some guy they have on a detainer . . . That's what I'm gonna find out. In the meantime the *Herald* has a terrific shot of her taken in front of the federal courthouse . . . No, in Miami . . . It wouldn't matter, it's a really terrific shot. Karen has style, and she's a knockout . . . You'll see. It's the kind of shot, if what she's doing here isn't a story, you could run it in 'Names & Faces' instead of whatever Madonna's up to . . . It'll have a cutline with it we can revise, add that she's picking up a prisoner, or whatever she's doing here . . . That's fine with me. Once you see the picture I know you'll use it."

▼▼▼

KAREN PHONED HER DAD LATE MONDAY AFTERNOON FROM her room in the Westin. He asked about her flight, hoping, he said, Northwest wasn't still serving that scrambled egg sandwich with the banana and yogurt, and the bagel if you got the sandwich down and were still hungry. A cold bagel, for Christ sake. He didn't wait to hear what she did have or ask about the weather.

"So what're you doing?"

"Right now?" Karen said, standing at her window. "I'm looking at Windsor, Ontario. You remember that movie *Stranger Than Paradise?*"

"No—who was in it?"

"Nobody. It doesn't matter," Karen said. "I went to see Raymond Cruz."

"The Homicide guy."

"He *was*. He's crimes against persons and property now, also sex crimes and child abuse."

"Detroit, he must be pretty busy."

"Home invasions are big, sexual assaults . . . They're after a gang that cruises around in a van raping women, four guys. They pick up a woman off the street or pull her out of her car, gang-bang her in the van and throw her out. Raymond says they're close to nailing these guys so he's staying on top of it. *But*, he knows who Maurice Miller is, the guy Glenn Michaels stayed with when he was here in November? Or said he did. They even had Maurice's case file out, looking at it—his priors, a lot of credit card stuff. They're checking him out to see if he's into home invasions. They had a wiretap on some guys who were hitting dope houses and heard Maurice's name mentioned as someone, it sounded like, they wanted to bring in."

"The bad guys."

"Yeah, to work with them."

"Has Maurice been picked up?"

"They haven't looked for him yet. I told Raymond maybe I could save him the trouble. He gave me Maurice's last known address, but doesn't want me to go after him alone. I said, 'Raymond, I'm a federal officer, I'm armed . . .' What it is, he wants to go with me, but he's tied up."

"Would this be like a date?"

Some of the things her dad said she ignored.

"I noticed in Maurice's case file," Karen said, "something that might interest you. He gave his occupation as prizefighter and his employer, the Kronk Recreation Center. You've heard of it, haven't you?"

"The Kronk? Sure, all the good Detroit fighters the last twenty years came out of there. Emanuel Steward's program, the guy who trained those fighters, Tommy Hearns . . ."

Her dad paused.

"McCrory," Karen said.

"Yeah, Milton McCrory."

"There was a lightweight, Kenty?"

"Hilmer Kenty. You remember those guys? You were a little girl. Your friends are at the mall, you're home watching the fights."

"Well, once in a while I did. And soaps," Karen said. "*General Hospital,* I almost became a nurse."

"What're you doing tonight?"

"Nothing. Watch TV if there's anything on."

"Monday night, Poirot's on followed by Miss Marple. You thinking of going to the Kronk?"

"I might, just to see what it's like."

"A place like that," her dad said, "the fighters are okay, they're in there working their tail off. Then there're the guys who want you to *think* they're fighters, they might even shuffle around like they're doing their footwork, hit the bags, but they never go in the ring. And you got the ones who hang out there 'cause it makes them feel like they're tough guys. You know, the atmosphere. But you can take care of yourself, right?"

"I'll call you tomorrow, let you know how I'm doing."

"I forgot to ask you," her dad said, "what's the weather like?"

▼▼▼

"WAS A TIME," MAURICE SAID, "YOU SEE A GOLD MERCEDES over in the parking lot has a license plate on it say HITMAN? You know Tommy Hearns is inside. Seeing the car would get our juices flowing."

Glenn said he thought there'd be guys hanging around outside or running, doing their roadwork. Man, it was a bleak, depressing neighborhood, trash blowing in the street . . . Maurice said it was too cold to be outside, the dude in his lilac do-rag and tailored black pea jacket, enough shoulders in the coat for White Boy Bob—White Boy wearing a wool shirt hanging out over his T-shirt—coming behind them up the ramp to the front door of the

Kronk Recreation Center at McGraw and Junction, a two-story red-brick building that looked to Glenn like a public library no one used in a poor section of town. The streets around here were a clutter of up-and-down two-family flats with porches, dingy cars out front narrowing the streets.

Inside at a table they signed their names, the time, and wrote "boxing" in the last column. Glenn could hear kids' voices, basketballs beating on a wood floor, in there where auditorium doors were closed, as they walked past to a stairway, went down to the basement and along a hallway that brought them to KRONK BOXING, lettered on a door painted yellow across the top and the rest of it a bright red, with more words on it that said THIS DOOR HAS LED MANY TO PAIN & FAME.

"More the one than the other," Maurice said, waiting for White Boy to edge past them and open the door. Going in, Maurice said to Glenn, "You feel the heat, uh? Hits you smack in the face." Maurice slipping off his pea jacket now, getting down to his black silk shirt and pleated trousers a shade of taupe. "Even how much they sweat in here, it don't smell bad, does it? Go sit over there on those benches. I be with you in a few minutes."

Some were like park benches, along the near wall facing the ring, a big one flat on the floor, its size taking up most of the gym. Four young guys, three black and one who looked to Glenn like an Arab, were in there shadowboxing, weaving, ducking, throwing jabs with their taped hands. Glenn had noticed a body bag over where they came in, pictures of fighters all over the walls, a sign above the ring on the other side that said TURN UP THE HEAT. Another one, THE BIGGER THE REWARD THE BIGGER THE SACRIFICE. Glenn stared at it a few moments thinking it should be turned around, lead with The bigger the sacrifice . . . In the space to the left of the ring were workout machines, a speed bag, a training table, athletic bags in jazzy colors on the floor. There were old black guys over there in yellow T-shirts with KRONK in red, the trainers, talking to kids working out, watching the ones shuffling around in the ring. Maurice and White Boy were over there now, Maurice approaching the trainers one at a time, faking jabs, rolling his bony shoulders, jiving with them, but not getting any kind of cordial response, no smiles; a trainer would shake his head and Maurice would move on to the next one. White Boy was on a workout machine now, shirts off, popping his muscles.

Glenn brought a cigarette out of his shirt, looking at another one of the signs. NO PAIN NO GAIN. No shit. He reached in for his lighter, the cigarette in his mouth, as one of the trainers, a big heavyset guy, came along from the other side of the gym—where the door was—shaking his head at him and pointing to a NO SMOKING sign. Glenn held his raincoat open to slip the cigarette back into the pack, chin on his chest to see what he was doing. When he raised his head again he was looking at two white guys in overcoats coming this way, the two guys looking right back at him.

Christ. Jack Foley and Buddy.

Buddy the one saying, "Hey, Studs, how you doing?" as they walked up, Foley with kind of a mild expression, neither one acting like a hard-on, except they sat down on either side of him, close. It gave Glenn only a few moments to deal with his nerves.

He said, "Jesus Christ, what're you guys doing here?" and it didn't sound too bad. Surprised, but not overdoing it, almost like he was glad to see them.

Foley said, "Weren't you expecting us?"

Getting to it right away. Glenn said, "Listen, I'll tell you what happened." It was awkward the way they were sitting, the three of them facing the ring, only two guys in there now. He said to Foley, on his right, "That broad you picked up—did you know she was a U.S. marshal, for Christ sake?" He turned to Buddy as Buddy stood up, took off his overcoat and sat down again. "She *knew* me, from that bullshit dope bust. She drove me to court. Twice. You know what she said, we're in the car on the turnpike? 'I never forget anybody I've cuffed and shackled.' "

Foley said, "Yeah? She said that to you?"

Glenn turned to see Foley, still with a mild expression, almost smiling. Glenn said, "She asked me if I had a gun," and saw a little more of the smile, not much, just a hint, but like Foley thought it was funny. "She told me to drive, leave you there, or I was going down for the rest of my life."

Foley said, "Then what happened?"

"I drove. What would you do?"

Foley didn't answer, his face close, deadpan now. Glenn turned his head and was looking at the two guys in the ring sparring, dancing around each other, ducking, throwing jabs, smacking each other's gloves.

"What happened after that?"

"She wanted me to get off the turnpike so she could take me in. No thank you, I had it on the floor. The next thing I know she wigged on me, grabbed the wheel and we spun out and piled up."

"What'd you do then?"

"Got out of the car and ran."

"She try to stop you?"

"She was out cold."

"How do you know she wasn't dead?"

"She was breathing."

"But she could've been hurt."

"What was I supposed to do, get help? She wakes up, she's gonna fucking put me away. I got out of there, man, I ran. I picked up a ride, drove to

Orlando and hung around Disney World, in crowds, man, I hid in crowds of people till I figured out what to do."

Foley said, "You hid out with Mickey Mouse, huh?"

"Yeah, Mickey and Minnie, that whole crowd. I thought about it and decided I could kill two birds, hide out up here and do the job I told you about at Lompoc. You know the one I mean?"

Foley nodded.

"So I called Maurice."

"Who's Maurice?"

"Snoopy," Buddy said, leaning over now to get his suitcoat off. "Snoopy Miller."

Glenn—it was weird—felt a sense of relief come over him hearing the name Snoopy. For some reason he thought of Snoopy the dog, saw him in his mind the way Snoopy appeared in the comic strip, before thinking of the other Snoopy who wasn't Snoopy anymore—the one over there with the trainers; no, talking to White Boy now and they were coming this way, White Boy carrying his shirts. Glenn had to wonder why only a few moments ago he'd felt cornered.

Leaning against Foley he said, "Here comes Snoopy now. You recognize him?"

▼▼▼

Foley wasn't sure. He had seen him fight only a couple of times at Lompoc, about the same time they began calling him Snoopy instead of Mad Dog and he quit the ring; and had seen him once in a while with Glenn, in the yard. Glenn got up and Foley looked over at Buddy.

"The guy in the do-rag."

"Yeah?"

"That's Snoopy."

"Little squirt," Buddy said. "What's he do now, tell fortunes?"

He was walking up to Glenn when Foley said, "Hey, Snoopy, how you doing?" and he stopped and looked over.

Standing at the edge of the ring apron, he looked from Foley to Buddy and back again, pretty serious about it. He said to Foley, "I'm suppose to know you?"

"Lompoc," Foley said, and waited for Glenn to say something, it was his party. But he didn't.

"Yeah, Lompoc," Maurice said, like he was remembering it now, picturing some part of it.

Now the big guy with him moved in closer saying, "We have a problem here?"

It took Foley back to the yard, guys sizing each other up, making judgments that could mean somebody's life. Foley didn't look at the big white guy, but kept staring at the Snoop he remembered as all show, had the moves, the weaves, the head fakes when he wasn't even near his opponent, doing that little jive skip and touching a glove to his head. He stared at the Snoop till he saw the man's face begin to relax and now he was smiling.

"Jack Foley. Am I right?"

Foley nodded.

"And Buddy. Yeah, I can see you two now in the yard, sure. Jack Foley, famous bank robber. It seem to me I been reading about you in the newspaper. Busted out of some joint in Florida, huh?"

"Low class of people there, Snoop. I got out with a little help from my friends." He saw Glenn about to speak.

But the big guy cut him off saying, "You call him that again I'll put your head through the wall."

Buddy said, "What? You mean Snoop?"

Foley watched the Snoop raise his hand to the guy as if to hold him off.

"Nobody calls me Snoop no more or Snoopy, is what White Boy's trying to say. He's a little crude, you understand. No, I left that Snoopy shit behind me."

Buddy said, "What do they call you now?"

"My name, Maurice. Nothing fancy."

Buddy said, "And you call this bozo White Boy?"

"White Boy Bob," Glenn said, putting his two cents in, and it sounded innocent enough, though not to Foley. Glenn telling them now, "White Boy used to be a fighter." Giving Buddy the bait.

Buddy said, "What's he do now outside of shoot his mouth off?"

Foley said to Maurice, "Like being back in the yard, huh?"

Maurice grinned at him. "Just like it. Nobody backing down. You back down you pussy. Tell me what you and Buddy doing up here in the cold."

"They think they're getting in on our gig," Glenn said, "but no one told me they were coming. I told you I had two guys and then told you I didn't? These are the two."

Maurice said, "Let's go outside to talk."

"What's the matter with right here?" Foley said. "It's nice and warm."

"*Warm?* Man, it's ninety-five degrees in here, sometime a hundred—the way Emanuel always kep' it so his boys'd sweat, get lean and mean like Tommy Hearns. No, I ain't talking any business in here. To me this is like holy ground, man. You understand? I got to be someplace anyway. Y'all want to talk, come to the fights Wednesday night, we'll sit down and look at it good."

Foley turned to Buddy. Buddy shrugged and Foley said, "Where?"

▼▼▼

OUTSIDE, WALKING TO THE CAR, FOLEY SAID, "YOU NOTICE, it's supposed to be Glenn's deal, but now it looks like he's working for the Snoop."

"Call him that again," Buddy said, "you heard that musclebound asshole, what he'll do to you."

"He was telling us who he is, that's all, making himself known."

"Yeah? Who is he?"

"A musclebound asshole. You know the thing that bothers me?"

"If the Snoop's been reading about you," Buddy said, "he knows you're worth ten gees."

"You recall did it say dead or alive?"

"I think it's for information leading to your being apprehended. They might pay off on your being dead, but I don't see how the Snoop'd work it. You know what I mean? It wouldn't be the same kind of deal as that bum giving up the Cuban."

"Lulu," Foley said. "I wonder if they got Chino."

"They might *have*. We been out of touch."

Crossing the street now, approaching the car, Foley said, "I kind of like that do-rag the Snoop had on. You know it? It looked cool on him."

"I ever catch you wearing one," Buddy said, "*I'll* turn you in for the ten gees."

▼▼▼

GLENN WAS TRYING TO GET SOME ANSWERS WHILE MAURICE watched the two guys sparring, poking at each other, and it was like talking to the wall.

"You said you could get a couple of guys for a hundred bucks each. Right?"

Maurice would yell at the one with RICARDO OWEN on the tank top he wore over his yellow T-shirt, telling him to jab, jab, telling him it was what he had the gloves on for. Keep 'em up and *jab*.

"If you can get the two guys, what do we need Foley and Buddy for?"

"My guys ain't here no more."

"Where are they? Did you find out?"

Maurice said, "Ricky, stick and move, man. Stick and move." And to Glenn, "They ain't allowed in here no more."

"What do you mean, they aren't allowed in here?"

"Stay tight on him, Ricky. Don't give him room. They fucked up their privilege, trainer caught 'em selling weed outside the front door. Ricky, you got to crowd him he does that."

The bell rang and the fighters moved away from each other to walk around on the canvas, their arms hanging.

Maurice said, "Come on," and brought Glenn away from the ring, away from the trainers looking over, to sit down on the bench nearest the door.

White Boy went over and began hitting the heavy bag.

"You tell me you bringing these people," Maurice said, "then you ain't bringing the people, but the people show up anyway."

"I told you I didn't know they were coming."

"But they here, they know about the deal and want to discuss it. Fine. Meantime the two I thought of getting I don't want now, they dirty. You understand? So what's wrong with using the bank robbers? We know they cool—go in as many banks as those two have?"

"You know," Glenn said, "you'll have to offer them a split, not any hundred bucks."

"Was that your deal with them?"

"We never got that far."

"Well, what we offer and what they get," Maurice said, "could be two entirely different things."

SEVENTEEN

Karen's phone rang at half-past eight. As soon as she heard "Karen, it's Marcie Nolan" she knew how her picture got in the paper, on the back page of the food section under "Names & Faces."

In the two-column photo Karen, in a tailored black suit, straight skirt, black bag hanging from her left shoulder, is holding a Remington pump-action shotgun, the butt of the stock resting on her cocked hip, the barrel extending above her on an angle, her right hand gripping the gun just above the trigger guard. Karen wears dark glasses and is looking past the camera, her lips slightly parted. The cutline reads:

LA FEMME KAREN

U.S. Marshal Karen Sisco guards the entrance to the federal courthouse in Miami during recent drug trials of Colombian nationals. Other assignments involve transporting offenders to prison and defendants to court for trial. Investigative work means tracking criminal offenders. Assigned to the Miami office of the Marshals Service, Karen was in town yesterday to meet with Detroit Police personnel on a special assignment.

"It was a mistake," Marcie said. "I mean they jumped the gun, they were supposed to wait till I interviewed you, see if there was a story."

"How'd you know I was here?"

"I saw you going into 1300 yesterday. I didn't know who you were seeing, but I thought I'd catch up with you sooner or later, so to save time . . ."

"That picture," Karen said, "was in the *Herald*."

"Yeah, I asked my editor to get it. Both papers are Knight-Ridder—tell them what you need and a few minutes later it's on your computer. I mentioned to my editor, if there isn't a story it might work in 'Names & Faces' and he put a note on it to that effect. But then when I couldn't find you, I got on another story and didn't get back to my editor. What happened then, the 'Names & Faces' guy saw the note, revised the caption in kind of a generic way and ran with it. Karen, I'm awfully sorry I wasn't able to talk to you first."

"It's okay. Don't worry about it."

"I was afraid you might be furious."

"I get pissed off sometimes," Karen said, "but I'm rarely furious. The FBI office and the marshal's might wonder what I'm doing here."

Marcie said, "They don't know?"

"I mean they might think I'm a publicity nut, that I called you. But I can't see them making an issue out of it."

"You didn't want them to know you're here," Marcie said, "and I blew your cover. I'm sorry, Karen, really." She paused. "Can you tell me what you're on?"

" 'Meeting with Detroit Police personnel on a special assignment.' What's wrong with that?"

"It doesn't say anything, though, really."

"I think more than enough," Karen said, wanting to get off the phone, but had to ask, "How did you know I'm at the Westin?"

"Inspector Cruz. I asked around till I found out he's the one you saw. Can't you tell me *any*thing? Even off the record?"

"Let's see what happens," Karen said. "How do you like Detroit?"

"Compared to what, the North Pole?"

"It's not as cold as I thought it would be."

"Just wait. I'd kill to get back to Miami."

"Well, if you do, I'll take you," Karen said. "And if I have any free time I'll call you. Okay?"

She phoned Raymond Cruz and had to wait almost two hours for him to get back to her, to learn that he was awfully sorry but would be tied up most of the day. She said, "Raymond, are you trying to avoid me?" And he got a little flustered because he was a nice guy, telling her no, never, he really wanted to see her, but . . . It made her feel a little better, even though now she had nothing to do all day. She could call Marcie Nolan back, make a lunch date or meet her for a drink after five. Or, she could forget about waiting for Raymond. She could quit wasting any more time and check out Maurice Snoopy Miller's last known address.

▼▼▼

FOLEY READ THE SPORTS AND ENTERTAINMENT PAGES, glanced through the food section and came to the back page . . . After he read the caption and stared at the photo for a while he called Buddy's room.

"You have the paper?"

"I saw it. What do you think?"

"It's a terrific shot of her."

"Outside of that."

"I don't know," Foley said, staring at the photo. "But I don't think her being here has anything to do with us."

"She came up here on her vacation," Buddy said, " 'cause she likes shitty weather."

"I think she's after Glenn."

"How'd she find out he's here?"

"You know Glenn, he probably told her he was coming. Can you think of a way she'd know we're here?"

There was a silence before Buddy said, "No, but if they're on his ass and we're seen with him . . . She wouldn't be up here by herself, working alone."

"The girl still with you?"

"They don't stay the night, Jack, 'less you pay for it."

"Let me give it some thought," Foley said, still looking at Karen Sisco holding the shotgun. "I'll call you back."

Even if Karen suspected they were here and checked the hotels . . . They had registered as George R. Kelly and Charles A. Floyd—making the names up on the spot—and paid cash for a week in advance, telling the reception clerk they'd just as soon not have a hotel showing on credit card bills that came to the house. "If you get my drift," Foley said to the clerk and almost winked, but the guy's bored expression stopped him.

He called Buddy's room and Buddy said right away, "If they got a tail on Glenn we're fucked. Tomorrow night at the fights we all get picked up."

"I understand that," Foley said. "I'm thinking maybe we can finesse around it, find out if they're on him or not before we go in."

"How do we do that?"

"I don't know yet. Let's drive by where they have the fights and look it over, the State Theater."

"That's what it is, a theater, a movie house."

"Yeah, but what's around it? We'd check it out anyway. How about later on we go for a ride. You can show me where you used to work."

"Did you see in the paper," Buddy said, and paused. "Here it is. 'Fight over tuna casserole may have spurred slaying.' This woman's live-in boyfriend, seventy years old, complained about her tuna noodle casserole and she shot him in the face with a twelve-gauge."

"I never cared for it either," Foley said. "Or macaroni and cheese. Jesus."

"It says police found noodles in the woman's hair and believe the guy dumped the casserole dish on her. They'd been together ten years."

"Love is funny," Foley said.

He hung up, looked at the photo as he thought about what he was going to do now and rang the hotel operator. "Ms. Sisco's room, please." He waited. The operator came back on to tell him there was no one by that name registered. Foley got out the Yellow Pages and opened the book to Hotels. He tried the Atheneum, a couple of Best Westerns, the Pontchartrain, skipped to a couple of Hiltons, looked at a list of five Holiday Inns, said "Shit," looked out the window at those giant glass tubes across the street and had to think for a minute.

The Westin, that was it.

He found the number and called it.

"Ms. Karen Sisco, please."

After a moment the operator said, "I'm ringing."

Foley waited. He had no idea what he would say, but he stayed on the line.

The operator's voice came on again. She said, "I'm sorry, but Ms. Sisco's room doesn't answer. Would you care to leave a message?"

▼▼▼

KAREN RANG THE DOORBELL AND WAITED, HANDS SHOVED into the pockets of her dark-navy coat, a long one, double-breasted with a belt in back.

The house on Parkside was in the first block off McNichols, a street the Westin doorman said everybody called Six Mile Road 'cause it was six miles from the river and the next roads after were named Seven Mile, Eight Mile and so on. Take the Lodge, get off at Livernois, go on up past the U of D and Parkside was a few blocks over to the right. Big homes in there, old but they're nice.

One right after another, most of them red brick and showing their age in the bleak cold, the street lined with bare trees. Karen had asked the doorman if it ever snowed and he said, "Mmmm, it should be starting pretty soon."

The door opened.

Karen said, "Moselle Miller?"

The woman, about thirty, light-skinned, sleepy-eyed, said, "What you want?" She wore a green silk robe and was holding her arms close against the cold.

"I'm looking for Maurice."

"You find him, tell him the dog got run over and I'm out of grocery money."

A male voice from inside said, "Moselle. Who you talking to?"

"Lady looking for Maurice."

"What's she want?"

"Hasn't said."

Karen said, "That's not Maurice?"

"That's Kenneth, my brother. He's talking on the phone."

The voice said, "Ask what she want with him."

"You ask her. Maurice's business," Moselle said, "is none of *my* business," sounding tired or bored. She turned from the door and walked into the living room.

Karen stepped inside, pushed the door closed and moved into the foyer. She heard Kenneth's voice and saw him now—in the study, a small room with empty bookcases—black male about six-one, medium build, twenty-five to thirty, wearing a yellow T-shirt and red baseball cap backward, talking on a cordless phone. She saw him standing in profile and heard him say, "How do I know?" Now he was listening, nodding. "Yeah, I can make it. The State, huh. Who's fighting?" He listened, nodding again, said, "What's this other deal?" turning to the foyer, and Karen walked into the living room.

Moselle was on the sofa lighting a cigarette. She said to Karen, "You like to sit down?"

Karen said thanks and took a chair and looked around the room: dismal, gray daylight in the windows, dark wood and white stucco, the fireplace full of trash, plastic cups, wrappers, a pizza box.

Moselle said, "What you want Maurice for?"

"I'm looking for a friend of mine I think Maurice knows."

"You not with probation, one of those?"

Karen shook her head. "No."

"You a lawyer?"

Karen smiled. "No, I'm not." She said, "Maybe you know him. Glenn Michaels?"

Moselle drew on her cigarette and blew out a stream of smoke. "Glenn? No, I don't know any Glenn."

"He wasn't here last November?"

"He might've been, I don't know."

"He said he stayed here."

"Here? In this house?"

"He said he stayed with Maurice."

"Well, *he* ain't even here that much." Moselle drew on her cigarette, let the smoke drift from her mouth and waved at it in a lazy gesture. "I like to know where he goes, but at the same time I don't *want* to know. You understand? I was with a man before Maurice, I knew his business, I knew everything he did, a beautiful young man, and it was like looking in the future, seeing how it would come to an end and, sure enough, it did. He got blown up."

Karen waited.

"He sat down in a chair this time . . . I spoke to him on the phone. He sat down in the chair and when he went to get up, he got blown to pieces."

Karen said, "You knew it was going to happen?"

"I knew too much," Moselle said. "I knew waaay too much. It's why I don't know nothing now. I don't know any Glenn, I don't know nothing what's going on. Understand?"

Karen watched her, Moselle's arms hugging the green robe closed.

"Your dog was killed?"

"Got run over by a car."

"What did you call it?"

"Was a she, name Tuffy."

"Where do you think I might find Maurice?"

"I don't know—the gym, the fights. He thinks he still in that business. I *know* he don't miss the fights. Having some tomorrow night at the State. He use to take me."

Kenneth stood in the arched entrance from the foyer. He said to Karen, "What you want with Maurice?"

Moselle said, "She looking for a man name of Glenn."

Kenneth said, "Did I ask you? Go on out of here. Do something with yourself." He waited until Moselle got up, not saying a word, and walked away from them through the dining room. Karen watched him coming toward her now in kind of an easy strut, the backward baseball cap low on his forehead, letting her know he was cool, he was fly, by the way he moved.

She saw the scar tissue over his eyes and said, "You're a fighter?"

"How you know that?"

"I can tell."

"I *was*," Kenneth said, moving his head in what might be a feint, "till I got my retina detached two times." He was standing in front of her now, so close Karen had to look up at him.

"What'd you fight, middleweight?"

"Light to super-middleweight, as my body developed. You go about what, bantam?"

"Flyweight," Karen said, and saw him grin.

"You know your divisions. You like the fights? Like the rough stuff? Yeah, I bet you do. Like to get down and tussle a little bit? Like me and Tuffy, before she got run over, we use to get down on the floor and tussle. I say to her, 'You a good dog, Tuffy, here's a treat for you.' And I give Tuffy what every dog love best. You know what that is? A bone. I can give you a bone, too, girl. You want to see it? You close enough, you can put your hand out and touch it."

Karen shook her head. "You're not my type."

"Don't matter," Kenneth said, moving his hand across his leg to his fly. "I let the monster out, you gonna do what it wants."

"Just a minute," Karen said. Her hand went into her bag, next to her on the chair.

Kenneth said, "Bring your own rubbers with you?"

Her hand came out of the bag holding what looked like the grip on a golf club and Kenneth grinned at her.

"What else you have in there, Mace? Have a whistle, different kinds of female protection shit? Telling me you ain't a skeezer, or you don't *feel* like it right now?"

Karen pushed out of the chair to stand with him face-to-face. She said, "I have to go, Kenneth," and gave him a friendly poke with the black vinyl baton that was like a golf club grip. "Maybe we'll see each other again, okay?" She stepped aside and brushed past him, knowing he was going to try to stop her.

And when he did, grabbing her left wrist, saying, "We gonna tussle first."

Karen flicked the baton and sixteen inches of chrome steel shot out of the grip. She pulled an arm's length away from him and chopped the rigid shaft at his head, Kenneth hunching, ducking away, yelling "God *damn*," letting go of her and Karen got the room she needed, a couple of steps away from him, and when he came at her she whipped the shaft across the side of his head and he howled and stopped dead, pressing a hand over his ear.

"What's wrong with you?"

Scowling at her, looking at his hand and pressing it to his ear again, Karen not sure if he meant because she hit him or because she turned him down.

"You wanted to tussle," Karen said, "we tussled." And walked out.

▼▼▼

MOSELLE CAME OUT OF THE DINING ROOM HOLDING HER ROBE together, shaking her head to show her brother some sympathy. She said, "Baby, don't you know what that girl is?"

Kenneth turned to her frowning, showing how

dumb he was from getting his head pounded in the ring.

"She some kind of police, precious. But nice, wasn't she?"

"You gonna tell Maurice?"

"You the one she beat on, not me."

"Maurice is coming by later. We gonna do a job."

"If I'm upstairs, tell him I need grocery money."

The phone rang. Kenneth went into the den to answer.

The doorbell rang. Moselle opened the door and there was Karen again, handing her a business card. Moselle looked at it as Karen said, "I wrote the hotel number on there—in case you run into Glenn."

Moselle slipped the card into the pocket of her robe. Kenneth didn't ask who it was at the door and she didn't tell him.

▼▼▼

WHAT FOLEY COULDN'T UNDERSTAND, FOR A BIG INDUSTRIAL city like Detroit there were so few people on the streets. Sunday, Buddy said it was because it was Sunday and everybody was home watching the game. Today was Tuesday, there still weren't many people walking around downtown. You could count them, Foley said. Buddy said he didn't know, maybe they built the freeways and everybody left town. They were on their way out East Jefferson in the Olds, a Michigan plate on it now, Buddy the tour guide pointing out the bridge to Belle Isle, the old Naval Armory, the Seven Sisters —those smokestacks over there on the Detroit Edison power plant, they were called the Seven Sisters. There's Waterworks Park. Buddy said, "You know Pontiac? Not the car, the Indian chief? Somewhere right around here he wiped out a column of British soldiers, redcoats, and they called the place Bloody Run."

Foley was half listening, looking around but seeing Karen, Karen's picture in the paper, Karen in real life coming out of the trunk saying, "You win, Jack," his favorite picture of her in his mind.

It was snowing now, pretty hard.

"We're coming to it," Buddy said, "there's the fire station." Now he was frowning, sitting up straight behind the wheel, windshield wipers going, Buddy squinting, trying to see through the snow coming down. He said, "Where's the plant? It use to come all the way out to the street, with a bridge across to the offices, the administration building; it's gone. There's something way over there. Jefferson North. You see the sign? Yeah, way over there, some stacks. It must be the new one. I mean this was a big fucking plant, took up blocks around here, six thousand hourly, and it's gone. You want to see where I lived?"

"That's okay," Foley said.

"We may as well turn around," Buddy said, guided the Olds into a gas station and came out again to go back toward downtown. "It keeps coming down they'll get the salt trucks out. The job I had in the old plant, I hooked up transmissions to the engines."

Foley had torn the picture out of the paper, Karen with her shotgun in the black outfit that looked familiar. He had it in the inside pocket of his suitcoat. He was imagining what would happen if he phoned her. She says hello and he says . . .

"The engine comes down the line, let's say it's for an automatic. Okay, I take this brace in my left hand—it's hanging from a track—work the hoist button with my right hand, get it in position so the pins in the brace line up with the holes they have to fit into in the transmission, jockey it around . . ."

He'd say his name. Hi, this is Jack Foley, how you doing? Like that, keep it simple. She'd ask where he was or how he knew she was here. No, she'd say she was surprised, or she'd say something he wouldn't expect. Either way he'd listen to her tone of voice.

"Then you hit the button on the hoist again and swing the transmission over to the line, rock it, get it in position with the engine. You let go of the hoist then and pick up your air gun and run four bolts into the top of the housing—tsung tsung tsung, fire 'em in."

Or go over to the Westin and call her room. She's not there, watch for her to come in the lobby. She had to come back sometime from whatever she was doing here. Unless she was through and she'd already left.

"But let's say you have the transmission on the hoist and the engine has moved past and it's already out of reach. You had to pick the transmission up in your two hands—honest to God, you pick up this fucker weighing close to two hundred pounds—hump it over to the engine and run it on to the shaft."

Foley saw her crossing the lobby, coming toward him. She looks up. She sees him and stops and they stare at each other and it would be up to her if there was such a thing in this kind of situation as taking time to talk, taking a time-out, and he thought of making the sign for it, one hand flat on top of the raised fingers of the other hand, whether it made sense or not, letting it happen.

"While I was working there the one-millionth car rolled off the line, a Chrysler Newport, buy one for forty-one hundred. It sounds like a deal, but that was a lot of dough then."

Foley listened to the wipers whacking back and forth.

"Man, it's coming down," Buddy said. "You can barely see the RenCen, just the lower part."

"There stores in there, shops?"

"Yeah, different ones."

"I think I'll go over and look around, maybe get a pair of shoes for this weather, some high-tops."

"It's easy to get lost in there. You have to watch or you're walking around in circles without knowing it."

"The hotel's right in the middle, huh?"

"Yeah, the tallest one there. The cocktail lounge I told you about's on top. Revolves around. You can eat up there. Or there're fast-food joints all around inside. You hungry?"

"I may just get a drink."

"I got to call Regina," Buddy said. "She's not praying for the Poor Souls since you don't hear that much about Purgatory anymore. She's still saying rosary novenas I don't fuck up. Twenty-seven days petition, what you're saying the beads for, and twenty-seven days thanksgiving, whether you got what you're praying for or not. I call, it means I haven't been arrested. I called her one time on the twenty-seventh day, she goes, 'See?' Regina's way of thinking, if I haven't been busted I must not've done any banks. In other words her prayers have been answered and I'm not going to hell. So, as long as she knows I'm out it gives her something to do. Hey, but who knows? Maybe what she's doing is saving my ass, or I should say my soul. Even though I'm not sure if there's a hell anymore or not. You think there is?"

"Just the one out in Palm Beach County that I know of," Foley said. "I doubt anybody's saying novenas for me, but I'm sure as hell not going back there."

"You can't be that sure," Buddy said.

"Yeah, well, that's the one thing I've made up my mind about."

"They put a gun on you you'll go back."

"They put a gun on you," Foley said, "you still have a choice, don't you?"

EIGHTEEN

THREE IN THE AFTERNOON, A SNOWSTORM BLOWING OUTSIDE, the restaurant on top the hotel was nearly empty, only one waitress, it looked like, on duty. Karen was ready to bet anything the waitress would seat her at a table near the three men in business suits having lunch, and she did: the young executive-looking guys talking away, laughing at something one of them said until Karen walked past, and then silence. Karen glanced over as she sat down next to the outside window wall of glass; for a moment she thought of asking for another table, not so close. But they were finishing with coffee and cognac, or something like it, and she was only going to have one drink. "Jack Daniel's, please, water on the side." She turned to see her reflection in the glass against an overcast sky, snow swirling, blowing in gusts, seven hundred feet above the city, down there somewhere. She heard one of them say, "Why not," and then to the waitress, "Celeste, do us again, please, and put the young lady's drink on our bill."

Karen remembered her dad reading a book, years ago, called *Celeste, the Gold Coast Virgin*. She turned to see them raising snifter glasses to her, smiling, pleasant-looking guys thirty-five to forty in dark business suits, two white shirts, the third one blue, as deep blue as his suit. She said, "Thanks anyway," and shook her head.

The waitress drifted back to Karen's table. "They want to buy you a drink."

"I got that. Tell them I'd rather pay for my own."

"They're okay," the waitress said, getting girl-to-girl on her, "they're celebrating a business deal."

"I'm not," Karen said. "But listen, make it a double while you're at it, Celeste. Water on the side."

She watched the three guys looking up at the waitress delivering the message. Now they were looking this way. Karen gave them a shrug and turned to watch the snow, thinking it was like the snow in a globe you shake and it swirls around, except that here you're in the globe looking out. Ten minutes passed before her drink arrived. She splashed it with water from a small carafe, took a good sip and the one with the shirt as dark as his suit and a pale, rust-colored tie was standing at her table.

He said, "Excuse me."

She liked his tie.

"My associates and I made a bet on what you do for a living." He smiled.

Not his friends or his buddies, his associates.

"And I won. Hi, I'm Philip."

Not Phil, Philip. Karen said, "If it's okay with you, Philip, I'd like to just have a quiet drink and leave. Okay?"

"Don't you want to know what I guessed? How I know what you do for a living?"

"To tell you the truth," Karen said, "I'm not even mildly curious. Really, I don't want to be rude, Philip, I'd just like to be left alone." She turned again to the snowstorm.

"You're having a bad day, aren't you? I understand," Philip said, "and I'm sorry."

She watched his reflection turn and leave. The gentleman, polite, concerned, understanding—all she'd have to say is let's go and they'd be out of here.

The next one said, "I think I know why you're depressed—if I may offer an observation."

So fucking sure of themselves.

"You called on an account today, asked for the order and they said well, they were going to have to think about it."

It was her black suit; she had to be here on business, but didn't look too happy about it.

"I have a hunch you're the new rep and your customer isn't exactly knocked out by the idea of a young lady, even one as stunning as you, handling the account."

Yeah, it was the black suit.

"Am I close?" Smiling. "Hi, I'm Andy."

Like that commercial on TV. Do you suffer the embarrassment of wetting your pants a lot? Hi, I'm June Allyson.

"By the way, we're simple ad guys. We flew in from New York this morning to pitch a major account." Andy hunched over to look out at the storm, maybe to get closer, be able to see through it. "Hiram Walker Distillery, it's right across the river, if Canada's in that direction. There's no way to tell, is there? Anyway, we presented a test-market campaign for their new margarita mix. We show this guy who looks like a Mexican bandido, the big Chihuahua hat, crossed bullet belts, and the headline says, 'You don't need no stinkin' bartender.' The client flipped. So, we're having a little celebration here before going back tomorrow."

Karen listened. She said, "Andy? Really. Who gives a shit?"

He frowned, and it was kind of a sympathetic expression, as he asked, "Why are you on the muscle? Want to tell me what happened?"

With these guys it had to be about business.

Karen said, "Beat it, will you?" and stared at Andy until he turned away. All she had to do was give in and they'd ask her to join them and she wasn't in the mood. Sit there and smile. Okay, what *do* you do if you aren't in sales? I'm a deputy U.S. marshal and you assholes are under arrest. No, they'd like that, so she'd have to keep it simple: tell them she was in law enforcement, a federal marshal, and they'd say wow, no kidding, and act sincere, interested—You're packing?—until they began to play off whatever she said, show her how clever and entertaining ad guys were, finally getting to: Are you staying at the hotel?

She was pretty sure the third guy would feel he had to make a pitch, or the other two would egg him into it. Sooner or later he'd be along.

Karen drank with friends. Alone, she might once in a while accept a drink from a guy she didn't know if he wasn't an obvious geek. She had met Carl Tillman that way. He bought her a drink and turned out to be a bank robber: the one she told her dad about—after Burdon let her know they had Tillman under surveillance—asking her dad what she should do, and he said get a new boyfriend. She would have learned soon enough, though, Tillman wasn't her type—even if he didn't rob banks. It was the little annoying things about him, like saying "*ciao*" instead of so long or see you later, or the way he called her "lady" and it made her think of Kenny Rogers.

If they'd leave her alone this wouldn't be bad, a new experience, to sit warm in the middle of a snowstorm, a blizzard, sipping sour mash. But as she thought this, and felt it, slipping into a relaxed mood, another dark suit appeared, reflected in the window wall, the third guy here to try his line. Karen waited for his opener. Finally he said:

"Can I buy you a drink?"

Without turning to look she knew who it was.

▼▼▼

EVEN HER INSIDES KNEW, A MUSCLE OR SOMETHING IN THE middle of her body had grabbed hold and wouldn't let go. What she had imagined and played with in her mind was happening, and she was afraid if she turned her head he wouldn't be there or it would be one of those guys. She stared at his reflection until she had to find out and turned her head. Karen looked up at Jack Foley in his neat navy-blue suit, his hair not quite combed but looking great. She said, "Yeah, I'd love one," and it was done, that easily. "Would you like to sit down?"

He pulled the chair out looking at her. Now he was across from her, close, his arms resting on the edge of the table, neither of them saying anything, not even about the weather, the three ad guys watching—Karen knew it without looking at them —wondering what was going on here. They see a man walk in: white male, forty-seven, six-one, one-seventy, hair light brown, eyes blue, no visible scars . . . No, they didn't, they saw a guy who looked a lot like them. Only different. Something about him . . . She had to try not to think of him with any reference to the past if this—whatever they were doing—was going to work. Not the past or anything happening beyond right now. But it was a fact, whether learned from reading his sheet or looking right at him, his eyes were a vivid blue. His teeth were white, white enough . . .

He offered his hand saying, "I'm Gary," and smiled.

She hesitated for a moment and then went along, said, "I'm Celeste," and had to smile with him, their smiles coming easily, in the mood to smile, sharing a secret no one else in the world knew.

When she lowered her hand to the table, his hand came down to cover hers. She watched his expression as she brought her hand out slowly, his eyes not leaving hers, and laid her hand on his. The tips of her fingers brushed his knuckles, lightly back and forth. She said, "It takes hours to get a drink around here. There's only one waitress."

He looked away for a moment and started to get up. "I can go to the bar."

"Don't leave me," Karen said.

He eased back in the chair. "Those guys bother you?"

"No, they're all right. I meant, you just got here." She picked up her drink and placed it in front of him. "Help yourself." She watched him take a sip.

He smacked his lips. "Bourbon."

"You're close."

He said, "You mean Jack Daniel's isn't a bourbon?" She smiled at him and he said, "No, I guess it isn't. You like Jim Beam, Early Times?"

"They're okay."

"Wild Turkey?"

"Love it."

He said, "Well, we got that out of the way."

She watched him take another sip and place the glass in front of her. "Did you ever see *Stranger Than Paradise*?"

He looked out at the snow and she knew he had.

"The two guys take the girl who just arrived from Czechoslovakia, someplace like that, to Cleveland to see Lake Erie? And there's so much snow you can't see the lake? That one?"

She was smiling at him.

He said, "Was that some kind of test question?"

"One of the guys gives her a dress," Karen said. "She takes it off, throws it in a trash bin and goes, 'That dress bugged me.' "

He said, "You like to act goofy, don't you?"

"When I have time."

"What do you do for a living?"

"I'm a sales rep. I came here to call on a customer and they gave me a hard time because I'm a girl."

"Is that how you think of yourself?"

"What, as a sales rep?"

"A girl."

"I don't have a problem with it."

"I like your hair. And that suit."

"I had one just like it—well, it was the same idea, but I had to get rid of it."

"You did?"

"It smelled."

"Having it cleaned didn't help, huh?"

She said no. She asked him, "What do you do for a living, Gary?" and saw his eyes change, become almost solemn.

He said, "How far do we go with this?"

It stopped her, threw her off balance. Karen said, "Not yet. Don't say anything yet. Okay?"

He said, "I don't think it works if we're somebody else. You know what I mean? Gary and Celeste, Jesus, what do they know about anything?"

She knew he was right, but had to take a moment before saying, "If we're not someone else then we're ourselves. But don't ask me where we're going with it or how it ends, okay? Because I haven't a fucking clue. I've never played this before."

The way he said, "It's not a game," she knew he meant it.

"Well, does it make sense to you?"

He said, "It doesn't have to, it's something that happens. It's like seeing a person you never saw before—you could be passing on the street—and you look at each other . . ."

Karen was nodding. "You make eye contact without meaning to."

"And for a few moments," Foley said, "there's a kind of recognition. You look at each other and you know something."

"That no one else knows," Karen said. "You see it in their eyes."

"And the next moment the person's gone," Foley said, "and it's too late to do anything about it, but you remember it because it was right there and you let it go, and you think, What if I had stopped and said something? It might happen only a few times in your life."

"Or once," Karen said. "Why don't we get out of here."

"Where do you want to go?"

Karen looked up. The advertising guys were getting ready to leave, dropping napkins, pushing their chairs back, taking forever. Philip looked over, and then Andy. Andy waved. Karen watched them leave the table finally and make their way out.

It was quiet. She looked at Foley in the slim-cut navy-blue suit, his white shirt with its button-down collar, his burgundy and blue rep tie—the conservative business executive—looked in his eyes and said, "Let's go to my place."

"Your room?"

"My suite. I showed my credentials and they upgraded me."

"You must do pretty well, in your business."

"I don't know, Jack. The way things are going I may be looking for work."

NINETEEN

THERE WAS MAURICE, WHITE BOY BOB, KENNETH AND THE new one, Glenn, in the living room getting ready, guns and boxes of bullets on the coffee table. Moselle stood watching them from the foyer. She got to meet this Glenn, but didn't mention anybody looking for him.

When he came, Maurice told him he was late and Glenn said, "Oh, is that right?" and told Maurice to look out the fucking window he'd know why. Glenn saying his hands ached from gripping the fucking wheel, hanging on, man, trying to stay in the fucking tracks. A car'd go by and all the slop and shit from the road would hit the windshield. Maurice saying, "You suppose to be the ace driver, *you* pass the cars, they don't pass you." Glenn saying, "Oh, is that right?" Snippy, Moselle thought, for a man. He told how he came up behind a salt truck and got blasted with it, like shrapnel hitting the car. He told how a woman pulled out in front of him and when he braked did a three-sixty, spun all the way around. He said you couldn't see anything and said driving in that ice and snow was fucking work, man, it wore you out.

"You done?" Maurice said. "If you done we can get on with business."

"I'm not driving," Glenn said, "so forget it."

"I hope to tell you you not driving," Maurice said, and looked over. "Moselle, you want something?"

"My grocery money."

"That's what we going to get. Put our mittens on, our masks, case we want to do some skiing . . . There. I look like a Ninja?"

"You going to see Curtis, aren't you?"

"We be back, oh, 'bout two hours," Maurice said. "Where's my little Tuffy dog? I want to kiss her good-bye."

"You going to see Curtis," Moselle said.

MAURICE WIGGED HEARING ABOUT HIS DOG AND GLENN thought for a minute he'd call off the gig, Jesus, ranting and raving. They got in the van Kenneth had picked up and Maurice sat in front with him, saying once he found out who it was ran over little

Tuffy that man's ass was his. He'd set fire to the man's house with the man in it. Kenneth was wired on crystal meth, talkative, asking Maurice how he was going to find the man in the first place. Maurice said don't worry, he'd find him, but never said how. He punched the dashboard with his fist a few times keeping himself primed, Glenn believed, for whatever was coming up. Kenneth would brake hard and as the van slid sideways would go "Yeaaaaah," and lift his hands from the wheel. Maurice didn't say anything to him until a couple of miles down Woodward Avenue—the streetlights making it weird-looking with the snow coming down—they turned on to Boston Boulevard, a street of homes bigger than Maurice's, the van sideswiped a parked car, bounced off it, and Maurice said, "What's wrong with you?" That's all, until they came to the house, a big dark place showing only a few lights, dim ones, and Maurice said, "Leave it on the street. We don't want to come out find we stuck." Kenneth said, "We shoveling away, here come the police," sounding as if he thought that would be pretty funny. Jesus, these guys. Maurice said, "We ready? Check your weapons." Glenn had a little snub-nosed .38 they'd given him. Kenneth had a shotgun. White Boy Bob had some kind of pistol and a fire ax. Maurice had a .45 because Huey P. Newton had said one time, "An Army .45 will stop all jive," and Maurice had been told about Huey P. and the Black Panthers when he was a kid. He said to Glenn, "You and Kenneth gonna come with me around back. White Boy goes in the front. We hear him busting in, we go in." Looking at the house he said, "Man, this is when to do it. They don't even see you coming."

Glenn said, "How many are *they*?"

"The man, Frankie, his wife Inez and a nigga works for them name Cedric," Maurice said. "'Less they have company, huh?"

As soon as they were out of the van they moved in a hurry, went past the side of the house single file, Kenneth making a path through the deep snow squeaking under their tennis shoes, all three pulling their ski masks down as they reached the back of the house. Right away they heard glass breaking, White Boy Bob smashing his way into the house, sounding like he was tearing it apart with his fire ax. They heard his voice, far away but clear, yell, "Police! Don't move!" Maurice said, "Go ahead," and Kenneth used the butt end of the shotgun to bust a pane in the French door, reached through to unlock it and Glenn followed them into the house and around a dining room table in the dark as a door swung in and Glenn saw a black guy with a gun, a shotgun, lights on in the kitchen behind him. They surprised him being so close. He tried to get back in the kitchen, but Maurice put the .45 in his face and told Glenn to take his shotgun. Maurice said, "Cedric, my man. You thought I forgot about you, huh?" He pulled Cedric out of the doorway to walk in front of them to the living room, telling Glenn, "This the nigga ratted me out the time I went down." Cedric said something over his shoulder Glenn didn't hear and Maurice whacked him across the head with the .45, like slapping him with the barrel. Cedric hunched his shoulders and put his hand up to his head.

White Boy was in the living room turning a lamp on, cold air coming in from a big front window smashed to pieces. He said, "They went upstairs." Maurice said, "White Boy, take Cedric here and put him in front of you." They went up a stairway that turned once to reach the second floor and now they were in a wide hallway of doors, all closed. Maurice poked Cedric with the .45 saying, "Take us to your leader." Cedric didn't say anything this time. He took them to the door at the end of the hall where Maurice called out, "Police! Y'all come out with your hands up!" But didn't wait to see if they would. He said, "White Boy," and White Boy swung his ax at the door to smash the lock and the force of it swung the door in. Maurice pushed Cedric into the room and with his .45 waved White Boy and Kenneth in after him.

Glenn followed Maurice expecting to see a bedroom, but it was like an office, an office, say, in a factory or a warehouse, old desks and file cabinets, cardboard boxes piled up, vodka bottles, ashtrays full of butts, a scale, a calculator. A white guy in shirtsleeves stood by an open window. A woman was coming out of the bathroom with the sound of the toilet flushing. Skanky, stringy-haired junkies was the way Glenn saw them, both holding their arms to their bodies now, rubbing themselves.

The man said, "Police, shit," sounding drunk or sleepy, in a nod. "Maurice, is that you, dude?"

Maurice lifted his ski mask. So did White Boy and Kenneth. Glenn left his covering his face.

"If it wasn't me, Frankie, it'd be somebody else."

The man said, "I'll tell you right now you won't find any product."

"You flush it down the toilet, we won't. No, I don't imagine. Inez, how you doing, girl? Not too good, huh? Man, you look like you been chewed up and spit out. Frankie, you gonna catch cold with that window open." Maurice turned his head to Glenn. "This is the gentleman I was telling you about use to be a customer, use to wear a suit and comb his hair; hell, use to be Frank, this scarecrow, Frankie and his lovely wife Inez. See what scag can do to a person? Now then, so we don't have to tear up your nice home," Maurice said, "get out the green from where you hid it. I'm gonna say forty fifty thousand and it's in this room. Frankie? Pay attention. You're gonna have to tell me where it is before I count to three. You ready? . . . One two three." Maurice raised the .45, put it on Cedric and shot him in the head. The impact sent him against the file cabinets and he seemed to hold on before sliding to the floor. Maurice stepped over to him and Glenn thought he was going to shoot him again, but all he did was stare at him—until Frankie spoke and Maurice looked up.

"You've been wanting to do him, haven't you? Shit, you *came* to do him."

"You think so, let's try Inez," Maurice said, turning to her as he raised the .45. "Ready for the count?"

Inez was looking right at him, all eyes, shoulders hunched, her hands tightened into fists. She said, "Give it to him!" raising her voice, the words sounding hoarse and scratchy and she began to cough saying, "Give him what he wants."

"He's gonna shoot you anyway," Frankie said, "he's gonna shoot us both," and looked at Maurice. "Aren't you?"

"Right this second," Maurice said, "you don't tell me where your money's at."

"It's different places in that file cabinet," Frankie said, "the one by Cedric."

Kenneth said, "You don't need Inez no more. Can I have her?"

"Go on," Maurice said, "but be quick." Kenneth took Inez by the arm and she went with him, eyes glued wide-open, tripping over her own feet, out of the room. Maurice, making a face, said to Glenn, "Would you fuck that woman? Kenneth, he don't pass up nothing has a pussy and it's free."

White Boy said, "Man, I wouldn't fuck her with your dick."

"All right," Maurice said, pulling the file cabinet open, "let's see what's in here." He poked through the files, finding currency he handed to Glenn who counted it, all small bills, and dropped the money in a cardboard box. It amounted to a few bucks over twenty-eight hundred. That was it. Maurice said to Frankie, "You gonna make us work, huh? You sure you want to?"

"Fuck you," Frankie said, "you're gonna kill me anyway."

Maurice didn't say if he would or not. He didn't say anything at all until they'd dumped all the files from the cabinets, looked in the boxes—some with little crack bottles in them—looked in the desk drawers, looked in the toilet tank, looked everywhere they could look, and when they were done Maurice said to Frankie, "You're right," and shot him twice in the chest—like that, *bang, bang,* nothing to it—Glenn watching Frankie almost go out the window, hit the sill and fall dead. Maurice said, "I guess we through here."

Glenn, with the money, followed Maurice along the hall wanting to get out of here, man, right now, run down the stairs and *out*. They came to a bedroom with the door open and there was Kenneth by the bed pulling up his pants, Inez lying on the bed with her knees still raised, her legs apart and Glenn said, "Jesus," the sight repulsive to him, this worn-out junkie showing herself, that dark wedge deep between her pure white thighs, it was ugly, and yet he felt himself becoming aroused.

Kenneth said, "Who wants a piece of this?"

Glenn stood there holding the carton of money; he was one of them, wasn't he? He said, "You leave any for us?" Like he was kidding.

Maurice said, "Look out," moving into the doorway and raised his big army pistol.

Kenneth saw him and held up his hand as if to hold him off. "Wait. What you doing?" Hurrying then to get his belt fastened.

Maurice extended his .45 into the room and fired and the white stick figure on the bed jumped and its legs came straight out stiff and hit the bed. Maurice fired again and the body jumped again, though not as much this time. Maurice paused. "She dead?"

Kenneth looked down at Inez, Glenn watching, waiting to hear.

"If she ain't, she ought to be. Man, I never been this close."

"Make sure," Maurice said.

Glenn followed him down the stairs and out the front door once they got it unlocked, down the walk through a foot of snow to breathe in the cold air, breathe it in and let it out slow, seeing his breath. Man oh man, these guys. He got in the van with Maurice, who sat looking at the house saying, "Come on, come on." They waited. When Kenneth got in behind the wheel Maurice said, "She dead?"

"She is now."

Glenn wanted to know what he did to her, but Maurice didn't ask so he kept quiet.

They waited, the engine running now but it was still cold, their breath coming out like smoke. Finally Glenn said, "Where in the hell's White Boy?"

"In there leaving his calling card," Maurice said, and Kenneth laughed. "White Boy's a shitter."

Kenneth kept laughing till Maurice told him to be quiet. Glenn sat there in the dark, cold in his wool-lined raincoat, wondering what he was doing here.

▼▼▼

WHEN THEY GOT HOME MAURICE PEELED OFF SOME BILLS FOR Moselle. She looked at the money saying, "This is it, huh? I can do better with the police. Was on the radio, they give you a hundred dollars for every gun you turn in, no questions asked."

"You believe that?" Maurice said. "You believe they don't check the serial numbers, see was any stole?"

"Was on JZZ just now. They wouldn't say it it wasn't true."

"Touch my weapons," Maurice said, "I'll trade you in." He turned to Glenn. "You gonna stay with me now, I can keep an eye on you."

Glenn frowned, squinting at him. "The fuck're you talking about?"

"So you don't disappear on me."

Glenn kept squinting, trying hard to show surprise. "Why would I do that?"

"Like he has the gift," Moselle said to Glenn, "can read your mind. I wasn't even there and I know what you're thinking. Was worse than you imagined, wasn't it? Baby, you with the bad boys now."

TWENTY

SHE WAS QUIET IN THE ELEVATOR, QUIET ONCE THEY WERE IN the suite and Foley had called room service and learned it would take about fifteen minutes. When he told her she said, "Oh," and looked around the room as if wondering where they would sit. He watched her turn on lamps and go to the window to tell him it was still snowing. He watched her cross to the bedroom saying she'd be right back, but knew room service would arrive before she came out.

The waiter delivered a fifth of Wild Turkey, a bucket of ice, a pitcher of water, two glasses and a dish of peanuts, placing the tray on the coffee table. Foley paid him. He was sitting on the sofa pouring drinks when Karen came out of the bedroom with a cigarette, still wearing the black suit. She said, "Oh, it's here. I hope you signed for it." He didn't say if he did or not. He was eating peanuts. He got up with a drink in each hand, walked over to her and she said, "Oh, thanks," taking the drink. He watched her sip from the glass and then raise her eyebrows to say, "Mmmm," as if she'd never tasted bourbon before.

"You're having second thoughts," Foley said.

She raised her cigarette and looked at it.

"I know what's bothering you and I can understand how you feel."

He waited while she took a deep drag on the cigarette and turned her head to blow the smoke away from them. When she was looking at him again he said, "You think I'm too old for you."

He waited again.

This time while she seemed a little surprised.

He waited with no expression.

She began to smile. Good. Not giving it much, but looking right at him and it was the right kind of smile, conspiring with him again, knowing something no one else did. She put on a serious look and nodded. She said, "Or I'm too young for you. Do you think we can work it out?"

▼▼▼

THEY WERE ON THE SOFA NOW WITH WHISKEY AND PEANUTS, no plan, letting it happen, gradually feeling a glow. Karen's shoes were off, her legs tucked under her.

Foley took off his jacket but not his tie; he felt good in the tie. He remembered the clipping, Karen's picture with the shotgun, and laid it on the coffee table. She said, "So it wasn't by chance. You found out I was here." He told her he'd called her room from downstairs. She said, "If I had answered, what were you gonna say?" He told her, well, he'd say who he was and did she remember him and ask if she'd like to meet for a drink. "If I remembered you," Karen said, "I came looking for you. I would've said sure, let's do it. But for all you knew I could show up with a SWAT team. Why would you trust me?" He said because it would be worth the risk. She said, "You like taking risks," touching his face with her hand, then kissed him, very gently, and said, "So do I, peanut breath." He felt her fingers brush through his hair as she kissed him again, still gently, and it was hard—aware of her scent, remembering it—it was hard to keep from eating her up. He put his arms around her, feeling her slim body in his hands, and she brushed his mouth with hers, saying, "What's the hurry, Jack? You have to be somewhere?"

▼▼▼

SHE KNEW HIS VOICE FROM THE TRUNK OF THE CHEVY AND the look in his eyes from before that, in a glare of headlights, the quiet look in his eyes as he said,

"Why, you're just a girl." As he said, "I bet I smell, don't I?" Conversational, covered with muck from a prison escape. If there was a moment, the kind of moment they'd talked about, that would've been it, in the headlights. Now he was clean, his face smooth and hard, her fingers touching his cheekbone, the line of his jaw, a tiny scar across the bridge of his nose. She said, "Sooner or later . . ." She stopped and he looked at her over the rim of his glass, about to take a drink. She loved his eyes. She said, "You have a kind look, trusting."

"That's not what you were about to say."

She shrugged, letting it go. But sooner or later she would ask him . . . Sooner or later she would begin saying things to him and not be able to stop. She said, "Remember how talkative you were?"

He said, "I was nervous," lighting her cigarette and then his own.

"Yeah, but you didn't show it. You were a pretty cool guy. But then when you got in the trunk . . ."

"What?"

"I thought you'd try to tear my clothes off."

"It never entered my mind. Well, not until—remember we were talking about Faye Dunaway?"

"I know what you're gonna say."

"I told you I liked that movie, *Three Days of the Condor*, and you said yeah, you loved the lines? Like the next morning, after they'd slept together, he says he'll need her help and she says . . ."

" 'Have I ever denied you anything?' "

"I thought for a couple of seconds there, the way you said it, you were coming on to me."

"Maybe I was and didn't know it. Redford tells her she doesn't have to help him and she says . . . You remember?"

"No, tell me."

"She said, 'You can always depend on the old spy-fucker.' "

"Why'd she say 'old'?"

"She was putting herself down."

"Would you call yourself that, a spy-fucker?"

"I think she was still scared to death, trying to keep it light but hip. Before they ever go to bed she accused him of getting rough. He says, 'What? Have I raped you?' And she says, 'The night is young.' I thought, Come on—what is she doing, giving him ideas? No, I wouldn't say that, definitely, or call myself a spy-fucker. Or any other kind." She said, "You know you kept touching me, feeling my thigh."

"Yeah, but in a nice way."

"You called me your zoo-zoo."

"That's candy, inside, something sweet. You don't hear it much anymore." He smiled and touched her hand. "You were my treat."

His sheet said no visible scars, but there was a white gash across three of the knuckles on his right hand and half the third finger was missing.

"You asked me if I was afraid. I said of course, but I wasn't really; it surprised me."

"I might've smelled like a sewer, but you could tell I was a gentleman. They say John Dillinger was a pretty nice guy."

"He killed a police officer."

"I hear he didn't mean to. The cop fell as Dillinger was aiming at his leg and got him through the heart."

"You believe that?"

"Why not."

"You said you wondered what would happen if we'd met a different way."

"And you lied to me, didn't you? You said nothing would've happened."

"Maybe that's when I started thinking about it. What if we did?"

"Then how come you tried to kill me?"

"What did you expect? You could've been dumping the car for all I know, hiding it somewhere, and I'm locked in the fucking trunk. I warned you first, didn't I? I told you to put your hands up."

"Yeah, after I said come on out. You knew I wasn't gonna leave you in there. You start shooting at us."

She thought of the gun and said, "That Sig .38 was my favorite." She watched him fixing up their drinks, the cigarette in the corner of his mouth. In that moment he seemed from another time.

"I've wondered about that," Karen said, "what you were gonna do with me."

"I don't know, I hadn't worked that part out yet. All I knew was I liked you, and I didn't want to leave you there, never see you again."

"You waved to me in the elevator."

"I wasn't sure if you caught that."

"I couldn't believe it. I was thinking of you by then, a lot, wondering what it would be like if we did meet. Like if we could take a time-out . . ."

He said, "Really?" He said, "I was thinking the same thing. If we could call time and get together for a while."

She wanted to ask, yeah, but for how long? Then what? But she said, "That day we met on the street, did you know it was me?"

"You kidding? I almost stopped."

"You didn't."

"I wanted to, but I was embarrassed wearing that tourist outfit. I didn't want you to think I dressed like that."

"The black socks with the sandals."

"Part of the disguise."

"I watched you all the way down the street."

"I could feel it."

"You were going to see Adele, weren't you?"

"I don't think we should get into that."

"No, you're right. Or Buddy. I won't ask if he's with you or what you're doing here. Or if you've run into Glenn Michaels yet."

He said, "Don't talk like that, okay? You scare me." He said, "I was trying to remember—Faye Dunaway and Robert Redford start kissing . . ."

Karen nodded. "As he's untying her."

"How did they get from there into bed?"

▼▼▼

FOLEY WATCHED HER GET UP FROM THE SOFA AND HOLD OUT her hand to him. She said, "Come on, I'll show you," and took him into the bedroom. He sat on the bed to take off his shoes, stood up to take off his pants. Got his socks off. She said, "Are you gonna leave your tie on?" Watching her undress, Karen getting down to a black bra and panties, he said he wasn't sure if the old ticker would be able to take this. When she got out of her undies and came over to him, standing close to help him with the tie, he was thinking he might've died already and gone to heaven. When his clothes were off he looped the tie around his neck again. Seeing her in lamplight before she turned it off he said, "My God, look at you." He had never seen a woman's body like hers naked. In magazines maybe, but not in real life. In the next few minutes he realized he had never met anyone under the covers like she was: man, all over him with her scent, touching, kissing, saying his name, saying "Oh, Jack," in a whisper that sounded sad. He asked her if she was having fun and saw her face in the light from the sitting room that filtered the dark, saw her smile, but even her smile was sad. They made love and she didn't speak or make a sound until she began to say his name again, "Jack?" He asked her what. But that's all she was doing, saying his name, saying it over and over until she was saying it pretty loud and then stopped saying it. No woman had ever said his name like that before.

▼▼▼

"WHAT AM I NOW?"

Lying in his arms in the king-size bed, light from the sitting room almost reaching them.

"You're still my zoo-zoo."

She moved away from him to sit up and swing her legs off the bed.

"Are you coming back?"

She said, "You can always depend on the old bank-robber fucker."

He reached her before she could leave the bed, and sat up, getting close behind her, his hand touching her breasts as his arm came around to hold her against him.

"Are you being funny?"

"I have to go to the bathroom."

"Are you?"

She said, "I don't know."

He let go of her, watched her get up and go into the bathroom. The door closed. He felt they were coming to the end of the time-out and he'd hear a whistle blow the way hacks blew whistles to tell you to stop doing something and start doing something else. He didn't know what to say to her now to get her back; he wasn't sure if he could put himself in her place to know what she was thinking. He did know how to listen and how to wait; he was good at waiting. If he couldn't get her back, at least for a while—there was no time limit—then he would become serious, not wanting to but knew he would, and they'd play it out.

But when she came back to the bed and stood naked looking down at him, he believed he could get her back.

She said, "I want you to know something. I wasn't looking for just a fuck, if that's what you're thinking?"

"Why are you mad?"

"Or I did it for some kind of kinky thrill. Score with a bank robber the way some women go for rough trade."

"What about *my* motive?" Foley said. "Now I can say I fucked a U.S. marshal. You think I will?"

She hesitated. "I don't know."

"Come to bed."

He raised the covers and she stood there making up her mind before finally slipping into bed and his arms took her in. He said, "I know of a guy—his wife held him down, wouldn't let him go out with the guys, wouldn't give him any money—he was a drunk. So he robbed a bank to get back at her, a bank where he was known and he'd be sure to get caught. The wife was humiliated and the guy was happy. He did fifty-four months, came out, patched things up with his wife and robbed the same bank all over again. Another guy, he goes in the bank holding a bottle he says is nitroglycerin. He scores some cash off a teller, he's on his way out when he drops the bottle. It shatters on the tile floor, he slips in the stuff, cracks his head and they've got him. The nitro was canola oil. I know more fucked-up bank robbers than ones that know what they're doing. I doubt one in ten can tell a dye pack when he sees one. Guys like—remember that movie, Woody Allen robs the bank?"

"Take the Money and Run."

"He hands the teller the note, she looks at it and says, 'You have a gub? What's a gub?' That's par, because most bank robbers are fucking morons. You've heard some of the nicknames they get? The B.O. bandit, the Chubby Cheeks bandit, Mumbles, the Laurel and Hardy bandits? A guy they call Mr. Pleats? Another one, the Sheik, guy wears something that looks like a turban? The Vaulter? Guy always jumped the counter for no reason. Robby Hood?"

She said, "What were you known as?"

"I don't think I had a nickname. But the point I'm making: to go to bed with a bank robber so you can say you did, you'd have to be as dumb as they are. I know you're not dumb, I know you're not looking for kinky thrills, as you say. So why would I think that? Why would *you* think I might think that?"

She said, "You're not dumb."

"You can't do three falls," Foley said, "and think you have much of a brain." He waited a few moments, lying there holding her, before he said, "If you get serious on me, it's over. You have to stop thinking."

Now Karen took time, holding on to him. She said, "I don't want to lose you."

"That's part of the feeling we both have. It's how we got here. But there's nothing we can do—you know that. You're not gonna give up the life you have and it's way too late for me. I couldn't if I wanted to. Change my name and look for work? You say 'work' to a con he'll go out the window, not even bothering to see what floor he's on. Look, we knew going in," Foley said, "when the time's up, it's up. I say that knowing I love you with all my heart, I sincerely do."

Her face came up to his; they began to kiss and touch again, Foley with a tender feeling he had never experienced before. Looking at her eyes he thought maybe she was crying or was about to. She said, "I can't go with you." She kissed him again, and in a voice so quiet he could barely hear her she said, "I want to know what's gonna happen."

"You know," Foley said.

▼▼▼

WHEN KAREN WOKE UP, LYING ON HER SIDE FACING THE bathroom, she didn't open her eyes right away. She wanted to; she wanted to look at the radio clock next to the bed and she wanted to turn her body enough to reach with her hand and, if he was there, touch him. As long as she didn't open her eyes or move he was still there. She could take her time, creep up on him and they'd make love again and she would hear his name coming out of her in the dark. So she lay there with the stale taste of whiskey in her mouth. All that was left. Until she said, Oh, for Christ sake, grow up.

And opened her eyes.

It was ten-fifteen. The bathroom door was open, the light off. She rolled to her back and turned her head. His side of the bed was empty; the room silent, the windows dark. She remembered looking at herself in the bathroom mirror and coming out to say things that were so fucking stupid now, hearing herself, her tone, and remembered him saying, "Why are you mad?" And later saying, "If you get serious on me, it's over." And that's what she did, became emotional and blew it because she was thinking too much, wanting to know how it would end. She thought, Well, now you know. And got out of bed.

Karen walked out to the sitting room with a sense of expectation. Foley was gone, but maybe he'd left a note. She looked around, at the desk, the coffee table. The newspaper photo he'd laid there was gone. But something wrapped in a napkin was lying by the half-empty bottle and the ice bucket. She picked it up and knew what it was as she unfolded the napkin.

Her Sig Sauer .38.

TWENTY-ONE

"I DROP YOU OFF," BUDDY SAID, "GIVE THE VALET GUY THE car, Glenn and a black kid by the name of Kenneth are waiting in the lobby. This is three o'clock in the afternoon, the snow's coming down, they want us to take a ride with them. I said you were buying a pair of shoes, and if they want to go look for you over there, good luck. We come out, White Boy's waiting in the car. What time did you get back?"

"About ten."

"It took you, what, seven hours to buy a pair of shoes?"

Wednesday morning now, Buddy had come to Foley's room frowning, wondering where he'd been.

"I saw Karen Sisco," Foley said. "She's staying at the Westin."

Buddy didn't say anything right away. First he

sat down at the table to look at Foley across his room service tray, Foley having the Continental breakfast in his socks and underwear, a bottle of Jim Beam close by.

"And she saw you?"

"Yes, she did."

Buddy said, "Oh, my," and watched Foley pour a shot of Beam into his coffee. "Well, we're sure casual about it, aren't we? You talk to her?"

Foley nodded.

"Buy her a drink?"

"We had a few."

"She knew who you were."

Foley nodded again, sipped his coffee and raised the cup. "You want some? You can use the glass in the bathroom."

Buddy shook his head. "Have a nice visit and then you left?" Buddy waited but didn't get an answer, Foley biting into some kind of Danish. "How's that work, a wanted felon socializing with a U.S. marshal?"

Foley said, "You know how I felt about her." He put his cup down. "The night I came out, we're in the trees by the highway, she's in Glenn's car? You kept asking why I wanted to bring her along. I said I just wanted to talk to her. Well, it turns out she wanted to talk to me, too, and that's what we did."

Buddy said, "Did you give her a jump? If you

did I might begin to understand where your head's at. I know the attraction pussy can hold for a man. What I can't imagine is risking your life over it, though I know it's done."

"It wasn't about getting laid," Foley said. "You told me out on the highway it was too late, you know, to have a regular life. I knew that. I still wanted to know what might've happened if things were different."

"You find out?"

Foley said, "Yeah, I did," not sounding too happy about it. But what did that mean? He was disappointed by what he found? Or was sorry now he'd robbed all those banks?

Don't ask, Buddy thought. He said, "What happens now?"

"We're back where we were."

"You don't want to move on?"

Foley sipped his laced coffee. He said, "If you want to, I'll understand, but I'm staying."

"Well, shit," Buddy said, "if you aren't worried —a big sensible fella like you . . . I think we ought to move to a different hotel, though, not be so close."

"It's all right with me."

"She know Glenn's here?"

"I think so, but I doubt she's located him."

"Glenn's nervous, being with those guys. White

Boy and this Kenneth, they're the kind probably can't write their own names but know everything. They took me by the State, it's a regular movie house on Woodward Avenue. If the snow wasn't up to our ass we could walk. Those salt trucks, they pile the snow up down the middle of the street and then haul it away, I believe dump it in the river."

"What time are the fights?"

"They start at eight."

"Let's go about ten. They say why Snoopy wasn't there?"

"Said he was busy. I'd call him Snoopy talking to Glenn? Glenn'd look at White Boy and I'd see White Boy in the mirror giving me the evil eye. We work with those assholes one time only, that'll be enough for me."

"We've come this far," Foley said.

"They took me past the Detroit Athletic Club, said Ripley goes there for lunch almost every day, comes out about midafternoon and goes home, takes the Chrysler Freeway. Glenn said they've been checking Ripley out since November. See, but Glenn wouldn't tell the Snoop what the score would be till he came back to De-troit this time."

"What do they need Glenn for?"

"That's a good question."

"What do they need *us* for?"

"That's even a better question."

"We watch each other's back," Foley said.

They'd been doing that for years. Buddy looked at the rolls in the Continental basket. "You gonna eat those?"

"Help yourself."

"I got your girlfriend's shotgun, but the only way I can get it out of the hotel's in a suitcase. Your Sig Sauer's no problem."

"I don't have it," Foley said.

Buddy was spreading butter on a croissant. He said, "What'd you do with it?" and bit off half the roll.

"I gave it back to her."

Buddy had to chew a few seconds before he said, still with a mouthful, "You want to forget the whole thing and go to California, I'll drive us."

▼▼▼

BURDON'S VOICE, SOUNDING PATIENT, SAID, "KAREN, I JUST spoke to our people up there, they tell me they haven't heard a word from you." Patient and then adding a note of surprise to the lilt in his voice. "Now how could that be?"

"I've been busy," Karen said. She held the phone between her shoulder and jaw, picked up the paper and turned to the Local News section. "Daniel? 'Three shot to death in home invasion.' Last night, during a snowstorm. Detroit Police think one of the invaders may be a guy I was over there asking about the other day, Maurice Snoopy Miller. The victims ran a dope house and this guy used to do business with them."

"Snoopy," Burdon said.

"Yeah, he's a friend of Glenn Michaels. They met at Lompoc and Glenn told DEA he stayed with Maurice last November when he was up here."

"Karen, you're ducking my question. How come you haven't been to see our people?"

"I don't have anything to give them. I walk in empty-handed saying I want to help, they'll say, good, why don't you put the coffee on."

"I told them you were coming."

"Yeah, and what'd they say?"

"They thought with something like two hundred agents in the state of Michigan and a bunch of marshals they had enough help."

"See? I don't want to go in until I can give them something, like pay my way, and I know I'm close to locating Glenn. In fact, I'm going to the fights this evening, and I have every reason to believe he's gonna be there."

" 'Every reason to believe' is like telling me you *think* he'll be there. All I have to say, Karen, you spot Glenn I want you to call for backup. You don't spot him, you come home and we'll find something for you to do. You took advantage of me, girl, caught me in a weak moment."

"How'd you do with the Super Bowl?"

"The point spread I had, I was doing fine till you came along."

"I won a new pair of shoes, off my dad."

"What about Foley? You hear anything?"

"I'm after Glenn, he's the key."

"Karen, you fuck up and I get sent to White Fang, Alaska as resident agent . . ."

"I'll go with you," Karen said.

"You bet your skinny ass you will."

Karen said, "Okay, then . . ."

▼▼▼

SHE SHOULD HAVE SAID, "YOU'RE HOPING I DO FUCK UP, aren't you?" She didn't believe she had, yet; because she didn't think of the time spent with Foley as morally wrong, and if it wasn't, and if she wasn't technically aiding or abetting but only violating a code of conduct, she could live with it and not feel guilty. When she was much younger she would go to confession and say, "Bless me, Father, for I have sinned. I stole a lipstick from Burdine's and I let a boy touch my breast but we didn't do anything." If she felt a need to tell more, she might add that she had smoked cigarettes after promising her mother she wouldn't. The priest would give her ten Our Fathers and ten Hail Marys, absolve her, she would be sorry for her sins, sort of, and whatever degree of guilt she had felt would be gone. Since then, for the past fifteen or so years, Karen hadn't been to confession because she seldom felt guilty about anything. If she had doubts, she would talk to her dad about it. Or, she would imagine talking to her dad, which to Karen was much the same thing.

Karen: I spent about seven hours with Foley.

Her Dad: Don't tell me everything.

Karen: Don't worry. Do you understand our taking a time-out?

Her Dad: The way you tell it, yeah.

Karen: There was no time limit specified.

Her Dad: But now you're back in play, out of time-outs.

Karen: I guess so.

Her Dad: You have to do better than that. You have to accept the fact.

Karen: Okay.

Her Dad: What are your options?

Karen: If I find him? Place him under arrest.

Her Dad: What else? What if he tries to get away? What if he pulls a gun on you?

Karen: He doesn't have a gun.

Her Dad: You want to do this or not?

Karen: I'm sorry.

Her Dad: What if he resists arrest, tries to get away, puts you in a position where you're trained to use your gun? Could you do it?

Karen: I don't think so.

Her Dad: What if he wants you to take off with him?

Karen: I wouldn't go. I told him that.

Her Dad: Would you let him get away?

Karen: No.

Her Dad: Then you'd have to shoot him, wouldn't you?

Karen: I don't know.

Her Dad: Would he shoot you, if he had to?

Karen: I don't know.

Her Dad: He told you he's not going back.

Karen: Yes.

Her Dad: So whose choice is it, really, if you have to shoot him?

Karen: Is that supposed to make it easier?

Her Dad: Why did you join the marshals?

Karen: Not to shoot people.

Her Dad: No, but the possibility is a fact you have to abide by. Can you do it?

▼▼▼

DURING THE AFTERNOON KAREN STAYED IN AND WATCHED A movie on television she had seen at least a couple of times before, *Repo Man*, because Harry Dean

Stanton was in it and he reminded her of Foley. Not his looks—they didn't look anything alike—his manner: both real guys who seemed tired of who they were, but couldn't do anything about it. Stuck, putting up with their lives the way people find themselves in jobs they care nothing about, but in time have nowhere else to go. She wondered if Foley ever had goals. Or if his idea of living was anything more than lying around the house, watching movies.

▼▼▼

BUDDY SAID HE WAS GOING OUT, SEE IF THERE WERE ANY whores around, maybe bring one up to his room. Foley imagined some poor girl standing in the snow in her white boots, bare thighs and a ratty fur jacket, shivering, getting hit by slush as cars went by; but doubted she'd be there in real life. He wished Buddy luck and pressed buttons on the TV remote until he found a movie. *Repo Man*, a winner he'd seen a few times before. Old Harry Dean Stanton getting the short end as usual. Fun to watch, though. This was the one, they open the trunk of the car and you see a strange glow. Like in *Kiss Me Deadly*, the strange glow in the case inside the locker, and they used it again in *Pulp Fiction*. Mysterious glow movies—some kind of radioactive material, but what it's doing there is never explained; if it was, Foley missed it. He liked this kind of movie. You could think about it after, when you had nothing to do, try to figure out what the movie was about.

TWENTY-TWO

MAURICE WOULD GET UP FROM THE TABLE AND WALK ALONG the apron of the stage yelling at one of the fighters, telling him, "Stick and jab, stick and jab." Not in the way of the audience, the ring up on the stage, but it was annoying and Glenn wished he'd shut the fuck up. Maurice would come back to the table and Kenneth would leave, go up on the side of the stage where guys were hanging out, big black guys, and Kenneth would hang with them between bouts, Kenneth dosed on speed and doing all the talking. Glenn had never seen so many big black guys in one place who weren't wearing football or basketball uniforms. Outside of him and White Boy Bob there were maybe five or six other white people in the whole theater. The waitress would bring a round and White Boy would throw his beer down in three or four swigs, give Glenn's shoulder a jab and tell him to come on, drink up, "You drink like a girl," and look to see if there were any other morons around thought he was funny. The black guys and their women at tables close by only stared, tolerating him because of Maurice.

Where movie seats used to be were rows of round nightclub tables: a row of them on each of four levels rising a step at a time up through the theater to the bar: a long one, and dark up there away from the ring lights. People hung out in the open spaces at both ends of the bar. Behind the bar was the aisle that crossed the theater from side to side, a stairway at one end that went down to the rest rooms. Beyond this area was the outer lobby with a small bar over to one side.

A fighter from one of the Kronk boxing clubs was announced, rap music came booming out of speakers and a procession of handlers and hangers-on appeared out of a door on the side aisle. Now women crowded in from the audience, jiving, waving as the fighter finally appeared to mount the stage and climb into the ring in red and gold to fight four rounds for two hundred bucks, the gold tassels on his high red shoes jumping now as the fighter worked his shoulders with quick jabs, shuffling around his side of the ring. Watching from the other side a white kid from out of town or some Mexican kid trying to look cool, unimpressed, would weave and do some footwork in his plain black shoes to be doing something, waiting for the rap show to end and the ref in his bow tie and latex gloves to motion them to the center of the ring.

Ever since they got here Glenn had been trying to think of a way to get the car keys from White Boy—Glenn listening to him and Kenneth talking about last night, grinning at each other, saying tomorrow, man, tomorrow was payday, talking about hitting Ripley's house. Glenn would listen to the two morons and watch Maurice bopping around from table to table giving brothers the brother handshake, touch fists in their ritual ways, Maurice the hipster, a dude black felt cap set on his head just right, and shades. "Maintaining a low profile," Maurice told him. "No do-rag. The fights, I'm all the way low profile."

They had come here in the Lincoln Town Car, White Boy driving, so White Boy had the keys.

Glenn had gone downstairs to the men's and neither of the morons was sent along to keep an eye on him; so he was pretty sure he could slip out of here, cross Woodward Avenue to where the Town Car was parked and if he had the keys, shit, he'd be out of here, on his way to California. He had boosted the car off a lot in West Palm: decided on the Lincoln—parked right in front, ready to go—and while the parking attendant was busy moving cars around, Glenn ducked in the shack and got the Lincoln keys off the board—he knew keys—then waited for the right moment to slip in behind the wheel and take off. He'd brought his tools along that day, not sure what method he'd use to pick up a car, and the tools were now in the trunk of the Lincoln, the car waiting for him right across the street. But White Boy had the fucking keys in his pocket.

Getting in the car wasn't the problem, it was unlocked. When they got here White Boy didn't know where the button was to lock the doors, so Glenn said, "Here, I'll do it," standing outside the car, the driver-side door open. White Boy walked away and Glenn reached in as though to press the lock button, saw the three of them already crossing the street to the theater, and all he did was close the door. He hoped to God if the doors were unlocked the glove compartment would be too, so he could get in there and pop the switch to open the trunk. Get out his tools, use the slap hammer to yank the ignition and he was off! White Boy could keep the keys. But if the glove box was locked, he was fucked. He'd have to find something to pry it open. But if he took too long—even if he could pop the trunk—Maurice would send the morons looking for him.

The glove box had to be unlocked. It would be his only chance of getting away from these people.

He'd wait . . . No, he'd better go right now.

There was the bell, a bout over with and Maurice was getting up, heading for the stage.

Glenn did wait a few moments before saying, "Man, that beer goes right through me. I got to go take a piss." He hesitated because he expected White Boy or Kenneth to look at him funny or one of them would say he had to go, too.

All White Boy said was, "What're you telling us for? You want somebody to hold your pecker?"

Glenn was glad to laugh. He said, "I have to use both hands, but I can manage."

As he walked away the moron said, "Hey, Glenn? Shake it easy."

Glenn had his back to White Boy by now and didn't have to laugh or even smile. He had to get out of here, fast, away from these morons. And if he couldn't pop the trunk and start the car, fuck it, he'd run to California.

▼▼▼

TWO YOUNG MEN IN RED-AND-GOLD KRONK JACKETS WERE working security in the outer lobby. Karen came along in her navy cashmere coat, a navy wool cloche covering her hair, jeans and hiking boots, and the security guys smiled and asked how she was doing. She said fine. They asked to look in her bag. She showed her ID and star and said, "This is all you need to know, right?"

They said hey and seemed pleased to see her, grinning, looking her up and down in the long coat, as she walked off through the lighted outer lobby and into the darkened theater. From the bar she scanned the descending row of tables and the stage, the ring empty, looking for white people, rap music coming out of speakers somewhere, a few women rising from their tables to make funky moves with the music. Karen saw a white couple off to the side and two guys down front, in the first row of tables. The bartender asked what she'd like and Karen said, "Just a minute." The smaller of the two guys at the table was getting up, the other one laughing. The smaller one turned, not laughing—it was Glenn—and started this way through the tables. Karen turned and looked at the bartender waiting for her. She said, "Not right now," and turned her head enough to see Glenn pause at the end of the bar and look back toward the tables, taking his time, before he moved off and was out of view. Going to the men's room—Karen was pretty sure—wearing a sweater, no coat. She was surprised then, once she came around the bar, to see him heading out through the lobby, hurrying. He couldn't have spotted her; there had to be another reason. She waited until Glenn was out the door and then went after him. Said, "I forgot something," going by the two security guys. Outside, she saw Glenn running across the wide avenue of packed, dirty snow, past car headlights creeping along, and into the parking lot, disappearing into the row of cars facing the street. Karen followed, reached the lot but didn't see him now. She put her gloves on moving in among the cars, stopping to listen, waiting to hear an engine start. The only sounds came from the street. She reached an aisle through the rows of cars and caught a glimpse of a car interior, almost right in front of her, the light on, and then off as she heard a car door slam closed.

Karen walked up to the front passenger side of the car. She saw his shape in the dark: Glenn behind the wheel half lying on his right side, his hair hanging . . . It looked like he was trying to claw open the glove compartment. His head jerked around as Karen opened the door and she saw the whites of Glenn's eyes, big saucer eyes looking at her in the light that came on, Glenn pushing himself up straight as she got in with him. The door closed and it was dark again.

"Glenn, are you trying to steal this car?"

He said, "Jesus. I don't believe it."

Pitiful. She almost felt sorry for him.

"I'm ruining your life," Karen said, "aren't I?"

He raised empty hands. "I don't have the keys."

"I see that."

"I mean I'm not stealing the fucking car."

"You're not?"

"I already stole it. Last week or whenever it was, in West Palm. I can't be stealing it again, can I? I can't even get my tools out of the fucking trunk."

"Let me see if I understand," Karen said. "You want to take off, get away from those guys. Is that it?"

"You see me in there?"

"And one of them has the keys."

He said, "Yeah," nodding, and said, "Listen, I have to take a leak pretty bad."

"The two guys you were with—that one, that isn't Maurice Miller, is it? I've seen Snoopy's mug shot and it didn't look like him."

"How could you know about him?"

The poor guy, bewildered; desperate, too, looking toward the theater. Karen glanced that way. All they could see from here, over the tops of cars, was the marquee and the name STATE in lights. Karen said, "Another one of those days, huh, nothing seems to go right? Glenn, I know your life history, who your friends are, where you've been and now, it looks like, where you're going."

"You're gonna bust me for picking up a car?"

"For the car, for aiding and abetting a prison escape, and conspiring to do whatever you came here for. Tell me, Glenn, are you getting into home invasions now?"

He said, "Jesus," shaking his head.

"Like the one last night," Karen said. "You were there, weren't you?"

"I'm not saying another fucking word, and I mean it. Jesus Christ, I don't even know what you're talking about."

"Put your hands on the top of the steering wheel."

"What for?"

"So I can cuff you."

"You serious? Listen, these guys, they're gonna be out here any minute looking for me. They're fucking animals, they're vicious. I'm not kidding. I was taking off and that's all I want to do, get as far away from those guys as I can."

"They scare you?"

"They scare the shit out of me, and I'm not afraid to admit it."

"Was Foley with you?"

"When?"

"Last night. About what time was it you hit the dope house?"

"I *said* I'm not talking to you. I'm not involved in whatever they're doing, the same as I didn't help Foley escape. You said so yourself."

"Yeah, well, I was wrong about that. Where do you suppose Foley is right now?"

"How do I know."

"You're telling me you haven't seen him?"

"What I'm telling you is I have to piss. I mean it, bad."

"What time was it you hit the dope house?"

"I don't know what you're talking about."

"Glenn, tell me what those guys are up to and I'll make you a deal."

"Like what?"

"I'll let you take a leak."

"That's some deal."

"Anywhere you want."

He hesitated. "You mean it?"

"Anywhere," Karen said. "Glenn, what time did those guys hit the dope house?"

He hesitated again. "It was early in the evening. I don't know, about seven."

Karen got a cigarette from her bag and lit it with hotel matches. She took a deep drag and blew the smoke out in a slow stream. At seven, and for at least the next couple of hours, Foley was with her at the hotel.

"Can I go piss? Please?"

The way Karen worked it, she let him urinate against the side of the car, the window down, while he told about Richard Ripley, the Wall Street crook, where they were going to pick him up and take him out to his home in Bloomfield Hills, late tomorrow afternoon. Karen nodded as she listened. She had heard of Ripley and knew he'd served time at Lompoc. She wanted to know exactly where he lived and then asked:

"What about Foley?"

"He's supposed to go with them," Glenn said, his shoulders hunched in the window. "But I don't know, he didn't show up tonight."

"You know where he's staying?"

"No idea."

"Where do you meet tomorrow?"

"Listen, I'm fucking freezing out here."

"Where're you meeting?"

"They haven't decided." He straightened to look toward the theater, then hunched over to look in the window again. "You might have something in your car to pop the trunk with. You know, with the jack?"

"You think Foley backed out?"

"I don't know—he doesn't exactly confide in me." Glenn straightened again, hugging himself. "I'm freezing my ass off."

"You want to get out of here," Karen said, "run, it'll warm you up. But listen, Glenn?"

"What?"

"If you're lying to me . . ."

"I know, you'll find me. Jesus, I believe it. I keep thinking, if you hadn't driven me to federal court last summer . . ."

"We wouldn't keep running into each other?"

"You wouldn't even know who I am."

Karen said, "If I didn't know you, Glenn, by tomorrow you'd be in jail or dead. Look at it that way."

▼▼▼

PEOPLE WERE LEAVING AS FOLEY AND BUDDY ARRIVED. THEY found the table, White Boy and a black guy sitting there. Maurice came down from the stage. He said, "Where you been?" an edge to his tone. "You miss the big boys, come in time for the walkout fights. Well, shit, you may as well pull up a chair." He said to the black guy, "Kenneth, this is Mr. Jack Foley and this is Mr. Buddy, famous bank robbers and jailbirds, say they want to help us out."

Foley put his hand on a raincoat draped over the back of a chair at the table. "Who's sitting here?"

"Your homie, Glenn," Maurice said. "Only thing, he went to the men's about an hour ago and never came back."

Foley gave Buddy a look.

White Boy, grinning at them, said, "I think he must've fell in."

"I sent these two looking for him," Maurice said. "They come back shaking their heads."

"Glenn have a car?"

"One he brought from Florida. We all come here in it this evening."

"Well, if he left his coat," Foley said, "and he's been gone an hour . . ."

"Hey, I *know* what you're saying. Glenn didn't want nobody to know he was leaving. Man, I *know* that. I sent White Boy back out again, see was the car still there, check it out. White Boy had the keys, but knowing Glenn's habits I thought it good to check. You understand? The car's still there and Glenn ain't nowhere to be found."

Foley said, "Everybody's somewhere, Snoop. Where's Glenn staying?"

"My house." Maurice turned his head toward the ring, watched a few moments and yelled, "Reggie, push off and hit, man. Push him off." He turned back to Foley. "Why don't you and Buddy sit down and have a drink with me. What you want?"

"We're leaving," Foley said.

"The fuck you talking about?"

"Snoop, if you don't know where Glenn is . . ."

"The man changed his mind, that's all, so he left. Decided he can't take the heat."

"Glenn's pussy," White Boy said. "He never done shit last night but watch."

Buddy said, "Where was this?"

A waitress came as he said it and asked if they'd like something. Foley shook his head; Buddy did too. The waitress dumped the little tin ashtray in a napkin and left and White Boy said, "You read the paper you'd have seen it."

Maurice said, "White Boy, that's another business. You understand? Has got nothing to do with us here."

"He keeps looking at me," White Boy said, nodding at Buddy.

"I can't help it," Buddy said. "I hear the Snoop call you White Boy, I'm trying to figure out why you let him."

"It's what they call me at Kronk, from when I trained there."

"You used to fight, huh?"

"Right here and out at the Palace."

"You any good?"

"You want to find out?"

Buddy said, "You ever done time?"

"He's asking do you gouge eyes," Maurice said. "Do you bite off ears. White Boy's got his own moves. But that's enough of that shit. Look," Maurice said, taking Foley by the arm and moving off a few steps to stand with their backs to the table. "What you worried about Glenn for? What's he know?"

"I thought everything," Foley said, watching the fighters jabbing and juking each other, one of them patient the way he moved in, the other taking wild swings and missing.

"Glenn knows everything we suppose to do tomorrow," Maurice said. "Snatch the man he comes out of his club, drive home with him. Glenn could tell somebody that, yeah, but it don't mean shit. You understand? I changed the plan. Glenn don't know it, 'cause while we waiting for you he left. For whatever reason it don't matter. It ain't happening tomorrow."

Foley, watching the fighter, said, "This fight isn't going four rounds."

Maurice glanced over. "Ain't even going two."

"You're not saying it's fixed."

"Don't have to fix nothing to know who's gonna win. It's in the matchmaking, how you match 'em up, who you bring in to fight the home boy. You understand?"

Foley kept his gaze on the ring.

"If it isn't happening tomorrow, when is it?"

"Tonight," Maurice said. "Soon as we leave here. Stop home to pick up what we need and go do it."

Foley said, "Give me a minute," and motioned to Buddy as he turned to the table. Behind him, he heard Maurice say:

"You got two minutes, that's all. Make up your mind."

Foley turned back to him to stand in close.

"I wasn't asking permission. Buddy and I're going up to the bar. We're gonna take however long it takes. We may keep walking. We do come back, it's understood this deal cuts fifty-fifty, half for us. How you cut your half is up to you."

"We can talk about it," Maurice said.

"No, that's the way it's gonna be, Snoop."

Foley walked away and Buddy followed him to the bar, this dark area away from the ring lights.

"He wants to do it tonight."

"What's the difference, tonight or tomorrow?"

"Glenn. He could be setting us up."

"Glenn's always a risk," Buddy said. "We've come this far."

TWENTY-THREE

KAREN TOLD HER DAD SHE COULDN'T SLEEP. HE SAID, "IS that right? I was doing pretty good myself, till the phone rang. There was nothing on the news about my little girl, so I guess I dozed off. Now I see I've missed Letterman. What's going on?"

She told about tracking down Glenn Michaels and getting him to tell what he was up to, her dad saying, "That's some deal you offered him. You let him go?"

"I bring Glenn to the First Precinct for stealing a car in Florida," Karen said, "have to explain to a lieutenant or a sergeant what I'm doing here? He could look at me and think—I don't know what, but probably think he should take over. You know what I mean? Not only he's never seen me before, I'm a girl waving a marshal's star at him, a fed trying to tell a street cop about a planned home invasion. He'd have to check me out. There'd be nothing to charge the other guys with; all I've got is a stolen car. So I let him go and called Raymond Cruz."

"The one you saw the other day."

"Yeah, and told him the whole story. I was concerned with jurisdiction. If these guys are breaking into a home in Bloomfield Hills, Oakland County, should I get in touch with the police out there, the sheriff's department or what? I didn't see anything federal about it, so why would I call the FBI. Right?"

"Sounds logical."

"I told you Raymond's an inspector, he's over crimes persons, crimes property and sex crimes."

"I recall that."

"He also heads the Violent Crimes Task Force and they're hooked into all the local police around, the county sheriffs and the Bureau. The Bureau's involved, also ATF, because in almost all of the home invasions they're busting into dope houses after cash and guns. That's all, in and out."

"But this one's different," her dad said.

"As far as we know or can assume, yeah. This guy Ripley's home in Bloomfield Hills isn't likely to be a dope house, even if he has done time. You remember Ripley?"

"Dick the Ripper, the inside trader. Yeah, I think he's the kind would have cash in his house."

"Anyway, Raymond said it wouldn't matter where the home was, the crime would come under the jurisdiction of the task force, and the feds would be involved because of the kidnapping in the plan."

"What kidnapping?"

"They pick up Ripley tomorrow coming out of the Detroit Athletic Club—it's downtown, right around here. One of them gets in the car with him and the rest of the guys follow. That's kidnapping."

"Would the cops alert Ripley? Tell him it's gonna happen?"

"Raymond said no, it could blow their surveillance. He said something like this, you had to make a judgment call. The ideal way, let the guys pick up Ripley and go through with the robbery, and then take them coming out of the house. But if you have reason to believe Ripley's life might be in danger, you'd have to move before that. I told Raymond it looked like these were the same guys who hit a house last night and killed three people. He said then they'd have to take them before they got to Ripley's home and he's brought inside."

"But get them for the kidnapping," her dad said, "as soon as Ripley's abducted."

"Right, and they can take them state or federal, either way. But this involves another judgment call. If these guys are too dangerous to let one of them get in the car with Ripley, then you don't have a kidnapping case. All you've got are some guys in probably a stolen car and probably with guns. But to get them even two years on a gun charge it has to be during the commission of a felony. So, do you let them go through with the kidnapping or not?"

Her dad said, "What if Ripley, for some reason, doesn't go to the club tomorrow? Or these guys decide to go directly to the house?"

"Tomorrow morning they'll scout the house, the neighborhood, and set up a surveillance, be ready for a change in the plan."

"And what will you be doing?"

"Raymond said I can ride with him tomorrow if I want. Be on the scene."

"But stay in the background?"

"Why do you say that?"

"When they're putting the cuffs on Olufsson, you want him to see you?"

"You're a riot."

"I mean Foley. I get him mixed up with that guy in Stockholm."

"Foley might not be involved."

"You hope."

"No, Glenn said Foley didn't show up for the meeting tonight, at the fights."

"How were they?"

"I didn't stay. I went back in to get a look at Snoopy Miller, so I could ID him, and left."

"Foley could still be there tomorrow."

"I don't know," Karen said, "he might."

"But you don't have to be there."

Karen said, "No," and paused. "What would you do?"

"It wouldn't bother me any to see him busted. I look at his picture in the paper, I can't say I'm impressed."

"Yeah, but he doesn't look like that. It's an old mug shot."

"Well, does seeing him cleaned up wearing a suit," her dad said, "change the fact he's a loser? A guy who's wasted his entire life? Yeah, I'd be there. I'd personally cuff his hands behind his back. And I'd make sure he hit his head getting in the police car."

"Thanks a lot."

"You asked."

▼▼▼

MOSELLE WATCHED FROM AN UPSTAIRS WINDOW. SHE SAW the Lincoln Town Car turn into the drive and pull up far enough for another car—an Olds, it looked like—to pull in behind it. The street had been plowed and cars left at the curb were buried in snow. She saw Maurice and White Boy come out of the Lincoln, and two white guys who looked like cops come out of the Olds. Where was Kenneth? Where was this Glenn?

Maurice came upstairs and turned the light on in the bedroom, acting like she wasn't there till he got down and pulled the suitcase out from under the double bed, where he kept his guns. Without looking at her he said, "The one in the dark overcoat's the jailbird with the ten gees on his head. I don't know it's gonna work or not, but I been thinking about a way to collect."

"Where's my brother?"

"Getting us a ride."

"Where's Glenn at?"

"Decide he don't want to go."

"You hide the body good?"

"Shame on you." Maurice brought pistols out of the suitcase, Moselle watching him, and laid them on the bed, the pistols and a box of 9-millimeter hollow points. "Glenn decide he don't want any parts of this business, so he left."

"And you let him?"

Maurice shoved the suitcase under the bed and stood up saying, "You keep talking you gonna risk getting hit in the mouth. Keep asking me questions. The one in the dark overcoat, has all that reward on his head and still talks like a con in the yard. You know what I'm saying? Like he's a man you don't mess with. Yeah, well, what I say to Jack

Foley is buuull *shit*. What I'm thinking is you gonna call the police. Say you heard him talking to his friend at the fights, sound like they going out to rob a man's house."

"How would I hear that?"

"You *did*, don't matter how. You say you believe it's the jailbird escaped from the place in Florida you read about and you want the reward."

"Where they gonna find him?"

"At the man's house he robbed."

"Dead," Moselle said, "from gunshot."

"It would look like it, yeah."

"What about his friend?"

"Same thing."

"Who killed them?"

"Nobody knows. Maybe the man from the house they tried to rob. Or the man's butler. Yeah, maybe the butler done it."

"They dead, too?"

"I 'magine it looks like Jack Foley shot them the same time they shot him and his friend, Mr. Buddy. Something like that. I get back I'll tell you how it took place."

"I have to say who I am," Moselle said, "to collect any reward. I do, it's like giving them your name, too. Don't you know that?"

"You like your grocery money, you like to weed out on that polio pot and become paralyzed, but you don't like to work for it." Maurice came over to the window to stand there looking out. "I *thought* I heard him. Yeah, there's Kenneth. Got a plumbing and heating truck. Look like we going out on this emergency call. Man's furnace quit on him."

Moselle watched him move back to the bed and pick up two of the guns. She said, "They three white men in the house. I try to collect this reward you talking about, they gonna be more white men in this house'n you ever saw before."

Maurice turned to her with a .38 Smith snub-nose and a Beretta nine. He said, "This one's for Jack Foley," handing her the Beretta. "And this one's for his friend Mr. Buddy. I like you to see they get them while I change my clothes. Would you do that for me?"

"I ain't calling any police," Moselle said.

"We talk about it when I get back."

"I don't care you beat me up, I ain't doing it."

"Honey," Maurice said, "getting beat up would be nothing."

Moselle had her hands in the pockets of her green silk robe, one of her hands holding the card Karen Sisco had given her, the hotel phone number written on it.

▼▼▼

When Kenneth came in, not paying any attention to them in the living room, White Boy got up and followed him through the foyer to the back part of the house, maybe the kitchen. Right after that the woman appeared, handed them each a gun and left. Foley said, "How come nobody wants to sit and chat with us?"

Buddy checked the .38, stood up from the sofa to stick it in his waist, and looked down at Foley holding the Beretta.

"You know how to work it?"

"I ought to, I've seen it used in enough movies."

Buddy took the pistol from Foley, checked the magazine, racked the slide to load the chamber and handed it back to him.

"It holds fifteen rounds. You have fourteen in there."

"You think that's enough?"

Buddy sat down again. "These guys are wacko."

Foley nodded. "I've noticed."

"They're gonna try to set us up."

"I believe it."

"Leave us dead at the scene. Look at the shit in the fireplace."

"I saw it."

Maurice came in the living room wearing white coveralls that looked custom tailored, a white sweatshirt showing at the neck. Foley said, "That what they're wearing these days to break and enter?"

"Take it and git, how it's done," Maurice said. "Don't waste any time. Stick a gun in the man's mouth and give him a count of three. Where's it at?"

Buddy said, "How's he gonna tell you with the piece in his mouth?"

"That's his problem," Maurice said. "Y'all want a drink? There ain't any hurry. I'd as soon wait here a couple hours." He looked at his watch. "Half-past twelve already. We wait and be sure the people snug in their beds. We come, they all sleepy-eyed. You know what I'm saying?"

Foley said, "You're not worried about Glenn?"

"If he told on us," Maurice said, "the police'd be here by now."

"Or they're waiting at the guy's house."

"Don't worry, we gonna check it out. Look around good before we go in."

Buddy said, "Maybe he's dead."

And Maurice said, "Yeah, got run over by a car. Or slipped on the ice and cracked his head. Glenn's gone on his own, that's all I can tell you."

Buddy said, "Well, we got to pick up another car. That Olds is fairly clean."

"No need," Maurice said. "We all go in the truck Kenneth got us. Man called us don't have any heat in his house. We come back, your car's here waiting."

Foley looked at Buddy. Buddy shrugged. Maurice watching.

He said, "Y'all have your ways of doing banks. I have my ways of doing this type of business. We in the house, we go right upstairs. Anything worth taking's gonna be in the man's bedroom, nine times out of ten. I tell you to do something, like check the other rooms first? See if they any guests in the house? It's on account I know my business. Understand? It ain't 'cause I want to boss you around. See, my boys know what to do, so I won't be telling them much. But I may have to tell you to go here, go there. Understand? What else? You say you want the cut to be down the middle. Well, even though we been doing all the work so far, I'm gonna agree to that, so we don't sit around here arguing about it. We move fast, in and out, and it's done. Y'all have any questions?"

Buddy said, "Where your guys at?"

"I 'magine they in the kitchen. You want to stir up White Boy again? Try to shame him and get him cross at you? For what? Think a minute. What good would that do us?"

"I just wondered," Buddy said, "if they were shooting up or what."

"Yeah, well Kenneth has some meth to keep him

all the way live. Some beer, that's all. Anything else you want to know about?"

Foley looked at Buddy. Buddy shrugged and Foley said to Maurice, "You have any bourbon?"

Maurice smiled.

▼▼▼

MOSELLE WATCHED FROM THE BEDROOM WINDOW: WATCHED them get in the big commercial van that had a company name on the side; watched until the van's red taillights were way up the street and gone. She went to the phone looking at the card Karen had given her, the card saying *Karen Sisco, Deputy United States Marshal,* sounding important, nice-looking card with a silver star on it in a circle. The clock by the bed was on 2:20. They'd been down there almost two hours talking and having drinks, Moselle waiting for them to leave. She knew what she wanted to ask this Karen Sisco, but didn't know what she'd say after, or how she'd answer any questions, knowing she'd be asked some. She had her hand on the phone. Then took it off, wanting to think about it some more. Get her words right in her mind. Have some weed first.

TWENTY-FOUR

FOLEY SAW HIMSELF PLAYING OUT THE END OF HIS LIFE AND was quiet, watching it happen scene by scene: in Maurice's living room, a half-gallon jug of vodka on the coffee table, watching Maurice duck and weave, telling how crafty he'd been in the ring; listening to White Boy's dumb remarks and the annoying way he laughed; listening to Kenneth speaking a language that seemed all hip-hop sounds, rhythmic, but making hardly any sense; Foley listening to sociopaths offering their credentials, misfits trying not to sound like losers, Foley realizing, shit, here was just a little more of what most of his life had been. He would hear Buddy make quiet comments that were meant to zing but fell flat, the same old same old, that stand-up talk you heard in the yard, but nobody here bothering to listen, busy thinking of what they'd say next. All us tough guys, Foley thought.

In the living room with the vodka, Maurice passing out knit ski masks before they left. Now in the back end of the big van full of plastic pipe and equipment: Kenneth driving, flying up Woodward Avenue past miles of dark storefronts and lit-up used-car lots, snow piled in the median, the road wide-open to them this time of night. Twice, Buddy told Kenneth to slow down. Kenneth grinned at the mirror. Buddy got out the .38 and touched the back of Kenneth's head with the stubby barrel. "Get ready to grab the wheel," Buddy said to Maurice, "when I shoot this asshole." Kenneth looked up at the mirror to find Buddy in there as Maurice told him, "Do like he says, man; slow down." They came to Long Lake Road, took it over to Vaughan and crept up and down the road twice, looking for security service cars or any kind of surveillance, before turning into Richard Ripley's circular drive.

▼▼▼

ALL FIVE OF THEM WERE IN THE BACK END OF THE TRUCK now, bumping into each other until Maurice let White Boy out the rear end and left the doors open enough so he and Foley could watch. "He's ringing the bell," Maurice said. "They open the door, we're in. They don't open it but ask what he wants,

White Boy says he's the heating man come to fix the furnace went out. They say they didn't call any heating man, White Boy asks can he use the phone, call his boss as he must've been given the wrong address. They look out the window, see the truck. Yeah, he must be telling the truth, he's a heating man, all right, and he's white."

They watched him ring the bell again. This time not a half minute passed before coach lights on either side of the entrance came on. "Get ready to go skiing," Maurice said, pulling his mask down. Now the door was opening and he said, "Here we go."

Foley had time to see a young guy in the doorway, his shirt hanging unbuttoned over jeans, in the moment before White Boy gave him a push and stepped inside the house with him. Maurice was out of the truck and Kenneth, with a shotgun, was scrambling to be next. Buddy caught him by his jacket collar and held him squirming until Foley was out. But then the moment Kenneth's feet hit the driveway he turned the 12-gauge on Buddy, still in the truck. Foley took the barrel in one hand and shoved it straight up in Kenneth's face, seeing the guy's eyes freaked with speed. Foley said, "Go on in the house before you get hurt." Kenneth had to put his face up close to Foley's and stare at him good before going inside.

Buddy said, "What're we doing here?"

Maurice had the young guy backed against a table in the foyer the size of a living room: good-looking young guy about eighteen with hair down on his shoulders; the pants and shirt he must've thrown on hearing the doorbell, but no shoes, barefoot on the marble floor. He looked scared and had to be, facing five guys in ski masks holding guns. Foley saw him trying to act natural, shaking his head.

"Honest to God, he isn't here."

Maurice said, "Out for the evening?"

Now the young guy looked surprised. "He's in Florida, Palm Beach."

Maurice hesitated. "When's he due back?"

Foley said, "Jesus Christ, what difference does it make? You want to wait for him?"

"Mr. Ripley's down for the season," the young guy said, "Christmas to Easter."

"Now tell me who *you* are," Maurice said.

"I'm Alexander."

Maurice said, "Boy, I don't care what your *name* is. I want to know who you are to the man, what you're doing here."

"I'm house-sitting."

"You by yourself?"

He seemed to hesitate before saying, "Yeah, just me."

Foley caught it and glanced at Buddy.

Maurice said, "What are you to the man, Mr. Ripley?"

"I don't know what you mean."

"How'd he come to hire you, watch his place?"

"Oh, he's a friend of the family. Him and my dad are old buddies."

"Your daddy a crook too?"

"No—I don't know what you mean."

"Where's Ripley's safe at, he keep his valuables in?"

"His safe? I don't have any idea."

"Let's go upstairs," Maurice said, and nodded to the house-sitter to lead the way.

Alexander said, "You know what? I think the safe's downstairs, in the library."

Maurice pushed him toward the wide staircase that took one turn on the way up to an open section of the hall with a railing.

"You just said you had no idea where it was."

"I mean I think that's where it would be."

"Yeah, and I think you don't want us to go upstairs. Go on, take us to the man's bedroom." On the stairway Maurice said, "Alexander?" and the young guy paused and looked over his shoulder. "You set off any kind of alarms, or how you turn on all the lights outside? You're a dead house-sitter. Understand?"

He said, "Yes sir."

"They any guns in this house?"

"Not that I know of."

In the wide second-floor hallway—lined with paintings of horses and fox hunts on dark oak paneling, upholstered chairs and lamps on bombe chests—Maurice said to Foley, "All right now, you and Mr. Buddy go on check the other rooms. Look at the wall behind any pictures hanging on it. Look at the wall in the closets, behind the clothes."

Foley said, "You check the walls, huh?"

"The man has a safe," Maurice said, "it's gonna be up here somewhere."

"How about his place in Florida?" Foley said. "If you'd called we could've checked his walls down there before we left. This is if you'd checked to see where he was. You follow me?"

Maurice took his time now. He said, "Jack, don't fuck with me. Understand? I don't have time right now to be fucked with." He turned to Alexander. "Where's the man's bedroom at?"

"This one," Alexander said. "Yeah, it could be in here," sounding eager. But just as Maurice gave him a shove toward the door, Foley saw Alexander look right at him, scared, worried—wanting to say something? Foley waited while Maurice and his guys filed into the bedroom. A light went on in there and he heard Kenneth's voice, Kenneth saying, "Hey, shit. Man, look at this."

As soon as they were alone Foley rolled his mask up on his head. "You ever wear one of these?"

"I don't ski," Buddy said.

"What do you bet," Foley said, "somebody else's up here?"

They opened the door to the next room, felt for a light switch and turned it on. A white satin spread covered the king-size bed. Foley started for the next room and Buddy said, "You don't want to check the walls?"

"You bet I do," Foley said. "Nothing I like better than checking walls. We'll come back. First I want to see where Alexander sleeps."

"He could be using Ripley's bedroom."

"I don't know, he could," Foley said. "He seems like a nice kid, huh? Trying like hell to act natural."

The beds were made in the next two rooms.

"Guy lives alone," Buddy said, "what's he need a house like this for?"

In the first bedroom they came to on the other side of the hall, the bed was turned down. "But hasn't been slept in," Foley said.

They came to the next room, the door open, the light off. Foley turned it on and saw stuffed animals on the dresser and a vanity, all kinds of little animals, birds, reptiles, and a bed that had been slept in, covers hanging down on one side, rumpled pillows, a pillow on the floor, a pair of sneakers . . . two pairs of sneakers, jeans and a sweatshirt draped over the arm of a chair. Foley picked it up, a dark blue one with UNIVERSITY OF MICH-

IGAN lettered on it in yellow. He went to the bed, leaned in close to the pillows and caught a soft powdery scent. He heard Buddy, close by, say, "You might've been a good cop." Foley moved to the bathroom door, a full-length mirror covering it, and tried to turn the knob. The door was locked from the inside. Close to it, his cheek against the glass, Foley said, "Honey, open the door. It's okay, I'm not gonna hurt you. I give you my word."

Silence.

He straightened and saw himself in the mirror wearing the overcoat, the white shirt and tie and the knit cap. He looked stupid. He took the cap off and shoved it in his overcoat pocket.

"Miss? Did you hear me?"

A woman's voice inside, close to the door, said, "Where's Alexander?" sounding fairly calm.

"He's okay."

"Tell him to say something."

"He isn't right here, but he's okay."

"What do you want?"

"Open the door, I'll tell you."

He waited.

"Miss, I can kick the door in. I don't mean to scare you, but you know I can do it." He waited again, looking at Buddy and saw Buddy straighten as they heard the lock click. Foley turned the knob, gave the door a push and let it swing into the bathroom.

The woman stood by the shower stall away from the door—not the cute little college girl Foley expected—no, this woman could be forty years old with thick red hair hanging free: a big woman with full breasts that were plain to see in her flimsy bra and low-cut panties, her navel centered in a little pot belly. She looked ready to take a swing at Foley if he approached her.

He said, "You're Alexander's girlfriend?" doubt in his voice, and she confirmed it.

"I work here. I'm the maid."

Buddy moved in closer. "Is this your room?"

She said, "Does it look like Mr. Ripley's?"

Buddy glanced at Foley.

Foley said, "How long've you worked for him?"

"Why do you want to know that?"

"Tell us where the safe's at," Buddy said, "and we'll leave you alone."

Foley said, "You and Alexander can get back to what you were doing. What's your name, hon?"

"I'm not your *hon*," the woman said.

Foley couldn't imagine her being tender, though she might be all a young guy like Alexander could ask for. He said, "I think you ought to stay in there. Get in the shower and don't make a sound."

She had her hands on her hips now, like no one was going to tell her what to do, saying, "Who do you people think you are?"

Scowling at them.

"You see the others," Foley said, "you'll know we're the good guys. I mean it, hide in the shower, for your own good."

She was asking, "What'd you do with Alexander? Where is he?"

When they heard Kenneth.

"Who's that?"

Before they knew he was in the room: Kenneth coming over to the bathroom with his shotgun, eyes bright in the ski mask, his eyes lighting up at the sight of the redhead in her underwear.

"Hey, shit," Kenneth said, "we gonna have a party."

TWENTY-FIVE

THE PHONE RANG AS KAREN, IN BED, WAS STARING AT LUMINOUS numbers in the dark: 3:45. She was sure it was Foley. In the moment it took to get up on her elbow and reach for the phone, no other name was in her mind. She said hello and felt a letdown as the woman's voice said, "I'm sorry if I woke you up."

"It's okay," Karen said, "you didn't."

"Reason I'm calling, I need to ask a question."

It was Moselle.

"Go ahead."

"If I know something's gonna happen—like a job is gonna be pulled and I don't tell the police I know about it? Am I, you know, could I be charged for knowing?"

"When is it supposed to happen?"

"See, I knew something this other time when a man was killed and I didn't say nothing?"

"You told me about it. You said a man was blown up."

"That's the one. They said if I told anybody I'd be dead, too. So I didn't. See, this time I been told the same thing. Only there's a reason I could get mixed up in it, too, and I don't want it to happen."

"Who threatened you, Maurice?" There was a silence. "If you're withholding information about a crime, yeah, you're complicit, participating in a wrongful act by association. You don't have to actually be there. When is this taking place, tomorrow?"

"Before that. Okay, I've told you and you know I'm not mixed up in it."

"But when is it going to happen?" Karen said, and waited. "Is Maurice there?"

"He left."

"You're alone?"

"I don't want to say no more than I have."

"Moselle, I'll be there as soon as I can. Will you wait for me, not go anywhere?"

She had hung up.

Karen called Raymond Cruz at his home, woke him up and stared at the clock while they spoke for a minute and a little more. He told her a car with a man from Robbery would be at the hotel by the time she was dressed.

▼▼▼

KENNETH WALKED UP TO THE REDHEADED MAID IN THE BATHroom saying, "What's your name, mama?" She wouldn't tell him, wouldn't say a word till he hooked a finger in the waist of her panties, pulled on the elastic as he looked in there and said, "Hey, shit."

The redheaded maid said, "Get out of there, you creep," and slapped his hand.

Kenneth, grinning at her, said, "Maurice got to see this," and took her by the arm out of the bathroom, past Foley and Buddy like they weren't even there.

"He's gonna jump her," Buddy said.

Foley kept quiet. They followed behind, along the hall to the master bedroom, Kenneth glancing around at them once; they didn't seem to bother him. He took the maid into Ripley's bedroom: the front part like a sitting room, full of fat, cushy chairs and a sofa, all white, everything white or black, a wet bar, a big TV, CD player, the man's king-size bed in there through an archway where Maurice, out of his coveralls, was taking suits and sport coats from the walk-in closet to look them over, drop some on the floor, lay some over a chair.

Alexander was in the sitting room part with White Boy. As Kenneth came in with the maid, Alexander yelled out her name, "Midge!" and started for Kenneth, telling him to leave her alone. Foley got to the doorway in time to see White Boy take

Alexander around the neck, rub the kid's scalp with his knuckles until he screamed and throw him on the sofa.

Kenneth had a finger hooked in her panties again, Midge holding on to his wrists, Kenneth saying, like he was making an announcement, "The bitch has a red puss on her. Y'all ever see a red one?"

Foley saw the maid let go of Kenneth's wrist and slap him across the face. Kenneth half turned from her, came back with his fist cocked and threw a left at her, a hook that jarred against the side of her face. She landed on the sofa, head bouncing against the cushion. Right away, as Foley watched, Alexander edged over to brush her hair from her cheek and take her hand, the woman looking up at Kenneth, stunned.

"I've seen 'em dyed blond on sisters," Maurice said from the other part of the room, "but I don't believe I ever seen a natural red one."

"This boy," Kenneth said, "been squirrelin' the maid, getting himself some house-sitting pussy."

Maurice said to Alexander, "How is she, boy, pretty good?"

Kenneth said, "I think she like to tussle with a man for a change. Get boned a way she gonna remember."

"Not till you done looking," Maurice said. "Will somebody please find the fucking safe?"

Out in the hall again Buddy said to Foley, "They're gonna gang-bang her. What're we supposed to do, watch?"

▼▼▼

MOSELLE WAS ON THE SOFA, CIGARETTE IN ONE HAND, HOLDing her robe closed with the other. Her gaze moved from the detective waiting in the foyer with his phone to Karen Sisco standing over her. More white people in the house these days than when white people lived in the house.

"I tell him it's none of my business. See, but he likes to brag on what he's doing. He *knows* I ain't gonna tell on him. But now this time he wants me to tell something. And if I do, I know it will mess *me* up good. See, there's two white men with him . . ."

"Tonight?" Karen said.

Moselle nodded and drew on her cigarette, wanting to tell it right, but not tell too much.

"Right now, this minute. They left with Maurice." Moselle paused, her gaze going to the foyer, then raising to Karen Sisco again. "But they not coming back with him." She watched Karen ease down to sit on the edge of the sofa, close to her.

"He's leaving them there."

She understood.

"You could say that."

"You know their names?"

Moselle shook her head. "Never was introduced."

This Karen said, "Are you playing with me?" Sounding irritated, not the nice person anymore. "What's your game? What're you telling me?" Getting a fierce look in her eyes.

Moselle leaned away from her. "I don't know the man's name till Maurice tells me. See, then I'm suppose to tell the police who this person is and where to find him, out at this rich man's house. Okay, if I *do,* it's gonna mess up my life good and I'll prob'ly go to jail. But if I don't, then I'm gonna be gone from this world, honey. *That's* what I'm telling you."

Karen seemed to ease back saying, "But why give up this particular guy?"

" 'Cause Maurice wants the reward you get for turning him in. Hoping, you understand, they pay off if the man's dead."

Moselle stubbed out her cigarette in an ashtray she held on the arm of the sofa, feeling Karen Sisco staring at her.

"See, the man's an escaped convict from Florida."

Feeling her staring and then feeling her get up and when Moselle looked, Karen in her long coat was across the room already, leaving.

▼▼▼

THEY HAD THEIR MASKS OFF AND HAD TORN UP RIPLEY'S bedroom: drawers pulled out and dumped, pictures off the walls, bed covers stripped, the mattress slashed.

Foley and Buddy, back from checking rooms, stood in the hall looking in. Foley said, "Would you hide walking-around money in a mattress?"

"I leave mine on the dresser," Buddy said. "This is a bunch of shit. These assholes are gonna end up with TV sets."

"You want to leave?"

"I'm ready anytime," Buddy said, "but what about the maid, and the kid?"

"I don't know," Foley said, looking at them now, on the sofa in the sitting room area. He did know, but didn't want to say. They seemed rigid, holding each other's hands, afraid to move. Kenneth, near them, was taking bottles of wine and booze from a cabinet and lining them up on the wet bar.

Buddy said, "I can see you don't have your heart in this."

"I never did."

"Before we go," Buddy said, "I think we're gonna have to settle with these assholes."

Foley nodded. "Yeah, I guess." He turned to Buddy then. "Listen, why don't you leave and I'll clean up."

"What're you talking about?" Buddy frowning.

Foley didn't answer because there was no way to explain what he felt, that these were the final scenes of his life playing out, that pretty soon it would be over and he was resigned to it happening. Here, not against the fence in some penitentiary. It was like if Clyde Barrow, driving along that county road in '34, knew he was going to run into all those Texas Rangers and there was nothing he could do about it. How did you explain that kind of feeling to anybody? Even to Buddy. Buddy was confused enough already and it made him appear restless. Foley said, "Take the truck and get out of here."

Buddy, still frowning, said, "I don't know what you're thinking, but we're going together, once I get the keys offa Kenneth."

They heard Maurice then, in there trying on clothes, say to Kenneth, "Put some music on," and saw Kenneth at the wet bar going through a rack of CDs.

"All he's got's Frank Sinatra," Kenneth said, "some others, little Sammy Davis, all ofay jive."

"Put Frank Sinatra on," Maurice said, looking at himself in a full-length mirror. "I can go Frank Sinatra."

"Hey, shit, the man's got Esther Phillips."

"Now you talking. Put Esther on."

" 'Confessin' the Blues.' "

"See has it got 'Long John Blues' on it."

Foley and Buddy, by the doorway, looked from Maurice to Kenneth.

"Yeah, number ten."

"Play it, man. Woman goes to see Long John, this seven-foot-tall dentist," Maurice said, looking at himself turning this way and that in the mirror, like the suitcoat might fit him if he caught it at a certain angle, not hang on him like a sack, the tips of his fingers showing. "Yeah, that's it, Long John telling the woman her cavity needs filling," Maurice watching himself, head bobbing slow motion, barely moving but on the beat. He caught Foley and Buddy in the mirror watching him from the doorway. "How y'all doing? You find anything?"

Foley held up empty hands. Then turned as White Boy brushed past them into the room, White Boy holding up a wad of bills in a rubber band.

"Six hundred, found it in the kitchen."

"That's a start," Maurice said, as Alexander came off the sofa.

"It's mine. Mr. Ripley gave it to me."

Alexander made a grab for the money and White Boy held it at arm's length above his head.

"Come on—I need it for school."

White Boy said, "Oh, okay, here," offering the wad of bills; but when Alexander tried to take it, White Boy raised his arm straight up in the air again, grinning at him, holding him off with his other hand.

"You rob kids?" Buddy said. "How about old women?"

"Anybody we can," Kenneth said, his head bobbing to Esther Phillips. "You a robber, it's what you do, man. You rob people."

Buddy started into the room and Foley took hold of his arm to stop him. They watched White Boy play with Alexander, waving the money at him, then raising it out of reach when he made a grab for it. They watched Midge get up to help Alexander and Kenneth right away step in front of her holding up his hands, feinting with them at her breasts. They watched White Boy drag Alexander by the hair to a closet, throw him inside and lock the door.

Buddy pulled his arm free and Foley said, "Stay out of it."

"I can't."

"Let's go see the Snoop."

They walked through to where he stood looking at himself in the mirror. "There's no safe," Foley said. "There's no cash or stones hidden anywhere."

Maurice studied his profile. "You look good?"

"Glenn was dreaming."

"Fucking Glenn," Maurice said. "Yeah, well, you take what you can get. You want a suit? You want a sport coat? The ones on the floor there, you can have any of those, I can't use 'em. You want shoes? The man has, must be twenty pair of shoes in the closet. Too big for me." He looked past their reflections and yelled, "White Boy! They's some cardboard boxes in the truck? Dump out the shit's in 'em and bring the boxes up here. We'll take the wine and the booze . . . Hey, and look in the kitchen, the freezer. See what looks good to you."

They saw White Boy in the mirror start out and then stop and look back.

"How about somebody helping me?"

Maurice said, "Y'all want to give him a hand?"

"We're leaving," Foley said.

"We all are, pretty soon now." Maurice turned and yelled at White Boy, "Get Kenneth!"

"He ain't here."

"Well, where's he at?"

"He took the redhead down the hall," White Boy said.

And Foley thought, Here it comes.

▼▼▼

TOWNSHIP AND SHERIFF'S RADIO CARS STOOD ALONG Vaughan Road, dull metal shapes in the dark, the sky overcast, unmarked cars against the snowbank, by the wall in front of the residence and blocking both ends of the circular drive. The detective from Robbery said, "Let me find out what's going on," and got out of the car. On the way here he had asked about the GCI prison break and that was pretty much what they'd talked about. The Robbery detective said he'd never heard of Jack Foley.

Karen was out of the car when he came back from the group standing by one of the sheriff's cars. He told her they were waiting for Inspector Cruz, he hadn't arrived yet. They walked to the nearer end of the circular drive and the Robbery detective pointed out the truck parked at the front entrance. He said they'd contacted the company and found out a truck was missing from their property and must have been stolen that evening.

Karen said, "It looks like the front door's open."

"It is," the detective said. "A guy came out just a minute ago. Got some boxes from the truck, went inside with them and kicked the door shut, but it didn't close all the way." Karen stared at the front entrance. The detective said, "Raymond should be here soon." He said, "You want to smoke? It's okay here by the wall." Karen shook her head. He had trouble with his lighter, getting it to flame. He lit his cigarette finally, looked up and said, "Hey, where you going?"

Karen walked up the drive to the front entrance, right hand in her coat pocket gripping the Sig Sauer .38.

▼▼▼

FOLEY SAW IT HAPPENING AS HE LOOKED IN THE MIRROR AND in a way it was like watching a movie:

"Kenneth's like a bullfrog: it moves, fuck it," Maurice said, turning this way and that to study his image, taking on a dead-serious look then as he stopped and said to Buddy, "Man, what are you doing with that?"

Now Foley was looking at the snub-nose .38 in Buddy's hand, holding it on Maurice, Buddy saying, "You guys are bad, Snoop."

And Maurice saying, "You know bad these days, man, is good," as Buddy stepped in and hit him in the mouth with his left hand and Maurice stumbled against the mirror and stood there with his hand to his face, his eyes taking on a shrewd kind of look.

"Watch the Snoop," Buddy said, "while I go find Kenneth."

Foley brought the Beretta out of his overcoat, saw Maurice's gaze follow Buddy for a moment and come back to him, Maurice touching his bloody mouth as he looked at the gun. Taking off the suitcoat he said, "Jack, you don't use a gun, do you?"

"Hardly ever."

"You nervous?"

"A little."

Maurice dropped the suitcoat on the floor and walked past Foley to the bed. Picking up his white coveralls he said, "This kind of setup, you don't have any idea what the fuck you're doing. Be honest with me—do you?"

"You're right," Foley said, extended the Beretta and shot him through the coveralls he was holding in front of him. "So I thought, why take a chance," Foley said, and shot him again and saw the Snoop's bloody mouth and his eyes staring, glazing over, saw him drop the coveralls and heard them hit the carpeted floor, something heavy in one of the pockets, and saw the blood in the center of the Snoop's white sweatshirt. He watched him sit down on the bed, then fall back with his eyes open and stay that way. Foley got the Snoop's piece, another Beretta, from the coveralls and ran out of the room.

He saw Buddy near the end of the hall looking back this way, his arm raised now, waiting for him. He said, "Two-gun Foley. What'd the Snoop do, pull on you?"

"He had it in mind," Foley said. "Listen, Kenneth's gonna be ready if he isn't deaf."

"I'm gonna bang in there and shoot him," Buddy said. "Something I've never done before, shoot anybody."

"You know he's got that shotgun."

"If you stand against the wall next to the door, reach over and turn the knob . . . You know what I mean?"

Foley slipped the pistol in his left hand into his coat pocket, put his back against the wall and looked at Buddy, standing now in front of the door. Foley's left hand reached for the knob. He turned it. Buddy kicked the door, going in with it, and the shotgun blast blew him back into the hall —past Foley already moving into the doorway. He saw them bare, both sitting up in bed, Kenneth racking the pump gun, Midge turned away from him, gathering up the covers hanging off her side of the bed, and coming around to throw them like a net at Kenneth as the shotgun went off and the covers caught fire and Foley was pumping one two three shots into Kenneth somewhere under there. Foley watched Midge, bare naked, jump up and drag the burning covers from the bed and saw Kenneth now, the bullet holes in his chest.

Foley knelt over Buddy in the hall, felt his throat for a pulse and said, "Shit." He looked up to see Midge—the woman not caring she was still naked, or maybe not even conscious of it—standing over him. "He's dead," Foley said.

She gave that a moment before asking, "Where's Alexander?"

"In the closet," Foley said, getting up. "But stay here. One of them's still around."

▼▼▼

KAREN STOOD INSIDE THE OPEN FRONT DOOR. SHE SAW CARDboard boxes lying in the foyer and a man on the staircase, a big guy with a gun in his hand. At the sound of the shots from upstairs he had stopped and now didn't seem to know what to do. Karen kept her eyes on him, both of them waiting, listening. She heard movement outside, hurried footsteps in the packed snow, and then silence, and then a voice calling to her, "Karen?"

She saw the guy on the staircase turn at the sound and saw Foley, in that moment, in the open part of the upstairs hallway, looking over the railing at her. She moved then, fast, to the foot of the stairs, put her Sig Sauer on the guy turned to her and said, "Police. Drop it or you're dead. Right now, drop it." She watched the guy stoop in a kind of awkward way to lay his gun on the stairs. He looked scared to death. She said, "Now come down," and saw Foley, at the top of the stairs now, watching her.

He said, "That's White Boy Bob. Honest, that's what they call him. The other two are dead." He paused. "So is Buddy."

Karen said, "Don't move."

She brought White Boy across the foyer to the open door, to the uniforms and detectives standing in the drive. She saw Raymond Cruz in the light from the coach lamps and said, "There's one more. Will you let me bring him out?"

Raymond hesitated. "Why?"

"I know him."

"He's a friend?" Sounding surprised now.

"I know him," Karen said.

▼▼▼

FOLEY HAD COME DOWN TO STAND WHERE THE STAIRCASE made its turn. As Karen crossed the foyer to the foot of the stairs she saw him pull his knit cap down over his face and now he was wearing a ski mask.

She said, "Come on, Jack—don't."

"Pretend I'm somebody else."

"You think I'd shoot you?"

Foley brought the pistols out of his pocket. "If you don't, one of those guys will. I told you, I'm not going back."

They were in the foyer now, behind her, Raymond Cruz and a half-dozen others lined up, watching.

"What're you now," Karen said, "a desperado? Put the guns down."

He raised them hip-high and she heard sounds behind her and was quick to raise her hand, though she didn't turn or look around. Karen took her time now. She said, "Okay, Jack," with almost a sigh, brought up the Sig Sauer in one hand and fired and he fell to the staircase, dropping the guns, grabbing hold of his right thigh. She turned to Raymond saying, "Wait, okay?" and went up the staircase to where Foley was lying. She sat on a step and carefully, gently lifted the ski mask and looked at his sad eyes.

"I'm sorry, Jack, but I can't shoot you."

"You just did, for Christ sake."

"You know what I mean." She said, "I want you to know I think you're a cool guy. I never for a minute felt you were too old for me." She said, "I'm afraid, though, thirty years from now I'll feel different about it. I'm sorry, Jack, I really am."

The poor guy, he looked like he was in pain.

▼▼▼

EIGHT IN THE MORNING TALKING TO HER DAD, KAREN SAID, "They don't know yet if they want to bring him up on the homicides. I doubt if they will. The Bureau's put a detainer on him, so when they're through with him here he'll go back to Florida."

"Wouldn't it be something if they sent you to get him."

"It's possible."

"Have a nice time with him on the plane—like picking up where your interlude, or whatever you call it, left off. And then throw him in the can."

"He knew what he was doing," Karen said. "Nobody forced him to rob banks. You know the old saying, don't commit the crime if you can't do the time."

"My little girl," her dad said, "the tough babe."

Read on for an excerpt from

ROAD DOGS

A NOVEL

ELMORE LEONARD

Available in hardcover in May 2009 from

wm

WILLIAM MORROW

An Imprint of HarperCollins*Publishers*

THEY PUT FOLEY AND THE CUBAN TOGETHER IN THE BACK-seat of the van and took them from the Palm Beach County jail on Gun Club to Glades Correctional, the old redbrick prison at the south end of Lake Okeechobee. Neither one said a word during the ride that took most of an hour, both of them handcuffed and shackled.

They were returning Jack Foley to do his thirty years after busting out for a week, Foley's mind on a woman who made intense love to him one night in Detroit, pulled a Sig Sauer .38 the next night, shot him and sent him back to Florida.

The Cuban, a little guy about fifty with dyed hair pulled back in a ponytail, was being transferred to Glades from the state prison at Starke, five years down, two and a half to go of a second-degree murder conviction. The Cuban was thinking about a woman he believed he loved, this woman who could read minds.

—

They were brought to the chow hall, their trays hit with macaroni and cheese and hot dogs from the steam table, three slices of white bread, rice pudding and piss-poor coffee and sat down next to each other at the same table, opposite three inmates who stopped eating.

Foley knew them, Aryan Brotherhood neo-Nazi skinheads, and they knew Foley, a Glades celebrity who'd robbed more banks than anybody they'd ever heard of—walk in and walk out, nothing to it—until Foley pulled a dumb stunt and got caught. He ran out of luck when he drew His Honor Maximum Bob in Criminal Court, Palm Beach County. The white-power convicts accepted Foley because he was as white as they were, but they never showed they were impressed by his all-time-high number of banks. Foley sat down and they started in.

"Jesus, look at him eat. Jack, you come back 'cause you miss the chow?"

"Boy, you get any pussy out there?"

"He didn't, what'd he bust out for?"

"I heard you took a .38 in the shank, Jack. Is that right, you let this puss shoot you?"

"Federal U.S. fuckin' marshal, shows her star and puts one in his leg."

Foley ate his macaroni and cheese staring at the mess of it on his tray while the skinhead hard-ons made their lazy remarks Foley would hear again and again for thirty years, from the Brotherhood, from the Mexican Mafia, from Nuestra Familia, from the black guys all ganged up; thirty years in a convict population careful not to dis anybody, but thinking he could stand up with the tray, have the tables looking at him and backhand it across bare skulls, show 'em he was as dumb as they were and get put in the box for sixty days.

Now they were after the Cuban.

"Boy, we don't allow niggers at our table."

They brought Foley into it asking him, "How we suppose to eat, Jack, this dinge sitting here?"

Right now was the moment to pick up the tray and go crazy, not saying a word but getting everybody's attention, the tables wondering, Jesus, what happened to Foley?

And thought, For what?

He said to the three white-supremacy freaks with their mass of tattoos, "This fella's down from Starke. You understand? I'm showing him around the hotel. He wants to visit with his Savior I point him to the chapel. He wants a near-death-experience hangover, I tell him to see one of you fellas for some pruno. But you got this stranger wrong. He ain't colored, he's a hundred percent greaseball from down La Cucaracha way," Foley looking at the three hard-ons and saying, "Cha cha, cha."

Later on when they were outside the Cuban stopped Foley. "You call me a greaseball to my face?"

This little bit of a guy acting tough.

"Where you been," Foley said, "you get stuck with the white-power ding-dongs, the best thing is to sound as dumb as they are and they'll think you're funny. You heard them laugh, didn't you? And they don't laugh much. It's against their code of behavior."

This was how Foley and Cundo hooked up at Glades.

—

Cundo said Foley was the only white guy in the joint he could talk to, Foley a name among all the grunge here and knew how to jail. Stay out of other people's business. Cundo's favorite part of the day was walking the yard with Foley, a couple of road dogs in tailored prison blues, and tell stories about himself.

How he went to prison in Cuba for shooting a Russian guy.

Took his suitcase and sold his clothes, his shoes, all of it way too big for him. Came here during the time of the boatlift from Mariel, twenty-seven years ago, man, when Fidel opened the prisons and sent all the bad dudes to La Yuma—what he called the United States—for their vacation.

How he got into different hustles. Didn't care for armed robbery. Liked boosting cars at night off a dealer's lot. He danced go-go in gay bars as the Cat Prince, wore a leopard-print jockstrap, cat whiskers painted on his face, but scored way bigger tips Ladies Night at clubs, the ladies stuffing his jock with bills. "Here is this middle-age mama with big *tetas*, she say to me, 'Come to my home Saturday, my husband is all day at his golf club.' She say to me, 'I give you ten one-hundred-dollar bills and eat you alive.' "

Man, and how he was shot three times from his chest to his belly and came so close to dying he saw the dazzle of gold light you hear about when you approaching heaven, right there. But the emergency guys see he's still breathing, blood coming out his mouth, his heart still working, man, and they deliver him alive to Jackson Memorial where he was in a coma thirty-four days, woke up and faked it a few more days listening to Latina voices, the nurse helpers talking about him. He learned he was missing five inches of his colon but healed, sewed up, good as new. When he opened his eyes he noticed the *mozo* mopping the floor wore a tattoo on his hand, an eye drawn at the base of his thumb and index finger, a kind of eye he remembered from Combinado del Este, the prison by Havana. He said to the *mozo*, "We both Marielitos, uh? Get me out of here, my brother, and I make you rich."

Foley said, "You thought you'd be cuffed to the bed?"

"Maybe I was at first, I don't know. I was into some shit at the time didn't work out."

"A cop shot you?"

"No, was a guy, a picture-taker in South Beach, before it became the famous South Beach. Before that he was a Secret Service guy but quit to take pictures. One he did, a guy being thrown off I–95 from the overpass, man, down to the street, the guy in the air, Joe LaBrava sold to a magazine and became famous."

"Why'd he shoot you?"

"Man, I was gonna shoot *him*. I know him, he's a good guy, but I was not going to prison for a deal this woman talk me into doing, with this dumbbell hillbilly rent-a-cop. I didn't tell you about it? I pull a gun and this guy who use to be in the Secret Service beats me to the draw, puts three bullets in me, right here, man, like buttons. I should be dead"—Cundo grinning now—"but here I am, uh? I'm in good shape, I weigh the same now as the day I left Cuba. Try to guess how much."

He was about five-four, not yet fifty but close to it, his dyed hair always slicked back in a ponytail. "A hundred and thirty," Foley said.

"One twenty-eight. You know how I keep my weight? I don't eat that fucking macaroni and cheese they give us. I always watch what I eat. Even when I was in Hollywood going out every night? Is where I went when the *mozo* got me out of the hospital, to L.A., man, see a friend of mine. You understand this was the time of cocaine out there. All I had to do was hook up with a guy I know from Miami. Soon I'm taking care of cool dudes in the picture business, actors, directors—I was like them, I partied with them, I was famous out there."

Foley said, "Till you got busted."

"There was a snitch. Always, even in Hollywood."

"One of your movie buddies."

"I believe a major star, but they don't tell me who the snitch is. The magistrate set a two-million-dollar bond and I put up a home worth two and a half I bought for six-hundred when I was first out there, all the rooms with high ceilings. I pay nine bills for another worth an easy four and a half million today. Both homes on the same canal, almost across from each other."

Foley said, "In Hollywood?"

"In Venice, California, like no place on earth, man, full of cool people and shit."

"Why do you need two homes?"

"At one time I had four homes I like very much. I wait, the prices go up to the sky and I sell two of them. Okay, but the West Coast feds see Florida has a detainer on me for a homicide, a guy they say I did when I was in Miami Beach."

Foley said, "The *mozo*?"

Cundo said, "Is funny you think of him."

"Why didn't you trust him?"

"Why should I? I don't know him. They say one time we out in the ocean fishing I push him overboard."

Foley said, "You shot him first?"

Cundo shook his head grinning just a little. "Man, you something, how you think you know things."

—

"What I don't understand," Cundo said, walking the yard with Foley, "I see you as a hip guy, you smart for a fucking bank robber, but two falls, man, one on top the other, you come out you right back in the slam. Tell me how you think about it, a smart guy like you have to look at thirty years."

Foley said, "You know how a dye pack works? The teller slips you one, it looks like a pack of twenties in a bank strap. It explodes as you leave the bank. Something in the doorframe sets it off. I walk out of a bank in Redondo Beach, the dye pack goes off and I'm sprayed with red paint, people on the street looking at me. Twenty years of going in banks and coming out clean, my eyes open. I catch a dye pack and spend the next seven in federal detention, Lompoc, California. I came out," Foley said, "and did a bank in Pomona the same day. You fall off a bike you get back on. I think, Good, I've still got it. I made over six grand in Pomona. I come back to Florida—my wife Adele divorced me while I'm at Lompoc and she's having a tough time paying her bills. She's working for a magician, Emile the Amazing, jumping out of boxes till he fired her and hired a girl Adele said has bigger tits and was younger. I do a bank in Lake Worth with the intention, give Adele the proceeds to keep her going for a few months. I leave the bank in the Honda I'm using, America's most popular stolen car at the time. Now I'm waiting to make a left turn on to Dixie Highway and I hear the car behind me going *va-room varoom*, revving up, the guy can't wait. He backs up and cuts around me, his tires screaming, like I'm a retiree waiting to make the turn when it's safe to pull out."

"You just rob the fucking bank," Cundo said.

"And this guy's showing me what a hotdog he is."

"So you go after him," Cundo said.

"I tore after him, came up on the driver's side and stared at him."

"Gave him the killer look," Cundo said.

"That's right, and he gives me the finger. I cranked the wheel and sideswiped him, stripped his chrome and ran him off the road."

"I would've shot the fucker," Cundo said.

"What happened, I tore up both tires on the side I swiped him. By the time I got the car pulled over, a deputy's coming up behind me with lights flashing."

"Tha's called road rage," Cundo said. "I'm surprise, a cool guy like you losing it. How you think it happen?"

"I wasn't paying attention. I let myself catch a dye pack in Redondo Beach, something I swore would never happen. The next one, seven years later, you're right, I lost it. You know why? Because a guy with a big engine wearing shades, the top down, no idea I'd just robbed a bank, made me feel like a wimp. And that," Foley said, "is some serious shit to consider."

"Man, you got the balls to bust out of prison, you don't have to prove nothing."

"Out for a week and back inside."

"What could you do? The girl shot you, the chick marshal. You don't tell me about her."

Karen Sisco. Foley kept her to himself. She gave him moments to think about and look at over and over for a time, a few months now, but there weren't enough moments to last thirty years.

Foley's conviction didn't make sense to Cundo. "You get thirty years for one bank, and I'm maxing out seven and a half for killing a guy? How come you don't appeal?"

Foley said he did, but the attorney appointed by the court told him he didn't have a case. "If I can appeal now," Foley said, "I will. If I have to wait too long, one of these nights I'll get shot off the wire and that'll be that."

Cundo said, "Let me tell you how a smart chick lawyer can change your life for you."

—

"I was told by the Florida state attorney, the federal court in L.A. gave me up 'cause I can get the death penalty here or life with no parole. But this cool chick lawyer I got—and I thank Jesus and St. Barbara I can afford to pay her—she say the reason L.A. gave me up, they have a snitch they don't want to burn."

"One of the movie stars," Foley said, "you turned into a drug addict?"

"Miss Megan say maybe because they like his TV show. Plays a prosecutor, busts his balls to put bad guys away. You have to meet her, Miss Megan Norris, the smartest chick lawyer I ever met. She say the Florida state attorney isn't sure he can put me away on the kind of hearsay evidence he's got. She believe he's thinking of sending me back to the Coast. They find me guilty out there I do two-hundred and ninety-five months, man, federal. You know how long that is? The rest of my fucking life. But Miss Megan say they don't want me either if they have to give up their snitch, the famous actor. So she say to the state attorney here, 'You don't want Mr. Rey?' She say, 'Even if he was to plead to second degree and does a good seven for you straight up, no credit?' Man, the state attorney is tempted, but he like me to do twenty-five to life. Miss Megan tells him she can get that out on the Coast where they have new prisons, not old joints full of roaches, toilets that back up. No, she sticks to the seven and adds, okay, six months, take it or leave it. She ask me can I do it. Look at me, I already done five years at Starke. It got crowded up there, the state prison, man, so they send me to this joint, suppose to be medium security, 'cause I don't fuck with the hacks or have snitches set on fire. Ones they can prove. Can I do three more less five months, all I have left of my time?"

"Standing on your head," Foley said. "What's the runout for the federal action?" He saw Cundo start to grin and Foley said, "It already has."

"They have five years to change their mind and bring me to trial if they want. But I'm doing my time here in Florida by then, safe from falling into federal hands. I said to Miss Megan, 'Girl, you could have made a deal, six years, I be almost to the door right now.' Miss Smarty say, 'You lucky to max out with seven plus. Say thank you and do the time.' "

"You get out," Foley said, "you're free, they can't deport you?"

"Fidel won't take us back."

"You glad you came to America?"

"I'm grateful for the ways they are to improve myself since I come to La Yuma. I respect how justice wears a blindfold, like a fucking hostage."

"Where'd you find Miss Megan?"

"I happen to read about her in the Palm Beach newspaper. I call her and Megan come to look me over, see if I can pay her. She like my situation, a way she sees she can make a deal. I tole her I pray to Jesus and St. Barbara. Those two, man, always come through for me. You ever pray?"

"I have, yeah," Foley said. "Sometimes it works."

"You want to appeal?"

"I told you one guy turned me down."

"Let me see can I get Miss Megan for you."

"How do I pay her, rob the prison bank?"

"Don't worry about it," Cundo said. "I want you to meet her. Ask what she thinks of me, if she goes for my type."

THE UNDISPUTED MASTER OF THE CRIME NOVEL

LABRAVA
A Novel

978-0-06-176769-2 (trade paperback)

Ex-Secret Service agent Joe La Brava gets mixed up in a scam involving a slew of eccentric characters.

SWAG
A Novel

978-0-06-174136-4 (trade paperback)

Used car salesman Frank Ryan has a surefire way to get rich quick: armed robbery.

OUT OF SIGHT
A Novel

978-0-06-174031-2 (trade paperback)

Minutes after pulling into a prison parking lot, a Deputy U.S. Marshal meets a legendary bank robber—that's when the fun begins.

THE COMPLETE WESTERN STORIES OF ELMORE LEONARD

978-0-06-124292-2 (trade paperback)

This collection is a must-have for every fan of Elmore Leonard.

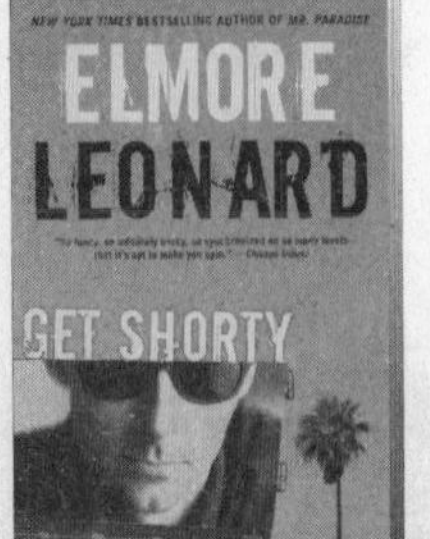

GET SHORTY

978-0-06-077709-8 (trade paperback)

A mobster goes to Hollywood—where women are gorgeous, men are corrupt, and no one can be trusted.

FREAKY DEAKY

978-0-688-16096-8 (trade paperback)

It's only after he transfers out of the bomb squad that Chris Mankowski begins juggling with dynamite.

BANDITS

978-0-688-16639-7 (trade paperback)

An unlikely trio targeting millions of dollars is sure to make out like bandits—if they survive.

BE COOL
A Novel

978-0-06-077706-7 (trade paperback)

Chili Palmer searches for his next big hit as murder blurs the line between reality and the big screen.

KILLSHOT
A Novel

978-0-688-16638-0 (trade paperback)

After witnessing a scam, Carmen and her husband must outrun two thugs determined to eliminate any living evidence.

WHEN THE WOMEN COME OUT TO DANCE
Stories

978-0-06-058616-4 (trade paperback)

Driven by terrific characters and superb writing, these short pieces are Elmore Leonard at his economical best.